THE ITALIAN OBSESSION

N.J. ADEL

The Italian Obsession

DEDICATION

To the real stalkers out there. Thank God you're not as disturbingly good-looking with big cocks as the fictional stalkers we write, read and fantasize about.
Or we're all fucked…
Ladies, stick to your book stalkers!
If you're stalked in real life, don't fall in love.
CALL THE COPS!
I'm serious!

WARNING
There are VERY disturbing scenes in this book. The hero is a psycho villain who does extremely SICK things, especially in the second half of the book. If you have any triggers, this book is definitely NOT for you.
Do NOT read.
Please.

Also by N.J. Adel

Contemporary Romance
The Italian Marriage
The Italian Heartthrob
The Italian Happy Ever After
The Italian Dom
The Italian Son

Paranormal Reverse Harem
All the Teacher's Pet Beasts
All the Teacher's Little Belles
All the Teacher's Bad Boys
All the Teacher's Prisoners

Reverse Harem Erotic Romance
Her Royal Harem: Complete Box Set

Dark MC and Mafia Romance
Furore
Tirone
Dusty
Cameron
Night Skulls Mayhem

Table of Content

DEDICATION IV

ALSO BY N.J. ADEL V

TABLE OF CONTENT VII

CHAPTER 1 1

LINA...1

CHAPTER 2 5

TINO 5

CHAPTER 3 10

LINA...10

CHAPTER 4 18

TINO 18

CHAPTER 5 25

LINA...25

CHAPTER 6 30

LINA...30

CHAPTER 7 37

LINA...37

CHAPTER 8 45

TINO 45

CHAPTER 9 49

TINO 49

CHAPTER 10 60

Lina...60

CHAPTER 11 ....**72**

Tino 72

CHAPTER 12 ....**75**

Lina...75

CHAPTER 13 ....**81**

Lina...81

CHAPTER 14 ....**91**

Lina...91

CHAPTER 15..**108**

Lina..108

CHAPTER 16..**116**

Tino 116

CHAPTER 17..**126**

Tino 126

CHAPTER 18..**139**

Lina..139

CHAPTER 19..**155**

Tino 155

CHAPTER 20..**164**

Lina..164

CHAPTER 21..**171**

Lina..171

CHAPTER 22..**186**

Tino 186

CHAPTER 23...**192**

    Lina...192

CHAPTER 24...**204**

    Tino 204

CHAPTER 25...**213**

    Lina...213

CHAPTER 26...**224**

    Lina...224

CHAPTER 27...**236**

    Lina...236

CHAPTER 28...**241**

    Tino 241

CHAPTER 29...**253**

    Tino 253

CHAPTER 30...**265**

    Lina...265

CHAPTER 31...**274**

    Lina...274

CHAPTER 32...**279**

    Lina...279

CHAPTER 33...**286**

    Tino 286

CHAPTER 34...**290**

    Tino 290

CHAPTER 35...**294**

Lina...294

CHAPTER 36...**298**

Tino 298

CHAPTER 37...**303**

Lina..303

CHAPTER 38...**316**

Lina..316

CHAPTER 39...**323**

Tino 323

CHAPTER 40...**329**

Tino 329

CHAPTER 41...**334**

Lina..334

CHAPTER 42...**343**

Lina..343

CHAPTER 43...**352**

Lina..352

CHAPTER 44...**361**

Lina..361

CHAPTER 45...**369**

Tino 369

CHAPTER 46...**376**

Lina..376

CHAPTER 47...**385**

Lina..385

CHAPTER 48..**399**

    LINA...399

CHAPTER 49..**408**

    TINO 408

CHAPTER 50..**418**

    LINA...418

CHAPTER 51..**427**

    LINA...427

CHAPTER 52..**433**

    LINA...433

CHAPTER 53..**441**

    TINO 441

CHAPTER 54..**445**

    LINA...445

CHAPTER 55..**456**

    ANGEL..456

ALSO BY N.J. ADEL **462**

AUTHOR BIO **463**

CHAPTER 1

Lina

The day my father was killed was the happiest day of my life.

It must be disturbing for anyone to say something like that, but when the man who was supposed to protect you was the one you needed to be protected from, *disturbing* became the definition of your existence.

They sat me next to my sister Nicky. Blankets warmed our shoulders as we leaned into each other. The sky cracked with lightning, thunderous rain pouring. She twined her fingers with mine and looked at me, saying nothing, but her eyes did all the talking.

The monster is gone.

It's not a dream.

He's never gonna hurt us again.

We're safe now.

Were we, though?

It was hard to believe safe was something my sister and I could be, even though I saw the body with my own eyes. The holes in his bashed skull where there were supposed to be eyes. His bloody, handless wrists. His mutilated groin. The police tried to shield me from the *disturbing* view, but I wasn't disturbed. Not by this. If anything, I was fucking happy.

Family and home were supposed to be safe. The shelter from the outside world and its horrors. Mine were quite the opposite, all because of the sicko who called himself our father.

Whoever killed—punished—Frank Baldi knew exactly what kind of man he'd been. What he'd done. To his own daughters. Why else would the murderer—our savior—chop off every part of my father's body he used to hurt us?

My eyes reached past the red and blue lights and into the blackness of the woods behind our house—the one we could no longer live in because Nicky was fourteen and the last of our family was murdered. Another reason safe wasn't a word that registered in my head. Foster care wasn't made of cotton candy and rainbows.

But that wasn't what I was thinking about when I squinted at the woods. I couldn't shake the feeling that whoever took my father's life was still out there, watching in the dark.

Had been watching.

The feeling started a few weeks before my father was killed. The constant alarm that someone was watching me. On the street. At school. At the mall.

In my own bedroom.

Nicky told me it was nothing more than the imagination of a frightened, twelve-year-old girl or just another bad dream. And just like I'd learnt with my father, I kept quiet and shut my eyes. Pretended it was another bad dream that I'd wake from soon.

I might have been twelve, constantly afraid and making believe, but I knew what I felt was real. Just like I needed a protector from the man that should have protected me, I'd need a savior from the man who saved me.

My father wasn't the only monster that visited at night.

CHAPTER 2

Tino

I'd watched her since the beginning.

Since I'd learned one of my men was a lowlife who liked to touch little girls. *His* girls.

With a job like mine and what I did to keep it over the years, a man like me wasn't appalled by many things. And my position required I didn't get my hands dirty anymore. But what that scum had done was enough to bring the darkest side of me to the edge. I'd gladly mauled the bastard with my own hands and enjoyed every tremor and scream that came out of his disgusting body.

For little Nicole and Angelina.

Everybody called the younger sister Lina, but in my head, she was Angel. *My* Angel.

From the moment I first saw her, I'd wanted to protect and care for her. She was twelve for fuck's sake. So innocent. So beautiful. So sweet she melted *my* heart when I didn't even think I had one.

Her mother was dead, and she had no parent but that fucker Baldi, with no one to protect her from him but her older sister, who was tough but a kid herself.

Who would hurt such an angel? How could a father do that to his own child?

As a father myself, there was nothing that I wouldn't do or sacrifice for my son and his protection. My Angel deserved a father that would do the same for her.

Nicole, too. She'd been looking out for my girl before I even knew what had been going on in their house, taking what no kid should have ever endured to keep Angel away from the monster as much as she could. For that she deserved to have the best.

I watched as Angel's sister lined up with her friends in graduation gowns, waiting with an excited smile for her name to be called to get her diploma. I was proud of her as if she'd been my own kid. Soon, she'd be off to college on a full scholarship I'd made sure she got. Just like the one my Angel would get in two years after she graduated.

After I got Baldi out of the way, I'd orchestrated everything in our lives so that I could give her the life she deserved.

So that, at the perfect moment, I would have her.

My eyes traveled to the most beautiful girl I'd ever seen as she cheered for her sister. My Angel was sixteen now. No longer a little girl but still so innocent and pure. Her light brown hair bounced behind her back as she jumped up and down, clapping with real joy, her green eyes and olive skin alight. When I saw her smile, the bitter taste always in my mouth turned into a sweetness I craved. Needed.

My body pulsed with the need to get closer. I never did though. A safe distance separated us as I always remained hidden from her sight. Even though Angel had been taking over all of my mind and heart for the past four years, I was making sure she wasn't aware of my constant presence.

At first, I had no intention she ever would be. I swore to protect her, even from myself. My life had no room for innocence or purity such as hers. But with the years, my obsession had worsened. Fighting it wasn't going to help me protect her. It was driving me insane, and that would only put her and everything around her in more danger.

She belonged with me. She was safe only with me.

For a second, my gaze locked on her lips. Pale pink painted the perfection that was her mouth, and my mind raced to a moment that belonged in the future. Our future that sometimes—most of the time—I ran out of patience waiting for.

I clenched my jaws, the urge to just go over there, put her over my shoulder and steal her away forever nagging. I was going to hell anyway. What was another sin to add to my long list? Or maybe I should just go ahead and propose to her. The state of Illinois allowed marriage at sixteen. I fucking checked—not that I cared about the law, man's or God's. I only cared about her. Not spooking her.

Like a stranger almost double her age kidnapping her or proposing to her out of nowhere won't make her run for the hills.

Chuckling, I dismissed my crazy thoughts. My Angel sucked all logic and sanity out of me. She did things to me that could start wars and destroy worlds.

I reprimanded myself, which I never did except when it came to her, dragging my gaze up to hers. *Not yet, my sweet Angel, but when the time comes, I will make you mine.*

CHAPTER 3

Lina

"**I** can't believe we're having our own apartment." Nicky squeaked, carrying the last of our boxes into the condo.

"I know, right?" In a haze, I stacked my box with the others in the living room that was bigger than our entire bedroom at Bellomo.

Not that I wasn't grateful for the amazing boarding school that took us in after the murder. Our home for the past four years was perfect. A private academy—community—for the rich elite we'd have never crossed paths with or even have known such establishments existed if the academy hadn't started that charity program for orphans and abused children four years ago. I couldn't believe how lucky we'd been to be one of the firsts who were accepted there. They only took one or two children in every grade every year.

We—program kids—had our own dorm and dining hall. We only met the other kids during classes and activities. Some of us didn't like that we were separated from the rich students, but I thought it was the perfect arrangement for our protection.

Bellomo—an academy named after and belonged to the most powerful family in Chicago—might have given us the best shelter and education people like us could have ever received, but it was built exclusively for the wealthy and powerful. The rich kids would have bullied us—had bullied, name called and fought with some of us already—and we wouldn't have stood a chance. It was their home, and we were the freeloaders.

However, Nicky and I never faced that challenge. No one had ever tried anything with us. Maybe because of Nicky. No one crossed that girl. She was tall and strong, and she'd spent every spare moment she got at the gym to get even stronger. She was my superhero.

Or maybe because everybody knew about the murder. How gruesome it was and that an unknown vigilante did it. I liked to believe they thought if they hurt us, the vigilante would come for them just like *he* had come for my father.

Or maybe it was just luck. The same luck that landed Nicky a full Bellomo scholarship to study Architecture at IIT Chicago. The same *luck* that got us into Bellomo in the first place.

I straightened up, my arms circling around my body reflexively, my eyes roaming the place. The condo had an open floor plan. The living room, dining room and kitchen all flowed together. There were two bedrooms down the only hallway, each with a private bathroom. We could have never afforded such a place if it weren't for Nicky's scholarship and the job she got at one of the coffee shops on campus. The money from our old house wasn't much to begin with. It was small and dingy and...haunted with our father's murder and his crimes when he was alive.

The condo was more than I could've ever dreamed of having, and yet I couldn't shake the same old feeling that someone was watching me. Even here.

A hand patted my shoulder, and I jumped. Then I sighed and swallowed as I realized it was just Nicky.

She rubbed my back. "Hey, what's wrong?"

"Nothing. I just…"

Her tender gaze traveled through the windows and among the stretch of skyscrapers that still didn't block any sunlight from reaching inside the new place. "You really think he's out there, don't you?"

I shook my head, laughing under my breath. "I know it's silly."

"There's nothing silly or funny about a vigilante killer stalking you, Lina."

I grimaced, sudden, inexplicable anger flickering inside me. I didn't like the way she described *him*, even though it might be true. "Stalking is a big word."

She gaped at me. "Lina!" Then her eyebrows shot high in shock. "Please don't tell me you… Did you… Have you actually seen him? Has he ever talked to you? Did he fucking touch you?"

"Oh my God. What are you…?" I shook my head fast. "I haven't seen or talked to anyone. This is probably all my stupid imagination, but if, and only if, *he* exists and is out there, I don't think *he*'s a…stalker." More like a dark guardian angel.

"No?" She crossed her arms over her chest and cocked a brow at me.

"Yeah. What if *he* just did it to protect us, you know?"

She snorted. "And now *he*'s out there keeping an eye on us in case another asshole comes our way?"

I busied myself with the boxes, escaping her taunting gaze. "Like I said it's silly. I just…"

"You're still thinking about how easily we got into Bellomo, aren't you? You still think that murderer has a hand—"

"Don't you ever?" I looked at her over my shoulder. "Things like that don't just happen to people like us, Nicky." That miracle—even though I was forever grateful for it—was too good to be true.

"Nobody does stuff like that for people like us without expecting something in return either. It's been four years. Don't you think *he*'d have showed up by now, asking for whatever the hell he wanted in return from us? From you?"

I stacked a couple of boxes to take them to my room and shrugged. "I guess so."

"C'mon, Lina. You know what? I think getting into that school was Karma's way of making it up for the shit we had to go through, but that's all the luck we've received. Everything else was our hard work or are you telling me that we haven't busted our butts to stay in that school, that I haven't studied my ass off to get that scholarship?"

I left the boxes and spun. Then I held her arms, holding her gaze. "Of course not. You worked really hard for this. You graduated first in your class for God's sake. You earned that scholarship fair and square."

"Then why are you still thinking that weird shit? There's no one out there, Nicky. There's only us. Baldi girls versus the world. We don't need saviors. Only each other."

I smiled and nodded in agreement. Nicky was everything to me. I had no clue what I'd do without her. My life without my sister was unimaginable even though we were so different. She was the organized, in your face, confident realist, and I was the quiet, all over the place dreamer. She kept me in check, and we balanced each other out.

I almost dismissed the whole *he* idea, borrowing her logic, when my gaze dropped to the violin case nestled in the top box of my stack. My mind drifted to my last birthday when I found it wrapped in my dorm room right on my bed. The most precious gift I'd ever received in my whole life. "What about the birthday gifts that miraculously appeared on my bed?"

"One of the perks of being born on Halloween. The guys at school were messing with you for a good spook." She went on with the story she'd told me every time my fears got the best of me. Every year our friends gathered money and got me a present, but instead of just giving it to me, they left it on my bed with no card or note or anything, made it look like it came from a stranger and then teased me about it.

I never believed that story. The gifts—a gold necklace with an angel pendant, a watch, a pair of silver earrings with pink tourmalines, and the violin—were really expensive, and said friends denied buying me any gifts when I confronted them. Nicky had always said it was part of the act, but no one was that good of an actor.

"There wasn't so much to do for fun at our school, and we barely got out. The guys did it for the kicks." She shrugged, as if stating the obvious. "Besides, Bellomo was a freaking vault. No stranger could have come in without getting caught."

"That I can't argue with."

She gave my arm a gentle squeeze and pecked my cheek. "I know what you're thinking, Lina, but we have no guardian angels or secret admirers looking out for us and giving us nice things. It doesn't work that way." She leaned in and whispered, "Especially if they're psycho stalking killers."

Anger bubbled in me again. At Nicky…and at myself. It was crazy how I wanted to shake her and demand she never call *him* that again, how I wanted to defend *him* even though he might have never existed, and if *he* did, *he*'d be exactly what she said *he* would be.

Why would anyone defend a psycho stalking killer?

Why would I want *him* to be real?

And above all, if *he* was, why couldn't I wait to meet *him*?

CHAPTER 4

Tino

As much as I loved Nicole, I didn't like that she took my Angel out of the dorm. I'd rather my girl had stayed there until her graduation, where I always kept an eye on her. Where she was safe.

Where I could visit whenever I pleased.

I could have made the academy insist she stay and reject her day school application, but I'd never seen my Angel happier when she knew she'd be living at her own apartment.

The things I'd do for your happiness…

When I stared at the three locks on their door, fury rumbled inside me, though. Like that was going to stop me from entering a condo in my own building. Yeah, I bought the whole thing when I knew they were going to move in and rented the penthouse in the building across the street so I could watch my Angel at all times.

Using my keys, I disengaged the locks one by one and opened the door. Then some relief washed over me as I realized I was overreacting. These locks were meant for my Angel's protection, to keep crazy strangers away. Certainly not me.

Good girl, Nicky. Keep my Angel safe like you always have.

The idea of sharing my girl with anyone, even her own sister, made me want to kill something. But Nicole really loved and looked after her. If Angel wasn't going to be sleeping in my school—or my bed yet—the next-best thing was for her to share a condo with her sister, where we could both protect her.

As I stepped inside, the smell of wood and cardboard filled my nostrils. The living room was a mess. Couch still in plastic wrapping. Table yet to be installed. Stacks of empty and unpacked boxes.

Was it the same inside the bedrooms, too?

I wished I could have helped my girl settle down, unpack the rest of the boxes for her, arrange her clothes in the closet, set her toiletries in the bathroom... I walked toward one of the boxes and opened it. It had some books and a folder with the name Lina written on it. My Angel's schoolwork.

If I unpacked them for her, would she notice or would she just assume she'd done it herself among the other stuff already out?

Unwilling to risk it, I put down everything the way they were and dragged my feet away. I fought so hard not to snoop inside more boxes and get a few things out myself. Maybe even take something that had her smell to keep at my place.

But no. I wouldn't want to freak her out. I clenched my fists and spun. Down the hallway, I took a deep breath, my heart fluttering, before I entered the second room. The one I saw Angel choose this morning.

Her scent tickled me the second I opened the door. Peach, licorice and honey with a touch of Jasmine. My Angel's room smelled like the sweet little girl she was.

The room was in a better condition than the living room. Almost ready to live in. I stared at the closet for a long minute. I wanted to go in and never come out, but I knew if I went in there, I'd do just that and everything would be ruined.

I sat at the foot of her bed, tracing the red floral patterns on the purple sheets. They weren't soft enough for her delicate skin, but that was the best she could afford for now. Soon, she'd have the largest bedroom she could ever wish for, and only the softest silk and cotton would touch her beautiful skin.

I took a whiff at the sheets. They smelled fresh and new. Her scent hadn't soaked into them yet. Disappointment coursed through me but immediately vanished when I spotted her violin case on the floor.

Carefully, I picked it up and got the instrument out. I held it in my arms as if I were holding a baby. As if I was holding her.

My eyes shut as I touched the strings her fingers played, Angel's image at her first recital at the academy vivid behind my eyelids. Fuck, she was perfect. A true artist in the making, destined for glory. I was there, of course, watching her in the dark without her knowing. I could have never missed it.

When I first got her the violin, she wasn't very happy about it. Her music teacher's files told me Angel was more enthusiastic about playing the piano, but I still got her the violin for her sweet sixteen. While she was talented at playing both instruments, I loved her with the violin much more than with the piano. When she played it, it looked like it was a part of her. She just hadn't understood it yet.

It was my job to help her choose what was truly right for her, help her see what she couldn't see on her own yet. It was my duty to clear out the obstacles that stopped her from following her path of greatness, from being where she belonged.

Just like I did when I got Baldi out of her way. Our way.

And I was right, once she got used to the custom made violin with the perfect chin rest for her—the one at the academy was *uncomfortable and itchy* as she'd told the teacher—she fell in love, and now they'd become inseparable.

My sweet Angel, I can't wait for the day you'll play for me. Only for me.

My chest contracted with the reminder of the time I still had to endure without her in my arms. Why did she have to be so fucking young?

The phone vibrated in my pocket, distracting me from my agony. I checked the text message I'd received. It was from Michele, the bodyguard that watched Angel and her sister.

Michele: They're leaving the mall.

Me: Everything ok?

Michele: Super.

I put my phone away and kissed the violin as I set it back inside the case. Then I rose to my feet and let my eyes travel around the bedroom for another moment. But the longer

I stared, the longer I stood in her room, the harder it was to leave.

One thought possessed me and wouldn't let go.

I could no longer wait two more years to make an appearance and ease my way into her life. Our meet had to be much sooner than that or both of us would regret the consequences of what would happen if I didn't feed that urge only she triggered inside me.

I inhaled her scent that lingered in the air one more time. "See you soon, my sweet Angel."

CHAPTER 5

Lina

Nicky kicked the door closed, her hands full of shopping bags. "You really should have gotten that rose gold dress. It looked dee-licious on you."

I rolled my eyes. "You're crazy. I have no idea why you dragged me into that store in the first place. Their cheapest dress was like five hundred bucks. That rose gold thing costs twelve hundred dollars, Nicky. Big fat WTF."

The plastic cover on the couch rumbled as she plopped down on it, tossing the bags aside while giggling. "Language, young lady."

I rolled my eyes again.

"How about you just wear it on Saturday with the tag on and then return it just like I'm doing with mine?" Her big eyes popped with a mischievous gleam. "It's not like we go to one of those parties every day."

The Bellomo Scholarship Awards Ceremony at IIT was a big deal. The society's crème de la crème would be there, and this year we get to be a part of that glamorous event because of Nicky's scholarship. It was dazzling and made my head spin with excitement and pride, but it didn't mean I'd *borrow* a dress from a store to attend.

"It's so wrong. I can't do that. Besides, it's your day. Nobody is gonna see me. It doesn't matter what I wear. Your dress, though…" I pulled it from the bag and marveled at its beauty, almost in tears. The fitted elegance of the sparkling purple and gold that showed her hourglass, athletic figure was mesmerizing. Unlike me, Nicky looked like Mom. Blonde with beautiful blue eyes and a fair skin, and that dress was made for her. "You have to keep it, Nicky. It's perfect."

A loud snort erupted from her. "We can't afford to pay eight hundred bucks for a dress. No way."

"You can wear it on my birthday, and your birthday, and everybody else's birthdays. I wish it could fit me or would ever look as good as it was on you so I could do the same. But you can still save it for your kids. It's worth every penny."

She giggled. "You're crazy? What kids?"

"The ones you're gonna have soon because you'll meet your future husband on Saturday. That dress brings boys to their knees. Guaranteed."

She pointed her index finger to her open mouth as if she wanted to vomit and then continued laughing as she rose, but not for long.

I shouldn't have said that. Boys had always been a tricky topic. I knew better. "Sorry, Nicky."

"C'mon." She waved a dismissive hand, looking at me as if I was silly for apologizing. "We don't need boys or husbands or any of that shit, remember?"

I raised my fist in solidarity as she marched to her room. "Yeah. Baldi girls versus the world."

When she slammed the door shut, I cursed. Putting down the dress, I jumped to my feet, and then I stalked to the boxes, taking my rage out at the cardboard, opening—tearing—

it with much more force than needed. My vision blurred with tears I didn't want to shed but fell anyway.

I took all the stuff I could carry and stormed inside my room. Then I crumbled on the bed, blubbering ugly. I didn't want her to see me like this. It wasn't like he'd hurt me more than he'd hurt her, and I didn't see her cry. Not in front of me, at least.

She never said it directly to me, but I knew what Father did to her. He might have done awful things to me, but he didn't rape me.

Over and over and over.

She took it all and never once complained, all so he wouldn't do it to me.

I needed to be strong like she always had been for me. I needed to show her she no longer had to take care of me or shield me from her pain. It was okay for her not to be tough all the time. It was okay to live and be happy and find love. It was time someone took care of my sister, someone who would love and cherish and treat her the way she was supposed to be treated. But if she couldn't let someone in yet, I'd be that someone until she was healed.

I wiped my tears and looked around me. Then my gaze wandered with the city lights through the windows. The old feeling that someone was watching me broke my skin into goosebumps. "If you're out there..." I shook my head, a hot sigh escaping me. "Thank you."

I knew it was crazy to be grateful for a vicious killer, but I couldn't help feeling any different. I hoped *he* could see where we were now, what we'd become. We were still damaged, but it could have been far worse. We'd been blessed, and none of it would have happened if *he* hadn't done what *he* had.

I grabbed my violin and sat by the windows, ready to play. "This one is for you."

CHAPTER 6

Lina

"C'mon, Lina. We're gonna be late!" Nicky yelled, banging on my bedroom door.

I rushed out of the bathroom—my own private bathroom—and hit the closet, hair and makeup done, excited to get out my new turquoise dress that cost only ten percent of that overpriced thing Nicky wanted me to *borrow.* "Just a minute. I'm almost done."

A strange shimmer took me by surprise when I reached for the hanger. Rose gold cascades of sparkle nestled right next to my dress. My jaw fell.

"Oh my God, Nicky!" My sister was the craziest and most amazing person in the world.

"Our ride will be here in three minutes, Lina. C'mon!"

I got out the gorgeous dress in freaking awe, and then I switched my gaze toward the door. Shaking my head, I convinced myself there was no time to argue with her, and I had no choice but to wear it. I couldn't disappoint her, not tonight, especially when she'd gone through all that trouble to get it and surprise me like that.

And—who was I kidding?—I really loved that dress.

Quickly, I put it on and complimented it with my pink tourmaline earrings and my heels. I twirled, immediately feeling like a princess.

Grabbing my purse, I opened the door. Nicky's fist was in the air, ready to bang on one more time, but it froze in the air when she saw me.

"Oh. My. God. Lina! You look amazing," she squealed. "I'm so psyched you agreed to wear it."

"I'd have never done it if it weren't for you. It's crazy." I grinned incredulously, but then I shrugged. "But so worth it."

"Yes, girl." She high-fived me.

"You look amazing, too. So hot."

She winked at my chest—at my boobs. "Back at ya."

My cheeks warmed. "It's too revealing, isn't it?"

"Nope. It makes the girls look perfect. And you should wear whatever you wanna wear. You should never be ashamed of your body or hide because of a bunch of assholes out there. If someone can't keep their eyes to themselves that's on them, not you."

I smiled with a nod. I was sure she was giving herself that speech before me. She ushered me out of the condo. "Let's go kick some ass."

At the entrance of Hermann Hall, my sister and I linked arms and went up the stairs. My heart thudded with every step. I'd never been on a college campus before, let alone gone to a party with seniors, college students and adults. "Man, I can't wait to finish high school."

Nicky laughed as we entered the lounge, and she presented our invitations with confidence to the nice lady outside the auditorium. We took our ID badges and ambled down the lounge. While Nicky kept her eyes forward, unfazed by the surroundings and the boys in tuxes doing double takes, I clutched her arm as if she were my mom and I were five again, and grinned like an idiot, noting how their eyes were all on my beautiful sister.

We were seated next to each other, but a few minutes before the scholarship awards segment, they asked Nicky to move to the second row with the other students.

She leaned in and whispered, "Be careful. If anyone makes a pass at you when I'm gone, kick them in the nuts and then holler for me."

I stifled a giggle. "Oh please. Like college boys are gonna hit on the junior? You take care of yourself. There are some hungry eyes for you here."

"C'mon, I'm serious, and you don't look like a high school junior," she winked at my boobs again, "not in that dress."

I didn't know why I kept blushing every time she did that or why Nicky was acting like we were at a bar, not at one of the most prestigious schools in town. But that was who she was. Always protective of me, and I loved her for it.

A man was wrapping up his speech, a representative from Bellomo. I wondered why the owners of such a huge organization—they didn't just own the academy. They technically owned Chicago—never showed up at any events or gave any speeches, not even at school or at a big ceremony such as this one.

It was so weird, and it made many of my friends believe the rumors were true; The Bellomos were the Mafia, and all this, the academy, the scholarships, the companies, the restaurants, was nothing but money laundering.

For me, it was so hard to believe. Why would the Mafia invest in elite education? Do charity? Make people's lives better? There were a thousand other ways to launder their money. It didn't make sense, but nothing was impossible. Maybe they did it to gain the respect of society, to create an unquestionable front and make it hard for the police to take them down, to confuse people like me and make them think the Mafia wasn't all that bad…

I shrugged, refusing to believe that our great benefactors were gangsters. I liked to think they truly cared about the future of Chicago's children. But what did I know? For someone who secretly believed the murderer of her father was a good man, I should never have a say in classifying who was good or who was bad. My villain-hero concepts needed adjustments.

When Nicky's name came up and she got to the podium, I was so proud and vibrating with joy and excitement I wanted to scream at the top of my lungs and get freaking pompoms to cheer for her.

I shoved my hands under my thighs to stop myself. I wouldn't want to embarrass Nicky with my fanatical pleasure in front of her future teachers and peers.

Suddenly, my stomach fell with the feeling that someone was staring at me. My heart did a backflip when I whipped my head to the side and saw there was a man one seat away, and his eyes were locked on my face.

Our gaze connected for a split-second before he broke it and hurriedly left his seat. What the hell?

Blinking after him—his back—I felt so cold like all my blood had left my body. Scared? Definitely. Why? Not sure, but there was something in his eyes that made my heart skip a beat and held me in place even after he was no longer looking at me.

Could that be…?

My eyes widened. The distance between us kept growing with every one of his strides. Shoot. I barely got a glimpse of his face in the dim light. I wouldn't be able to recognize him if I ever saw him again. And if that was...*him*...

I wanted to go after him, ask him who he really was and why he was staring, but my legs wouldn't budge. I swallowed, balling my hands into fists under me, closing my eyes for a second to get a grip. I couldn't just let him disappear. I needed to know if it was *him*.

I took one glance at Nicky and trailed my eyes back on the man about to vanish in the dark. Summoning every shred of courage I had inside me, which wasn't much, but was enough to get my butt off the chair, I followed him.

CHAPTER 7

Lina

My feet raced the air as I followed him outside the auditorium, but I couldn't keep up. His long legs allowed him wider strides. Any second now, he could slip away from my sight.

Afraid he'd vanish, I took off my heels to gain more speed. I must have looked like a crazy person, running barefoot at a sophisticated event such as this, but I didn't care. I had to see his face. I had to know.

How I was gonna talk to him, I had no clue. What exactly was I supposed to say? *Hey, are you my father's killer? Have you been following me for the past four years? Are you a stalker like my sister says?*

Like if he were, he'd simply confess? And what if he was just some random guy stealing a glance at the girl next to him? What if it wasn't *him* at all?

What if it was?

My mind and heart raced, but I kept running. I just had to meet him to end all doubt. To put an end to my confusion. My fear.

The more I ran, the darker the halls became, and the crowd thinned with every corner. A sudden awareness in the form of Nicky's voice kicked in.

What the hell are you doing? What if he was a stalking psycho killer, luring you into a dark, isolated area? Are you thinking at all?

My breath caught, and I had to slow down for a second or two as I realized it was really dark in here, and there was no one here but me and—

My eyes darted around the emptiness surrounding me and then squeezed shut. My heartbeat pulsed in my temples, anger and panic taking over me. Was he gone?

"Hello?" I asked the silence, desperate. "Are you here?"

I waited for an answer like an idiot, but after a few long seconds, it was clear there was no one here but me. Dammit.

Why did I have to be such a coward and slow down? I couldn't believe I lost him just like that. I was so fucking close. I tilted my head back and swore again.

Maybe it was for the best. Maybe he was truly a bad guy I should have never chased into the dark like that. But in this moment, I didn't care if he was. Nothing bothered me but the fact that I missed my chance to really see *him*.

I shouldn't think that way. It defied all logic. For some reason, though, I knew in my heart, *he* wouldn't hurt me. Not like that.

My lips puckered as I spun, cursing my luck, not even sure how I'd get back to Nicky. I was totally lost in this deserted part of the hall. I started walking away, but I glanced over my shoulder one last time and sighed, no idea what I was hoping for. He was long gone. "If that was really you, I wish I could've seen you."

Then I rolled my eyes at the heels in my grip, as if I'd forgotten I'd taken them off. I bent to put them back on. When I straightened my back, something warm and soft fell on the side of my neck.

A breath.

A gasp fled my throat, and I froze for what seemed like an eternity.

"Don't move," he barely whispered. His low voice was strained and hard. His breath kept falling hot on my skin.

Everything in me shuddered, and all the air escaped my lungs. A Horrible wave of fear crippled my mind, and the ridiculous thoughts about *him* not hurting me shattered with his command. I should try to run. I should scream. I should do anything other than just stand there and wait for his next move. Whatever that might be.

But I obeyed him. I didn't move. I couldn't even if I wanted to. My limbs had gone cold, unmoving just like they were at the auditorium when he looked at me.

"A-are yo-u…gonna…?" I couldn't finish, tears choking me.

"Am I gonna what?" he asked with the same low, hard voice. So deep and masculine and terrifying.

Kill me? Rape me? Kidnap me? All three? I didn't say anything so I wouldn't put ideas in his head. Besides, I was hiccupping through the tears I could barely breathe, let alone speak. I closed my eyes, pretending this was a bad dream like I always did.

"Shhhh." His breath came closer, sending a stronger shiver through me. Then I felt something pointy and scruffy on my shoulder. A bearded chin? *His* bearded chin? The confirmation came as the scruffy hair pressed to the side of my neck. Lightly, gently.

Suddenly, I was no longer cold. I was burning hot. The heat coming from his body seeped through my pores with his simplest touch. Oh my God, he was touching me.

And I was letting him.

Fear snaked down my spine, crippling me further. What the hell did I do? Why did I have to follow him? Why did I have to say what I said? I literally told him I wished I could've seen him, and here he was. What had I just gotten myself into?

And why the hell was I just standing there, unable to say a simple word such as no while he allowed himself to touch me without permission?

It's just a bad dream.

Refusing to let me pretend, my senses crawled back into my foggy brain. He wasn't exactly touching me. His hands and body were nowhere on mine. It was just his chin on my shoulder, and the side of his face on mine. So light and careful, as if he was afraid to break me, but it did make me quake.

Then I felt it. His hand. On my…hair.

Another gasp flew off my throat. He touched my hair so casually, so possessively, without hesitation. Like he had the right to do it. Like I belonged to him.

"What a-are y-you doing?" I stammered.

I heard him inhale deeply, and then he exhaled with the same intensity, inducing another shudder from my body. "You smell so good."

Did he just sniff my hair? That was so creepy and sick…and so incredibly intimate.

"You're so beautiful," he whispered and took another deep breath.

Both my lashes and heart fluttered. Nobody had ever touched me in that way or said things like that to me before. Nobody except…

The horrible memory slapped me out of the trance *he* put me in. "Please stop," I gasped.

He mumbled something in a foreign language. Spanish maybe or Italian? It sounded native but he didn't have an accent when he spoke in English. Then, just like that, the strand in his hand dropped on my back. "I'm not like your father," he reprimanded, as if he read my mind, as if he knew exactly how I felt.

My hands trembled harder, and my heart pounded in my throat. This was no random guy. He knew about my father. He knew who I was. *Oh my God. Is it really him?*

"Ci vediamo, my sweet Angel."

His warmth on my face was replaced by an unbearable coldness, and I heard him step back. He was letting me go, even though someone like him, someone that obviously didn't play by the rules, someone that was probably the most dangerous man I'd ever met, could have gone further. From what I'd glimpsed earlier, he was twice my size. I wouldn't stand a chance in a fight against him.

But he was letting me go.

I should run now, grateful that he was. I should find my way back to Nicky and never look back. Why the fuck was I still standing here?

"Can I please see you?" I asked under my breath, shaking, unable to begin to understand what the hell was wrong with me. Why did the urge to see him outweigh my self-preservation? Why would I want him to stay longer when all I should be doing was running for my life, praying I'd never see him again?

One more time, I waited like an idiot in the dark for his answer, but I could no longer feel or hear his breath. He'd left. So long for putting an end to my confusion and fear. If anything, they'd multiplied.

He wouldn't even let me see his face.

Just like he didn't wait for my permission to smell my hair, I should have turned, not waiting for his, and seen his face. I was so angry at myself, at how much of a coward I was. For God's sake, I was still frozen in place, not even moving my head to look at him over my shoulder.

Finally, I did. Then I strained my eyes into the darkness. He wasn't there. All I was left with was tears, a frightened heart and a dark promise.

Ci vediamo, my sweet Angel.

That was Italian, and I understood it very well. Many of the students at Bellomo said it to each other. It meant *until we meet again.*

CHAPTER 8

Tino

I kept smelling my hand like I couldn't get enough of her scent. It lingered on my beard, too, filling my mouth and nose with every breath, lick and swallow. Honey, peach, licorice and jasmine.

I should have left after she caught me. I should leave now, but the amount of willpower it took me to walk away from her when she was that close to me was all I had for the night. I hid in the shadows, close to the hall exit waiting to see her one more time. She looked so beautiful, so elegant in that dress. A princess soon to be a queen. All the time when we were alone together, I wanted nothing but to hold her and never let go.

You were born to rule, my sweet Angel, and so you will by my side.

She shouldn't wear that dress in public again, though. Some of the kids—and fucking men—were looking at her. At her chest. Didn't they know she was mine, and she was too fucking young? Even *I* hadn't allowed myself to claim my rights and enjoy what was mine.

How many men am I supposed to murder for you, Angel? Because I'd have killed them all for just looking at her. But she didn't know she was mine yet, and so the world couldn't know.

I was counting the days…

People streamed out of the hall. I weeded them out until I found my girl. She looked…distant. Even when her sister spoke to her, she barely responded. I knew I shook her tonight, but I couldn't keep my distance anymore. She had to know our time was coming soon. She had to know I was there, waiting. I had to occupy her mind like she invaded mine. I needed to make her think about me like I thought of nothing but her.

For years, I cared about nothing but La Famiglia and my duty toward it. I knew nothing but. I'd been a made man since I was fourteen. After I'd seen Angel, it was as if my life had been split into two halves. Before her and after.

Nothing mattered to me anymore but her and my son.

My phone vibrated in my pocket. I got it out and stared at the name of the caller. Il Figlio. Speak of the devil.

Without taking my eyes off Angel, I picked up the call. "Piccolo."

He grumbled. "When will you stop calling me that?"

"You know when." When he stopped being a dick and became a made man himself so I could make him my underboss.

Another grumble. I could easily picture the eye roll and the finger he was giving me now. "Anyway, I'm at the house, but they're telling me you haven't been staying there all week. You good?"

I smirked at the reason. She was climbing into her ride home with Nicole, Michele ready in the car behind them. "Yeah. You?"

"Same. I just…um…wanted to check on you, old man."

I chuckled. That was code for *I'd spent all my allowance and needed more money*. He had issues with being part of one of the oldest Mafia families but no problem spending its *blood money*. "Tell you what? Let's have some good old father son time like we used to. I'll text you an address. Stop by in an hour."

CHAPTER 9

Tino

She locked herself up in her room since she'd returned home. Violin in her hand, she sat by the window. Was she going to play for me again? That other night, I'd felt she was playing only for me, as if she knew I was watching, as if she knew how much I loved listening to the music she made.

But she wasn't playing. All she seemed to be doing was staring out, looking for something or someone.

"I'm right here, my sweet Angel. I'm always here."

Her fingers wiped under her eyes, and I narrowed my gaze in my dark bedroom to get a better look at her. Was she crying? She used the hem of her pink tank top to wipe her face now. She was crying.

"Why, Angel? Please, no. Your tears are so precious. Is it because you miss me? I know. I miss you, too. But not for long, my beautiful girl. We'll be together soon enough, and we'll always be together. Nothing will ever come between us."

Her hand moved to the top of her shoulder, feeling where my chin had rested. I smiled. She was thinking about me. She was missing me. Her fingers moved up to the side of her neck and back down to her shoulder, as if she was remembering the feeling of my skin on hers.

Her fingertips drifted along her collarbone and slowly, *sensually*, slid down her—

I tore my gaze away and stared at the blank walls. The demons in my head tugged hard at my forbidden desires, begging me to watch what I, what no man should ever watch. I knew I'd kill anyone who would.

She's not a child. She's almost seventeen.

You said yourself you could marry her right now, and it'd be legal.

Your mother had you when she was sixteen.

Your late wife was Angel's age when you married her.

It's not like she belongs to someone else. She's yours, so go ahead and—

Squeezing my eyes shut, I groaned and practically ran outside of the room before I did something I'd never forgive myself for. This was the first time I'd ever seen her do something...womanly. My sweet, innocent, pure girl was no longer a girl. "But I'm not a fucking pervert."

Yes, you are. You're a fucking stalker. You've been stalking her since she was fucking twelve.

"To protect her. I've never once—" I cursed and stormed toward the minibar. Then I poured myself some prosecco. "If my Angel wants to...touch herself...thinking of me," a delightful, smug feeling washed over me, "that's her business. She has needs." Needs only I would satisfy. Now if I'd been young and free like she was. But I wasn't, and we had to fucking wait.

If she'd been any other girl, if her prick of a father hadn't brutally hurt her, mentally scarring her for life, I'd have just taken her without giving a single fuck, giving her everything she ever needed or wanted as long as we both fucking lived.

My eyes betrayed me and stole a glance at the windows. I could still see her room from the hall. My Angel was in bed now with the lights on, and by the way her body moved, there was no doubt what she was doing under the sheets.

I swore and downed my drink. "I'm gonna need something stronger than that." And I was definitely going in first thing in the morning, taking all the clothes she was wearing now before she got a chance to wash them.

A buzz snatched me out of my thoughts. A text message from one of my bodyguards letting me know my son was here. I went to the door and saw my son in the security panel camera. Then I punched in the code and buzzed him in.

My arms wide open, I smiled. "Piccolo."

"Ugh." He rolled his eyes but hugged me. "Old man."

I slugged him on the back, and then subtly searched him for guns, hoping he'd fucking listen and walk with one. "I'm only thirty-seven, and why the hell aren't you packing?"

"Because I'm not a made man, remember? I'm piccolo," he taunted as he sauntered inside.

"This isn't funny, Leo. I have enemies, and you're my only son. They can hurt you to get to me. How are you gonna defend yourself? You won't even have your own bodyguards."

"I'm sure the ones you appointed to follow me around anyway will take care of the job." The fucker winked at me, sinking in the couch, rolling his arms around its back without a care.

I returned to the bar and poured us some drinks. Bourbon—his favorite—for him, and whiskey for me. I put his drink on the coffee table and sipped from mine as I sat across from him.

"I'm not old enough to drink," he mocked.

As if he hadn't been for years? "You're fucking eighteen. That's old enough to do many things. I married your mamma when I was eighteen, already top of my crew—"

"Dad, please. Can we for once not have the Mob talk every time I visit?"

"Why the fuck not?"

"'Cause it'll lead to the Mom talk," he said as a warning, "and we'll both be upset."

My eyes narrowed at him, my jaws clenching. His dark blue eyes held mine in a dare. I took in his face that I'd missed for months. My own son was the spitting image of me, but he was doing everything in his power not to be like me.

He was, though. In so many ways. He just didn't want to admit it.

Violin music streamed in, and my heart immediately banged, dancing to my sweet Angel's melody. My lips twitched with a smile as I turned my gaze toward the window.

"That's nice. Where's it coming from?" Leo asked.

Reflexively, protectively, I rose, and then I gave him my back to block the view before he found out. I didn't want him to see her. I didn't want him to listen. I didn't want anybody to see her or listen. She was mine, and the music she was playing now was for me. After she thought about me while she pleasured herself. Only me.

"A little girl in the opposite building. She's good." She was a lot more than good, and she was no longer a little girl, but he didn't have to know that.

"She is. Does she play every night?"

"Not every night." But I hoped she would.

"Is that why you rented this place? To listen to free music whenever she did?"

I froze for a second. Then I spun, meeting his eyes, reading him. Was that a simple joke or was he trying to drag words out of my mouth? Did he know or suspect anything about me and Angel?

He chuckled. "I mean, look at this place. City line view. Free show. If I had your money, I'd do the same just for those."

"You know damn well you can have my money and more if you want to, but enough of that *talk*." I took another sip from my whiskey. "Since when do you like classical music, Leo?"

"Since now." He winked. "Is she pretty?"

My face burned with rage. My hand clenched around the glass, almost shattering it. "Who?"

"The little girl with the violin."

"The fuck I know? She's *little*."

"For you, old man, but probably not for me." He squinted playfully, cupping the air in front of his chest as if it were tits. "How little are we talking about here?"

Brutto stronzo! I forced a smile on my face when all I wanted was to punch him speechless. I loved him to death, but talking about my girl like she was a piece of meat, talking about my girl at all, even from him, simmered my blood. If he was someone else, he'd be missing, at least, a tongue now.

"Speaking of little girls, are you with anyone?"

"Not really. I mean…nothing serious."

With Leo, that was always a good thing. When things got serious, he… I pushed away the memory of how he ended things with his last girlfriend. "Allora, when are you gonna announce your engagement to Claudia? The Lanzas are waiting for you to set a date."

He pinched the bridge of his nose. "I can't believe you right now."

"Did I say something wrong? She's been promised to you since she was born. The poor girl loves you to bits, and she finished school this year. Her family expects a wedding very soon."

He downed his drink in one go. "I'm not marrying the Lanza girl or any other Mafia princess. Haven't I made that clear months ago?"

A surge of fury burst through me. I went back to my seat and leaned forward. "The *Lanza girl* is Enzio Il Tagliatore Lanza's cousin." Half-sister actually. That family had always been fucked up, but who cared? They were our best allies, and I fucking loved Enzio. He was like my best friend. "When it came to family honor, he had no trouble killing his own twin brother. Do you have any idea what's gonna happen if you don't marry Claudia?"

"Her heart will be broken for a couple of days, but she'll live. The Lanzas will have no trouble finding her another prince, one who is a kiss ass that cares about nothing but Mob power."

I slammed my glass against the table, and he flinched. "Che cazzo?! You think this is a joke? You're not a kid anymore, Leo. Anything you say or do has consequences. You might reject our ways, but you damn well know how it is in our families. She's been engaged to you. No other man has been allowed to think of her as a wife. Leaving her now means one of two things. She's not good or pure enough for you or you've already fucked her. Either way, it'll be a scandal. She won't be good enough for anybody else because nobody likes a hand-me-down."

He shook his head, swearing under his breath.

"A man doesn't break his promises, Leo, and certainly doesn't do something that shameful to a Mafia princess. Bellomo's son won't treat an innocent girl from one of the best families out there with disrespect."

"I didn't make that promise. You did." He got to his feet. "So why don't *you* fucking marry her?"

"Basta!" I hurled my glass against the wall, smashing it to pieces. "I gave you your freedom before because I had no doubt you'd come back to your senses with age, but obviously, you're abusing my patience."

His eyes, no longer mocking, widened at me, his chest heaving.

I ran both my hands in my hair, taking a deep breath. "If this is about college, fine. I'll entertain that, but you're going to become made first before you go. You'll take your omertà, you'll go through with the ceremony, and then you'll marry Claudia after you finish freshman year."

"Or what?" He infuriated me again with his reckless indifference.

"There will be fucking war!" I lunged at him and squeezed his arm. "You think the Lanzas will let you ruin their daughter's reputation without blood?"

He jerked his arm out of my grip, his eyes in flames. "Listen to me, *Don Bellomo*. I'll go to college. I'll have a decent job when I graduate that isn't remotely related to any of our precious family business. I will marry a girl that has nothing to do with mobsters of any kind and the blood that comes with them. If a war is bound to happen because of a promise I never made, so be it. It'll be on your hands, not mine." His mouth curled with a snarl. "Just like Mom's."

CHAPTER 10

Lina

In the shower, as I worked the lather on the side of my neck, the feeling of *his* beard on my skin revisited me. As if it'd left me all night or this morning. *His* scent—masculine, expensive cologne I imagined only celebrities and models in those brand commercials wear—and the brief memory of our encounter stayed with me until I fell asleep, invading my dreams, waking up with me and wouldn't leave my head—and my body—yet.

Closing my eyes, I licked my lip at the heavy throbs between my legs I'd only started to have since last night. To say I was confused was an understatement. How I was feeling about meeting *him* was messing up my mind. I should have been scared, and I was, enraged and alarmed, too. *He* was a dangerous stranger that lured me to a dark corner to do only God knew what before *he* managed to stop or change *his* mind. *He* was older than me. I didn't know how old, but judging from *his* beard, *his* voice, the way *he* spoke, the clothes and cologne, I'd say much older, like *he*'d go to jail for a long time if *he* touched me older. But the main, dominant emotion that climbed on top of everything else was dangerously depraved. For the first time ever I felt...turned on.

As if they had a mind of their own, my hands slipped down to my soapy boobs, feeling my painfully erect nipples, the throbbing and sticky wetness between my thighs intensifying. I'd heard cold showers cooled people off, but even that wouldn't conquer the horny spell a stranger—*my stranger*—had put me under just by breathing on me.

I moaned a swear, my fingers sliding down my hips and then touching the insides of my thighs, the urge for another release too loud to resist. I'd never...*masturbated* before last night. Never wanted to. Never had the privacy to try it even if I had. Just the mention of the word sent me blushing, and in all honesty, shaking. The idea of being touched, even by myself, had been terrifying. Because then I'd have thought of the only man who had ever touched me, and that was horrid.

Yesterday, things changed. Even though *he* didn't really touch me, I found myself thinking of how it'd have felt if *he* had.

God, that was wrong. I shouldn't fantasize about an older murderer guy. A stalker like Nicky said. But I was. The throbbing wouldn't fade. It was increasing, aching.

Don't move.

I trembled as I remembered *his* words, *his* voice, picturing *him* here in the shower with me, water cascading on both our bodies. My finger rubbed over my wetness, and I imagined it was *him*, holding my hand and rubbing it against me, ordering me to stay still while making me come. For *him*.

You smell so good. You're so beautiful.

Gasping hard like I'd been when I felt *his* breath on my skin, when *he* sniffed my hair, now because of the pressure building down my belly, not because of fear, I imagined *his* free hand on my boobs, and *his* mouth I had yet to see on mine.

The orgasm hit me hard and fast. I stifled my moans so Nicky wouldn't hear, but I so wanted to scream. To come was the best feeling ever, and if that was how I felt while I touched myself, how would it feel if a boy was touching me? If a man was making love to me? If *he* was that man?

A knock made me jump. I almost slipped. "What's taking so long? You can't stay in there all day. We have to run to the mall to return those dresses before they close," Nicky said.

I turned off the water and evened my breath, trying to sound as cool and not guilty as possible. "My dress is in the closet, Sis. Just take it and go. You don't have to wait for me."

"You still need to come with me."

"Don't you have the receipts? What do you need me for?"

"I don't have *your* receipt. You never gave it to me."

What? Why would *I* give it to her? She was the one who bought it so she must have had it. Did she lose—

The panic of having to pay twelve hundred dollars because my sister lost the receipt crashed into me for a second before a bigger wave of panic replaced it.

I was too taken by how beautiful the dress was on me to notice yesterday, but the realization came rushing in now. When I wore it, the tags weren't there.

What the hell did that mean?

A loud gasp escaped me. *Could it be…?*

"Lina, you okay? What are you doing in there?"

My heart thrashed, and my body trembled as I grabbed a towel. I covered myself, and my feet faltered their way to the door. When I opened it, her brows were shot high up, her quizzical expression scrutinizing me.

"Nicky…I'm gonna ask you something really stupid, but I want you to answer me anyway."

She snorted. "Okay."

"Who bought my dress?" I held my breath.

Another snort. "You did, silly. You finally succumbed to temptation and did it." Her giggle radiated through her face.

My head spun like I was about to pass out.

"Lina? What's going on? Did you just start your period? You don't look so hot. Is that what it was all about yesterday?" My panic suddenly reached her but for all the wrong reasons. "Oh my God. Is the dress ruined?

Please don't tell me it's ruined." She sounded like she was about to cry.

"No. Don't worry. It's as good as new. But… Yeah, I just…um… I'ma make myself some anise tea and rest a little bit for the cramps to pass." I tried to swallow, but my mouth felt like a rock. "Why don't you go ahead and return your dress, and I'll do mine later today?" I couldn't bear another second of this. If she asked one more question or gave me one more examining look, I was gonna collapse.

"Okay. Yeah sure. I'll go make you that anise tea then I'll go."

I allowed myself to breathe. "Thanks, Sis."

When she left the room, I was out of breath again. Rapidly, I tore through my closet and checked the goddamn dress for the tags, for a note, for any fucking thing left with it.

Nothing.

My heart sank to my knees. Nicky didn't buy me this dress. Someone else did. Someone who had been following me to know I wanted to buy this dress. Who knew where I lived. Who could get in and out our condo without being noticed, whenever he pleased.

Him.

Nicky's footsteps boomed closer. I hid the dress in the closet and sat on the bed, trying so hard to stop shaking.

She set the cup on the nightstand, and then she kissed me. "You're gonna catch a cold like this. Get dressed, sweetie."

I faked a smile and nodded once.

"Are you sure it's just your period?" she asked, concern dripping from her voice. "You've been acting really strange. Did something happen? You never told me where you went on your own last night when I left you."

I thought about telling Nicky the truth. I hated lying to her, and after knowing that *he* could break into our condo that easily, I was more scared than ever. But if I told her, she'd freak out. She'd do anything to keep me safe, including leaving everything behind and go somewhere else where she might think *he* couldn't find us.

My sister was finally happy. New home. New school. I couldn't ruin things for her now.

"I went out for some air and got lost. It was just for a few minutes." That felt like a lifetime. "Then I found the signs and followed them back to the auditorium."

Disappointment crossed her face as she nodded. I could tell she didn't believe me. "Okay. Just know that you can tell me anything. I'm always here for you."

"I know. I'm here for you, too."

She smiled and kissed me again. Then she left, and I crumbled on the floor, sobbing, panicking. "I'm such an idiot. How could I think of *him* in any other way than *he* was? A freakin' psycho stalker."

A horrible thought flickered in my head. What if *he* was watching me right now?

I bolted upright, my eyes darting around, right and left, up and down, searching for cameras. "Can you see me? Are you watching me in my own bedroom?" Fear turned into rage as I rose to my feet. "You're a coward. Do you hear me? You're a fucking coward." I held my towel tight to my body, afraid it might fall, afraid *he*'d see me naked. Afraid *he* might already have. "Show yourself, you piece of shit!"

My head and I spun in endless circles, silence and fury my only company. "Is that what I am to you? A game you watch? A toy you dress up and undress for your amusement? A property you plan to buy? You think you can buy me with a dress?" I stormed inside the closet and yanked the stupid thing out. I tossed it on the floor and stomped on it. "Here it is. Your precious gift." It wasn't just the dress, though. It was all the other birthday presents, too. I touched my ear, pulling the earrings, almost tearing my earlobes, and threw the expensive, disgusting jewelry at the window.

The violin peeked from my chair, and I grabbed it. In a full swing, my arms rose behind me to smash it, but I froze, my heart shattering. This instrument was more than an object. It was my only solace. My best friend. I couldn't just kill it.

Instead, I crumbled again on the chair, tears burning my face. "Why? How could you do this to me? How could you hurt me like that? I thought you were my savior, my protector. How could you violate me like that?"

It wasn't like *he* hadn't broken into my bedroom before. I had no doubt now *he* had broken into our old house, and *he* was the one leaving me the presents in my Bellomo dorm. As crazy and wrong as it may sound, I didn't mind that *he* did. I even liked it. Loved every moment of *his* attention. Adored that *he* cared. I believed that was *his* way of telling me *he* still remembered me. Letting me know that I mattered to *him*, and *he* was still out there watching over me.

The little girl *he* had to save.

But breaking into this condo for God knew how many times, leaving me a sexy dress that made me look like a woman, not a little girl…

Yesterday showed me how much of an idiot I'd been. All this time I was nothing but a body *he* thought *he* could buy when it was ripe enough.

Tears flowed in abundance now. The pain tightening my chest was almost as bad as the ache my father carved inside me. Nicky was right. Her words echoed in my head. *Nobody does stuff like that for people like us without expecting something in return either. It's been four years. Don't you think he'd have showed up by now, asking for whatever the hell he wanted in return from us? From you?*

He did. *He* showed up yesterday to claim what *he* thought *he* owned.

I did owe *him*. A lot. *He* saved me from the sicko monster that was supposed to protect me. From guys like *him*. How fucking twisted was that?

And now, even though *he* didn't say it or make any clear demands, I knew exactly how *he* wanted me to pay for *his* favor. *He* didn't need words. The heat in *his* breath, in *his* voice, in *his* almost touch that even now was wreaking havoc on my body was enough.

He killed my father to save me. *He*—not a miracle—put me and my sister in a good home and school. *He* bought me expensive clothes and jewelry. Even my violin. All this to have one thing.

Me.

No. My body.

"Why did you stop? Why didn't you make me pay? Why didn't you collect your debt?" I asked the emptiness, the silence driving me crazy. "I need answers goddammit."

Ci vediamo, my sweet Angel.

His dark promise rang in my head, taunting me. Then it suddenly hit me. *He* was toying with me, messing with my head. Yesterday wasn't about a claim. It was another battle in *his* psychological war that *he*, again, won.

The gifts—one of them was an *angel* necklace because that was how *he* liked to call me for God's sake —were to gain my attention, to make me know *he* was there, to make me think about *him* and never forget. Last night was to make me know what *he* desired.

To mindfuck me so I'd desire *him*, too.

To make me explore that side I didn't dare tread until *he* opened its door for me. To do it while I thought of *him*. My dark, forbidden fantasy.

And it worked. *He* knew I'd never been touched by anyone but my father. *He* knew I was desperate to replace the horrible memories with better ones that involved another man.

Him.

He made sure of it. *He* fucked my mind so when the time came, when we met again like *he*'d promised, when *he* decided to claim me, I'd be ready for *him*. Wanting *him*.

I fell into *his* trap like a moth to a flame. I did everything *he* wanted me to do. Consciously, and now unconsciously, my body would always associate *him* with desire. I'd always want and crave *him* even if *he* was the last person I should ever think of in that way.

Little had I known four years ago I wasn't really saved. Life had only replaced one monster by another.

CHAPTER 11

Tino

I should punish her.

She was being a brat, destroying my gifts, comparing me to that fucker…

I didn't install any bugs or cameras in her room, and I didn't listen to a word she was saying when she threw that tantrum, but it wasn't hard to guess. Why else would she be so upset? It couldn't be the dress. It was just another one of the presents she was well aware I was the one bringing, one she annoyingly ruined.

Didn't she know how much I loved her in it?

I did have access to a live feed of her room now. After she bought a nanny cam to keep me away, she left me no choice. I had to make one of my soldiers hack into her feed, broadcast whatever the fuck I wanted her to see when I was in the condo.

"Nothing is going to keep me away from you, Angel." I almost snapped my brush in half as I told the unfinished painting. The face that had been haunting me awake and asleep.

I hadn't touched a brush and a palette in years, not since my wife died. The moment Angel and I had together was worthy of my time, though, worthy of being captured and framed eternally.

Anger wouldn't leave me be, though. How could she think I'd hurt her the way her father did? "Haven't I told you I'm nothing like him? What else can I do to prove to you no one will ever treat you better than I will, no one will ever protect or care for you or your needs and desires like me?"

She deserved a nice, heavy spanking for what she did. However, I must admit it wasn't entirely her fault. Part of it was mine. I shouldn't have talked to her the other night. I shouldn't have talked to her at all until the time was right for me to take her. She was nowhere near ready.

Still, she should have believed me.

For that, she deserved the spanking and more. But I wouldn't punish her for it. Not yet.

I'd always been with her, even when she didn't know. Everything I'd done was so that she could have the best, yet somehow that night, I left her in ruins.

I wouldn't make the same mistake twice.

"The next time you see me, Angel, there's no slowing down or turning back." I stroked the colors of her beautiful hair. "You'll be melting in my arms. You'll finally know it's the only place where you belong. I'll make sure of it."

CHAPTER 12

Lina

My seventeenth Birthoween—like Nicky liked to call it—couldn't come any slower.

When we used to live at Bellomo, I never waited or cared for my birthday. Being born, to a father like mine, wasn't something to celebrate or be happy about. Besides, everybody was busy with Halloween costumes and silly pranks. It was one of the few days they got to leave campus. Nobody cared that it was my birthday, too.

Except for two people. Nicky…and *him*.

My sister would always bring my favorite cupcakes, chocolate with rainbow frosting, and we'd devour them along with whatever candy our friends would donate to our party for two at the dorm. She'd give me her present. Then we'd go for a walk and watch people have their fun. We never joined, though. Wearing scary costumes, watching horror movies and telling scary stories weren't our thing. We'd had enough horror to last a lifetime, and I knew Nicky wanted to make that day all about me. A celebration of the living, not the dead.

Then I'd go home and find *his* gift on the bed.

This year was different. Nicky took me out to an expensive restaurant where her new friends at college once had invited her. The place was far more elite than we'd ever be. One look at the menu, and my heart shrank. A meal here cost more than what we both spent on food for a whole month.

When I looked at her, moon-eyed, she just giggled and told me to order whatever I wanted. This birthday was special because we were finally free to do whatever we wanted. We were no longer locked in a boarding school with a curfew.

I did as she asked without arguing so I wouldn't disappoint her, but I didn't want any of that. It seemed like I didn't appreciate my freedom as much as she did. I'd happily go back to Bellomo. At least, *he* remembered me there.

It was pathetic by all means. After the awards ceremony, I was mad and scared. I'd spent weeks looking over my shoulder, having a mini heart attack every time I opened the closet or the locker or the bathroom. I checked my nanny cam feed around the clock. I looked under the bed every night like a child before I managed to sleep. I was living in a constant state of fear.

Then months passed, and the fear changed into something more awful when I realized nobody was watching me anymore. There was no sign of *him* anywhere. *He* was gone. And I was no longer afraid. I should have been happy, at peace, able to return to my fear free life, but I was angry and miserable that *he* left.

Because I fucking missed *him*.

Pathetic and stupid and crazy and awful, but I couldn't help it. I missed my murderous stalker who wanted me as his fucktoy.

"Why aren't you eating, Lina?" Nicky asked with a mouthful of steak.

I stared at my plate of salmon pasta that I barely touched. I didn't have much of an appetite. I just wanted my cupcake, and the reminder that *he* didn't forget me.

How could *he* abandon me just like that? How could *he* forget all about me all of a sudden when *he* did everything to carve *himself* in my memory forever?

Part of me—all of me—had been waiting for today because maybe, just maybe, when I'd go back home, I'd find *his* gift on the bed. I'd know that *he* didn't abandon me. I'd know *he* still cared and remembered.

"I'm sorry, Nicky. I'm just not that hungry."

"It's okay. Save room for dessert. That you're eating. You can't say no to cupcakes."

I managed to smile. "Now you're talking."

She gestured for the waiter, and he brought the chocolate with rainbow frosting cupcake, a candle in the middle. He lit it and wished me a happy birthday before he left.

Nicky sang for me and asked me to make a wish. I blinked for a second. I didn't make wishes. I wasn't a girl that her wishes came true. Not even when that wish was as twisted and crazy as wanting a psycho stalker to break into her home.

But I did anyway, wishing for what no normal person wished ever, and then I blew out the candle.

"I won't ask what you wished for so it'll come true." She winked and waved for the waiter to bring the check.

"It's been taken care of, ma'am." He smiled and wished me a happy birthday again.

Nicky frowned at him. "What do you mean? Who took care of it?"

"It's our thing at Leo's. Ladies who have birthdays on Halloween dine for free."

"Why was it never mentioned before?"

"We don't advertise it so it won't be abused. Excuse me, ma'am. Have a nice evening." He hurried away.

"Wow. That was just wow. You lucky dog." She linked arms with me, giggling. "Aren't you a little bit more psyched that we came here tonight? Now we don't have to live on noodles and mac and cheese for the rest of the year. Is that what you wished for? A free meal?" She giggled again.

I chuckled humorlessly, checking the nanny cam feed on my phone and seeing everything was just as I'd left it. "No. I didn't wish for that." I slipped the phone back in my pocket as we exited the restaurant, kids and teenagers in Halloween costumes, jack-o'-lanterns and thunder greeting us. Gosh, I hated thunderstorms.

"Well, I bet whatever you wished for wasn't better than a free meal at Leo's. Did you know this place is owned by Sebastiano Bellomo himself? He named it after his son. It's really weird that a man like him has only one child. They say his wife died a few years ago in a shooting."

"That's so sad," I mumbled, waiting for our late Uber. *Please arrive before it rains.*

She droned on about how she believed the Bellomos were really the Mafia and that shooting was a retaliation of sorts. She also believed that even if the wife was dead, a handsome guy like Sebastiano Bellomo must have had many bastards.

I didn't argue about her source of information. She'd never seen the guy to know whether he was handsome or not or to be so sure he was a gangster. I no longer cared whether our benefactors were the bloody Mafia or angels sent from heaven, though. Who was I to judge when I'd wished for a stalker to come stalk me back and was upset he didn't?

All I wanted was to go home and cry myself to sleep.

My dark stranger was gone forever.

CHAPTER 13

Lina

The next morning, I woke up with the decision to never think about *him* again. Of course, I betrayed myself an hour later when I opened my locker, hoping that *he* might have left my present here instead of at home.

When I found nothing, I swore at how stupid I was and went to class.

He was really gone, and it was for the best. I was finally safe—the safest I'd been in seventeen years—and free to live my life however I wanted. I'd focus on my lessons, rehearsals and maybe replace my unhealthy fantasies with more normal ones about that cute boy I kept seeing around. At the mall, at the bakery, at the Laundromat a few blocks from our building, and here at Bellomo.

He never spoke to me, but he always stared, giving me a smirk.

At first, with everything that had been going on, I thought he was just another creep. Then, because of how desperate I'd become, I thought it could be *him, my creep*. Except that boy was about Nicky's age—he couldn't have killed my father when he was only fourteen—and he didn't have a beard.

Putting all paranoia and craziness aside, I convinced myself he must have been just a boy who lived close by to be around so often. When I saw him at Bellomo, I guessed he must have had a brother or a sister here. Or a girlfriend. A boyfriend?

That would be such a waste. He was so beautiful with dark, thick, hair that curled at the end in the sexiest way ever. Dark blue eyes. A nose and cheekbones that belonged on a Roman coin. Strong jawline and lips that danced with mischief every time he gave me that smirk.

For months after my birthday, our continuous, accidental, silent encounters sedated my sadness and took my mind off *him*, but I never forgot. *He* could forget all *he* wanted, but I would never forget.

Sometimes, despite the promise I'd made myself, I still played for *him*, even though *he* wasn't listening. Today was one of those days. When I held my violin to play at Bellomo's junior recital, I didn't see the students or their parents or the teachers or Nicky. I closed my eyes and pretended *he* was sitting in the front row, wearing a dashing tux as if we were at the opera, not at a school theatre, *his* intense eyes I'd barely seen before were on me, only me. I imagined they were ocean blue, drowning, dangerous and ever so inviting like a deadly siren, and they'd twinkle with how much *he* loved my music. How much *he* loved…

I shook my head, my fingers turning firmer on the strings, angrier. I didn't open my eyes, but in my head, I, too, was holding *his* gaze, telling *him* everything I'd been stifling for months with my violin. Every note spilled a forbidden secret. Every stroke was an unspoken emotion. Every slur was me and *him* and the dark.

My heart squeezed with the final note, my eyes, too. As if they were afraid to open so *he* wouldn't disappear. As if they were saying, "One more moment, please."

My breath snagged in my chest, and something wet dropped on the back of my hand. My own tears.

Great. I was crying, in front of all these people who were actually watching me. I forced my eyes open, and a round of applause along with a standing ovation received me. The people were real, and they loved my performance, and I was crying, terribly missing a horrible man that, to most people, only existed in my head.

I took my bow and ran to hide backstage. In the pitch black darkness, I rested my back against a wall, banging a fist. Tears wouldn't let me be. I hadn't cried in months, not since my birthday, and now they flooded out of my eyes.

"I hate you," I whispered. "Why don't you fucking leave me alone?"

"I'm sorry."

A gasp ripped from my chest, my heart pounding frantically. I was so startled I couldn't focus to recognize the voice. Was it *his*? Was *he* here?

My head whipped right and left, my entire body tingling with anticipation. "Who's there?"

"A big fan." The voice oddly carried the same depth of *his*, only more cheerful, playful.

Footsteps approached, and suddenly I was blinded by a burst of light. "What the hell?"

"I'm so sorry again. I didn't mean to scare you."

That was definitely not *him*. *He* would never apologize like this. *He* did whatever *he* wanted, took whatever *he* wanted without permission or care.

The light moved away from my face and became a spot on the floor. Ridiculously expensive, black, Italian shoes and a pair matching of slacks appeared. As I looked up, I saw flowers, and then a familiar smirk hit me.

The cute boy's.

Only now he wasn't cute at all. He looked so creepy with the flashlight from his phone focused on his face, like he'd just come out of a cheesy horror movie.

"You sure? Looks like it's exactly what you're trying to do here," I said nonchalantly, disappointment dulling my senses.

He laughed. I didn't mean to say what I said as a joke, though. "Can we please move somewhere more…" He laughed again, nervous now.

"Yeah." Wiping my face, I led him to the spot next to the dressing rooms where there were enough lights to make an elephant sweat.

"These are for you." He handed me the bouquet, a charming smile on his face. No more mischievous smirking.

Dazed for a second—nobody had ever brought me flowers before—I stared at the beautiful arrangement of white and red roses. Then I took them, my hand shaking. "Thank you so much." It was weird that when he was acting like a creep I could look him in the eye, and now that he was being nice, my cheeks burned, and my gaze fell on the floor. "Is that the part when I smell the roses and it turns out you sprayed them with chloroform so you could kidnap me?"

When he didn't respond, I looked up. His smile had vanished, and his brow inched as he swallowed.

"Actually *that* was a joke." I shook my head. "I'm terrible at it. Obviously." *Nice work, Lina.*

"It takes at least five minutes of inhaling something soaked in chloroform to become unconscious. You need something else mixed with it like alcohol or diazepam to make it work."

"And the fact that you know that is not creepy at all..."

"Oh my God, I was just trying to... I'm..." He threw his hands in the air, chuckling. "Can we start over?"

"Yes, please."

"Thank you." He wiped his forehead, sweat beading it. "I came today to listen to your recital. I loved your performance. You were amazing out there."

"Thanks...um... You came to watch *my* recital? Like specially?"

"Yeah."

"Wow. Okay. I thought you were here because your relative is playing, too."

"What relative?"

"The one you come to Bellomo for...or is it a girlfriend? Don't say it. Boyfriend?" *Shoot me now.*

He just gaped at me, and then he rested his hands on his hips, his suit jacket moving a little to the back, and now I noticed the defined chest and abdomen muscles under his white shirt. "I haven't met any girl that rendered me speechless quite often like you have, Miss Baldi."

I blinked, not sure what he meant. "Lina. My name is Lina."

"I know, and Lina, you should know I've been single for about eight months. I never had, never will have a boyfriend because I'm not gay, at all. I come here because I'm an alumnus, not because I have any current relatives in Bellomo…and to be completely honest, I use those alumni meetings and events to come see you."

The heat from my cheeks and the lights traveled all over my body. "Oh."

"You look even more beautiful when you blush." His voice dropped an octave, and I somehow managed to blush even more.

I stammered—no, I uttered incoherent sounds that must have made me look as if I was choking.

"Are you okay?" he asked.

"I…I just…I wasn't prepared for this. I'd never been with a boy or…" I should just die right now. "I can't believe I'm saying this out loud. I'm gonna shut up. Forever."

"Are you telling me that no one has ever told you you're beautiful before?"

Two. Both of them said it to take something that should have never been theirs. Both of them broke me beyond repair. My eyes burned, so I pushed the thought before I'd cry in front of him. I'd embarrassed myself enough. "Why do you use the alumni meetings as an excuse to see me? It's not like you don't see me around outside school."

His eyes grew dark. "It's not enough."

A strange tingling hit my spine, pleasant yet uncomfortable. "What?"

His smirk returned. "Like I said, I'm a big fan. I plan to be at every one of your performances, and by that I don't just mean recitals."

"What else?"

"Walking to class, eating, going shopping, anything and everything," he stepped forward, his fragrance a blend of a forest and something delicious, something you felt guilty to crave, "because everything you do, Lina bella, is art."

"You are…" Intense? Weird? Confusingly hot? "…Italian."

He flashed his teeth. "And your biggest fan ever."

Smooth. I had zero experience, but I had no doubt he was a player. And creepy. The guy could smooth talk his way out of anything, obviously. He didn't need the recital as an excuse to talk to me. Why did he prefer to wait all this time, staring, *accidentally* appearing everywhere I went? Creepy. Exactly my type. "What do I call my *only* fan?"

"Leo."

"Just Leo?"

"For now."

Definitely creepy. It seemed to be the one trait I couldn't *not* be attracted to in a guy. "Secretive much?"

"I'd be more than happy to reveal my secrets to you, one for every time you give me the honor of taking you out."

I blinked until I got a headache. "Take me out?"

A shadow crossed his dark blue eyes, and for some reason they resembled the image I'd created for *his* eyes. Drowning, dangerous and incredibly beautiful. "Unless my suspicions are right, and today's performance was meant for a special someone. Someone you want to be with."

My chest heaved, and tears blurred my gaze for a second, the reminder heavy on my heart. "I… I gotta go." I turned and started down the hall. I waved the bouquet without looking at him. "Thank you for the flowers."

CHAPTER 14

Lina

On Sundays, Nicky didn't get up until noon. We didn't have breakfast. Brunch was more like it, and it was on me. She worked so hard at school and at the coffee shop. Even though her scholarship paid for everything, she always worked extra shifts, trying to save enough money for the next few years. Architecture school was going to get much harder and time consuming, and she wouldn't be able to keep the job with her studies.

She never took more than half a day off—on Sundays. It was the only time she rested. The least I could do was make her a nice meal. Well, buy her one with my allowance. My cooking skills were disastrous.

It wasn't raining this morning, thank God, and Sunday farmers market was on. I picked up some strawberries, avocados, cottage cheese and organic eggs, Nicky's favorites for toast four ways, along with a beetroot and a couple of radishes for the shaved salad. That I could make.

I headed to the bakery for salmon bagels, dark chocolate cannoli and Nicky's pineapple upside-down cake. I hated pineapples, but she could live on them for the rest of her life. They were sweet, but whenever I ate them, they never stayed down.

The door chimed with more customers coming in as I stood in line. This place was always busy. It was good I got here before ten. Last week, they were out of cannoli by then. Asking the cashier to add one piece of cherry cobbler for me, the smell too yummy to resist, I opened my purse and got out the cash.

"Put our orders together."

My head jerked up, and Leo's smirk met me. His arm extended toward the cashier with a credit card in hand.

I shook my head at the cashier. "Please don't."

"Scusi. It's already done," he said with a heavy Italian accent, smiling at Leo.

Leo took the bags and his coffee. "Grazie, Giuseppe."

I glared at them both. "So you know the cashier, and he lets you cut in line like this?"

"Something like that." Leo gestured for me to follow him to a table.

I moved to the side only so I wouldn't hold the line. "I'm not sitting with you, and you can't keep doing this."

"Doing what?"

"Bumping into me wherever I go."

"Then you shouldn't turn me down every time I ask you out. You leave me no choice."

I rolled my eyes. "Can you give me my stuff please? I gotta go."

He held the bag up as high as his arms allowed, which was way beyond my reach. "Come get it."

Sometimes I hated it when boys had to be a foot taller than the girls they were interested in. It was sexy and even necessary, but now it was just unfair. "You know I can't unless I borrow a ladder, so please…"

"I'll give it to you on one condition."

"I know the condition, and I can't. Please stop being a douche."

"Why can't you? You're single. I checked. And you obviously like me, too."

"You're so full of yourself, Leo *For Now.*"

He chuckled. "Look me in the eye and tell me, without lying, that you don't like me, and I'll never ask again."

I wasn't that good of a liar, and one dip in these blue eyes would ruin my chances before I uttered a single word. "Why are you going through all this trouble for a girl like me? It's been like what, six months now since you started our accidental, silent meet-cutes? Aren't you tired? Since the recital, you've asked me out eight times already, and my answer has always been no. Why won't you go date someone…like you?"

"I'm not tired, and I don't want someone like me or someone not like me whatever that means." His arm dropped, and his gaze, dark and intense, held me in place. "I only want you."

I faltered back a step, his fragrance overpowering the delicious smells of the bakery, his gaze sending a sweet shiver down my spine. "I…um…" I closed my eyes, snapping myself out of his invisible hold. "Unlucky for you, I don't date. And don't ask me why. It's just the way it is."

It wasn't like I didn't want to give boys a try. I wasn't like Nicky. I needed to give normal a chance, for my sanity, at least. To get over whatever the hell *he* did to me. I couldn't even put a name to it, but it ruined me. A healthy relationship would be nice. Therapeutic.

But I just didn't know how to do normal or if I'd ever be ready. A boy like Leo, an experienced, rich, college boy who was obviously out of my league, couldn't be my first.

When he said nothing for a while, I reluctantly opened my eyes to measure his reaction. He just stood there, staring at me, studying me, and then he breathed out. "Va bene. You don't date, so we won't date."

Relief brushed me for a second before he opened his mouth again.

"But you do drink coffee, so you can have that with me." He didn't wait for my response. He walked and set his cup and my bag on the table, mumbling something in Italian—I understood enough to gather it was a coffee order—at the cashier.

"C'mon, Leo. Take a hint."

"I did. I stopped asking, didn't I?" He pulled a chair out for me. "It's just coffee, Lina. Doesn't mean anything."

I knew it did, but one coffee wouldn't hurt. Right? It might finally convince him I was a lost cause, and he'd stop trying. I hated how I had to turn him down every time. It needed to end. "I can only stay for ten minutes." I took the seat he offered.

A server brought my coffee, and I thanked him, keeping it in the space between Leo and me as a shield on the table. He gave me his usual staring, not drinking his either.

"Are you gonna say something?" I wasn't planning on doing the talking, but this was weird. The staring, even though I'd gotten used to it and maybe even started to like it, made me nervous and self-conscious. There was no way a boy like him would notice a girl like me, let alone like her that much. He was the full package, and I was…well, me.

"I like to look at you. You're the most beautiful girl I've ever seen."

My face warmed despite me, and he smiled. He loved to say things like that so I'd blush for his amusement.

I cleared my throat. "Where do you go to college?"

"I study Economics at UChicago."

"And why have I never seen you at Bellomo before this year if you're an alumnus?"

"Because I'd probably left before you joined. How long have you been there?"

"Five years."

"Yeah, I transferred a year before that. I…" He let out a deep breath. "Something terrible happened to my family that year. I needed to get away. My father and I moved to San Francisco for a while."

I can relate. "I'm sorry. Family tragedies are the worst." I didn't want to pry or ask for more details. That might lead him to ask about *my* family tragedy. I wasn't ready to share.

He stared back at me, but this time it was different. It was knowing.

"Oh my God." I looked down, shaking my head. "You know about my father, don't you?"

"There's nothing to be ashamed of, Lina. With all due respect, he was a scumbag that deserved to be brutally murdered."

I gritted my teeth, grabbing my bakery bag to leave. "I'm not ashamed of it. It was just nice, for one freaking second, to talk to someone who didn't know about the worst thing that ever happened to me, the one thing that defined me everywhere, made everyone see me as *that* girl."

"It doesn't define you, not to me," he said fast as if that would stop me from leaving my chair. "Lina, please, you have to believe me. This isn't what I see when I look at you."

I cocked a brow in a challenge, lifting my chin. "Then what do you see in the poor, orphaned and abused program kid, rich boy?"

He leaned forward, countering my move with equal determination to win. "Not that either. I see a girl, smart and beautiful inside and out, one that deserves to have anything and anyone she wants because she's no less than any other girl, one that deserves to be loved for who and what she is. The only problem is, she doesn't see herself the way I see her, but I won't stop until she does."

My lips twitched and my nostrils flared. This could be one of the most beautiful things any girl wanted to hear, but for me, it was infuriating and condescending. Nicky's words echoed in my head. *We don't need boys or husbands or any of that shit. We don't need saviors. Only each other. Baldi girls versus the world.* "So what, you think you can save me? From myself?" I mocked, but on the inside, I was shaking like a leaf with fury and pain.

"Do you need saving? I would if you did, and not just from yourself."

"What the hell is that supposed to mean?"

"There's something that scares you, Lina. I don't know what it is, and it's driving me crazy. It's the real reason you don't want to let someone in or open up your heart."

If only he knew… "You don't know what you're talking about."

"I know I can protect you. From anything."

"Not from *him*." I mumbled under my breath, the words falling out of my mouth reflexively yet fortunately too low for anybody to hear.

Or so I thought.

The darkness that swam in his gaze meant he did hear it. "Who's *him*?" he seethed.

My eyes widened, fear crippling me. I'd never told anyone before about the day we met. I'd been lying to Nicky about it for months so she wouldn't know. Why the hell did my tongue slip now? I should have never mentioned *him*. Ever. Especially when Leo reacted that way. I knew he was intense, but he gave the word a new level.

"Nobody." I gulped, stepping away. "I gotta go."

"Lina, wait," he said as a warning, his hand grabbing my arm before I could leave the table.

My bulging eyes dropped to his grip. "Let go of me." I trembled with fear and rage, ready to scream if he didn't comply.

Swiftly, he removed his hand and put it in the space between us in surrender. "I'm sorry. But you can't just say something like this and leave. You gotta tell me who he is so I can protect you."

"Protect me? Who the hell do you think you are? What, your wealthy family is friends with some cop and you think they can keep any bad guy away because of it?" I snorted. "The cops didn't save me from my father, Leo. It was the bad guy who did. If, and only if, there was another bad guy out there I was scared of, it'd take someone even worse to save me from them."

Much to my surprise, he nodded, unfazed. "I agree. That's why *I* can protect you."

"What do you mean?" I asked warily, my eyes tightening at him.

"When you asked me about my last name, I didn't answer you because…maybe you'll get the wrong idea. You're not the only one that is defined by her family, Lina." He wet his lips and sighed. "My dad is…" He trailed off suddenly, his gaze wide, staring at something over my shoulder. "Dad?"

I glanced at the spot distracting him. There was nothing but the other customers at their tables and a bearded man in a coat and suit, sunglasses covering half of his face, looking for a free table I presumed. My gaze returned to Leo. "Yes? Who's your dad?"

"That will be me."

My heart jumped in my throat at the voice startling me from behind. A voice that sounded a lot like Leo's but deeper, older, and just like Leo's voice once reminded me of *his*, this one did the same cruel trick.

I whirled, and the man with the sunglasses was standing a few inches away. He took a couple more steps closer, and suddenly there was nothing I could hear but the echo of his footsteps, everything moving in slow motion. He was one of those people that owned the space they were in by just existing. My heart thrashed when, standing this close to him, I noticed he was about the same build as *he*, and he did have a beard like *he* did.

Could he possibly be…?

A small smile tugged at the corners of his mouth as he took off his shades and the scarf on top of his coat. "Good morning."

His Italian—steamy hot—accent snapped me out of my delusions. *He* didn't have an accent when *he* spoke in English, and this man's voice wasn't as dark and crippling as *his* whisper. Just because he was over six feet and had a beard didn't mean it was *him*.

I shook my head, swearing at my own brain that was tricking me to believe *he* was still there, looking for *him* in every man I saw. First Leo and now his dad.

This is Leo's dad? He looked too young to have an almost twenty-year-old. He, despite the crazy resemblance, was more like Leo's older brother, who somehow was even hotter.

His gaze shifted toward Leo. "Is she all right?"

I realized he'd greeted me, and I didn't say anything. How rude! So much for leaving a good first impression. "I'm sorry. Good morning to you, Mister…Leo's dad." *Mister Leo's dad? People like me should never speak. Ever.*

He cocked a brow at my silliness, but this was his son's fault. Had he told me, I wouldn't have sounded so clueless.

He looked at Leo again, reproach darkening the breathtaking blue of his eyes, and set his scarf and shades on the table. "I see what's going on here. Are you going to properly introduce us or should I?"

Leo took a breath before he gestured between us. "Dad, Lina. Lina, this is my dad…Sebastiano Bellomo."

Shut the front door! "Be-bellomo?" My eyes widened until they hurt. "Like…our Bellomo Academy Bellomo?"

"Yes, your Bellomo. The one and only," Mr. Bellomo said tightly. Then he took my hand ever so gently and lifted it to his mouth, taking me by surprise. His lips sent a jolt of tingling heat all over me as they brushed the back of my hand with a lingering kiss.

I shuddered, and he smirked in response. It wasn't like Leo's mischievous smirks but rather…mesmerizing. "Piacere," he said.

Lightheaded, my jaw fell. "Huh?"

His smirk turned into a full smile that made my heart flutter. "It means pleasure to meet you."

I giggled. I freaking giggled. I never giggled. Clearing my throat, I realized my trembling hand was still in Mr. Bellomo's. I should withdraw it and take my eyes off him. I should do anything other than pretending to forget my hand in the warmth of his, staring at him like I'd never seen a guy before, and giggling like an idiot.

"Yeah…sure…yeah…me too…Mr. Bellomo." My voice rose with his name, a reminder he was the owner of my school for God's sake, the man that made our lives and many other kids' lives better, much better…and Leo's father. God, Leo. I forgot he was even there.

My head jerked toward him, pulling my hand away, but Mr. Bellomo put his other hand on top of mine with the same tenderness, ruining my chance to withdraw now that my hand was caged between both of his. I noticed his visible tattoos, an angel covering the back of his hand and little birds one on every other finger. More shapes extended on his wrist, but most were hidden under his sleeve for me to make out what they were. Mr. Bellomo was cool and badass. Must have been a bad boy when he was young.

"I see my son has left that tiny little detail out when he introduced himself. He has the habit of doing that quite often."

"Dad, what are you—"

"Please sit," Mr. Bellomo interrupted Leo, ignoring his son as if he was air, looking at me. "I hope you don't mind if I sit with you for a few minutes. This is probably my only chance to get to know my son's girlfriend."

"I'm *not* his girlfriend…I…uh…" I jabbed a thumb back at the door, the bag crumbling and crunching in my grip, "was just leaving."

"Lina, please, we're not done," Leo pleaded, but I didn't want to listen. I was mad at him for invading my life like this, knowing everything about me when he wouldn't even tell me who he was. He wasn't just some rich boy. He was a Bellomo for fuck's sake. No matter what he said or how hard he'd try to convince me, I was literally *that* girl to him. The poor, orphaned and abused charity case his own father sponsored.

Now he wanted to find out the only secret I had left? No, thank you. I'd keep that to myself.

"Yes, we are. There's nothing to talk about." I'd storm out of here if his dad wasn't holding my hand hostage. Why the hell hadn't I pulled it away yet? I didn't even like to be touched. When Leo gripped my arm, I freaked out, and now his father was holding my hand for probably a whole minute, and all I wanted was for it to last even more?

"Listen, if you don't wanna tell me, fine." Leo switched his gaze toward his father, pursing his lips. He seemed to be struggling with something. "But you can tell Dad."

"What the..." I bit my tongue on a curse. I wanted to scream. Was he out of his mind? I was beyond embarrassed and angry. "You have no right to do this. You don't even know me, Leo. Why would I tell your dad…anything?" I finally managed to get my hand back. This was so weird. This family was weird. I was weird.

"As much as I hate to say it, *he* can actually help," Leo said through his teeth.

"Help with what?" Mr. Bellomo asked, taking my hand again, this time leading me back to the chair I was sitting in. I had no choice but to sit, out of respect, forever in debt to his generosity. He took the seat next to me, and again he cradled my hand inside his firm yet gentle ones. "Are you in trouble, young lady? Because if you are, I'd very much like to help. It's what I do."

Great. Just great. Assuming I could ever tell anyone about *him* without flipping my world upside down, risking everybody's lives—*he* was a psycho murderer whether I liked it or not—Mr. Bellomo would be the last person I'd tell. He'd tell the people at school. I'd live the rest of my junior year and my senior year in endless shit.

Much to my dismay, Mr. Bellomo's caring gaze and tender touch, those of a concerned parent, those I'd never seen or felt with my own father, tugged at me, urging me to spill my heart out and confide in this man.

No. I couldn't do that to him. I owed him a lot. I couldn't jeopardize his life. "I appreciate it, Mr. Bellomo. You've helped us more than anyone ever has, but I'm not in trouble or—"

"She's afraid of someone, a man, so much she wouldn't dare tell anybody about," Leo interrupted, and I fixed him with a death glare. I'd never wanted to slap someone more than I wanted to slap him right now.

Mr. Bellomo blinked once, and then he leaned back, abandoning my hand. Okay. I understood. Nobody should get in trouble on my account. Even if I was asking for his help and he backed down, I couldn't blame him. Just the mention of *him* was enough to make any sane man, even a powerful one like Mr. Bellomo, bail.

"Please excuse my son." He, too, glared at Leo. "I think I taught you better than to interrupt a lady like that." He shook his head, his incredible gaze returning to me. "However, if that is true…Angelina…then Leo is right." His eyes grew hard, dark, and suddenly dangerous. "I'm the only man you can tell."

CHAPTER 15

Lina

My gaze traveled between Leo and Mr. Bellomo back and forth as my head spun with questions and assumptions.

Why would Mr. Bellomo say he was the only one I could tell? Why did Leo say he agreed when I told him only a bad guy could save me? Why would he think his dad and he could?

My mind ran in circles, reaching one conclusion every time. Could Nicky be right? Could the rumors about the Bellomos be real?

Oh my God. The Bellomos were the Mob, and I was sitting at the same table with them.

"Can I please go?" My voice shook. Cold sweat trickled down the back of my neck.

"No," Leo said, and my heart sank. My eyes darted around, looking for help. Then I remembered Leo knew the Italian cashier who obeyed him without a second thought. Fuck. The Bellomos probably owned this whole place, like they owned everything else in the city.

"Oddio. What are you doing? Can't you see what's going on here? You're scaring her more than she already is." For the second time Mr. Bellomo—Don Bellomo—scolded Leo for me. His eyes locked on my face, tender and caring. "Nobody is keeping you here against your will, Angelina. But if you're in danger, young lady, I can't just let you leave. You're a student at my school. Your protection is a part of my responsibility."

How could someone so beautiful, so kind, be a notorious criminal? Why would my heart skip a beat when he said my name in that accent? How the hell did he know my name? "How did you know my name is Angelina?" Lina was short for so many names. He couldn't have just guessed it.

Here came the smirk again. "The academy recitals. Your name and photo were on the brochures. Our little prodigy. You and your sister are the pride of Bellomo. Like Nicole, I have no doubt you'll win a scholarship next year." His smirk grew into a smile. "I knew I've seen you before. Your face is impossible to forget…so is your music."

"You've been to my recitals?"

"Each one of them. How could I miss it? You play like an angel." The admiration in his voice, genuine and heartwarming, put my fear aside for a second. "Have you ever heard her play, Leo?"

"Yes. I'm Lina's biggest fan," Leo said, smiling at me.

"Doesn't seem like it. Looks like I have a bigger fan than you," I countered.

Leo opened his mouth, his face smug like he had a good comeback, but his dad beat him to speaking first. "I've never heard anyone play so beautifully like you. Except for the girl that plays at night. She's your only match."

"The girl that plays at night? Is that a stage name?" I asked, intrigued, my fear retreating further, my mind working with more clarity. The Mob wasn't stupid to harm anyone in broad daylight with all these witnesses around. And I was a student at their school, they couldn't just take or hurt me, not when everybody saw us together and could tie them to it.

"No. She's a neighbor. A little girl that plays the violin at night sometimes. I've never seen her face to face, but she, too, plays like an angel. Leo heard her once and immediately became a fan of classical music."

Leo cleared his throat, nudging his dad with his elbow.

Don Bellomo rolled his eyes. "Che cosa?"

"The girl that plays at night...is Lina," Leo said.

"Cazzo?"

I didn't understand much Italian, but I clearly understood that one word. The fuck was the right thing to say. "Hold on a sec. What?"

They both just looked at me, Leo growing pale. I cocked a brow at him. "Can you explain?"

He ran a thumb over his eyebrow. "Dad rents the penthouse in the building across from yours. I visited him once, and you started playing..."

"And?"

He opened his mouth and snapped it shut a couple of times, and then he shook his head and shrugged. "This is gonna sound... When I left that night I was...not in the best mood, and you were still playing. The music soothed me somehow, so I..."

Mind spiraling, I quivered. "You wanted to know who the girl was, so you've been following me…for months…" My chest contracted with a sob that threatened to burst out. "How long have you been stalking me, Leo?"

"Stalking? No, Lina, no. I wasn't hiding somewhere watching you where you couldn't. You saw me everywhere. I was only trying to get you to notice me."

"But how did you know where to find me? I thought you first saw me at one of those accidental meets, and it kept happening because you lived close by. *Then* you did it to get me to notice you. But you…"

"Oddio, what did you do now?" Don Bellomo mumbled and pinched the bridge of his nose.

Leo swallowed. "I didn't do anything. I might have done a little digging before—"

I jumped to my feet, unable to listen to another word, and darted toward the door. He yelled after me, but I shoved the door open with my palm and shoulder. Pain instantly seared me. That would leave a bruise by tomorrow.

Walking as fast as I could down the street, tears flying in the cold air, I could hear his shouts after me approaching. Then feet scurried close, and he was in front me, blocking the way.

"Stay away from me!" I warned without a speck of fear in my bones. I didn't know where I got the courage, but I wasn't afraid of the Mob boy who'd been stalking me for months. Maybe it was the surge of fury talking, and I might regret it later. I didn't care, though.

Enough.

What the fuck was I? A psycho stalker magnet? The only guys interested in me had to be monsters? One would vanish from my life so another would appear?

A more disturbing thought sent me downhill spiraling. What if all this time Leo wasn't another monster? What if it was *him* after all?

My eyes bulged at him, and my chest heaved, all the air knocked out of my lungs. "When did you start? When was the night you first heard me play?"

"I don't remember exactly, but it was around seven months ago."

"Give me the date, Leo. Stalkers don't forget these things," I gritted but kept my voice down so people on the street wouldn't hear. Why the fuck was I still protecting him?

I should just yell it at the top of my lungs so everyone would know.

"For God's sake, I'm not a stalker. That night I went to visit Dad because I needed some money. He texted me that address. I didn't even know about the new place he'd rented. That night we had a fight. I was so angry when I left I didn't even take the money, and your music was the only thing that soothed me. It was like…magic."

"I won't fall for this shit anymore. When. Was. It?"

"June last year. Maybe the fifth. Why does the date matter so much?"

My blood froze in my veins. "Nicky's ceremony. That was the night he came and then disappeared."

"Who are you talking about?"

"The vigilante," I whispered. "My stalker since I was twelve. The one who vanished in June, on that particular night after he messed with my head, only to appear a few days later with a shaved beard, pretending to be a boy with a huge crush on me."

"What the… I have no clue what you're talking about, and I never had a beard, Lina. You can ask."

"Stop lying to me," I sobbed. "I thought you were too young back then to be the one who did it, but you're in the fucking Mafia. Fourteen isn't too young to be a killer for you." I stepped back, hiccupping through the tears. "It's been you all along, and this is another one of your mindfucks."

He pressed his palms together under his chin in a plea. "I swear to you I knew nothing about you till that night. Why would I tell you I'd protect you from that person if I were him? Why would I ask my dad to help you? Why would I say anything about knowing you were the girl that plays at night, knowing you might think I was stalking you, risking everything only to tell you the truth? To make you trust me so I can protect you?"

"I don't know. I don't know anything anymore." My pulse throbbed in my temples as tears blinded my vision. "All I know is that you need to stay the hell away from me. I don't wanna see you ever again. You hear me? Ever."

CHAPTER 16

Tino

Nobody touched what was mine. Nobody. Not even him.

I'd been watching him from a distance, hovering around her like an annoying insect everywhere she went. I could've sent him to the end of the world for doing just that—perhaps I should have—but I knew my son better than anyone. He was like me. Once he got fixated on something, he wouldn't let go. At the last recital, I almost had it. But if I forced him away, he'd flip, and it'd be the same with Gloria, his last girlfriend, all over again.

The second I saw his hand on Angel's arm, though, *I* flipped. I didn't care if I was risking it all. I couldn't let him touch her. I couldn't stay in the shadows to honor my promise. I'd vowed the next time she saw me she'd be melting in my arms and finally know it was the only place where she belonged. But again, she forced me out before time.

How could you do this to me, Angel? Of all the people in the world…

My fists clenched until my knuckles turned white. She'd been pushing him away as she should have, but today she was giving him a chance. She was letting him get close. Another mistake I'd punish her for. Hard.

How could she do this to me?

I let the lingering feeling of her soft hand in mine calm me down. If it hadn't been for their indiscretion, I wouldn't have had the pleasure of touching her hand without triggering her suspicions. A blessing in disguise.

I'd kept our touch as long as I could, never wanting to let go. I'd missed her so much, more than I could stand. It took me everything to play my little game of the concerned father when my own boy was trying to steal away my Angel.

Leo returned, grim and furious as I expected. I'd lied through my teeth, and I'd lie some more until the damage was done. I'd thrown the bait, and they took it. This little adventure he thought he could start with my girl had to end before it began.

His heart would be broken? So what? *Anything to make you mine, my sweet Angel.*

It wasn't like he didn't deserve it. He was lucky it was the only thing in him that would break. Leo should have come nowhere near Angelina, and not just because she was mine.

She'd suffered enough. She deserved much better than my son. My Angel was innocent, and Leo was no saint. He'd broken so many hearts before, and that wasn't the worst in his long list of sins.

I could say the same thing about myself, but the devil's son sometimes was worse than his father. It was hard to believe, and I'd denied it for so long, but it was the truth. I knew him better than anyone, better than himself. He'd have never taken care of her like me. He could have never protected her like I could. No one could or would.

Angelina Baldi was mine. End of story.

I had to be extra careful from now on, though. She heard my voice before, and she might have learned the smell of the cologne I wore that night. I wore a different one today, and I spoke with my original accent, careful not to speak as quietly as I had when I stole that precious moment before our time.

"She said the vigilante that killed her father was stalking her. That's why she freaked out. She thought I was him," Leo babbled, huffing and puffing like a wounded animal.

"What did she exactly say about him?" I was dying to know what she thought of me, how she felt about me.

"She said he disappeared after her sister's scholarship party. But she was talking about him as if…as if she was angry he did."

I looked away for a moment, hiding my smile. She missed me like I missed her. Despite how mad she was before, she still missed me.

"Dad, are you listening?"

"Si, piccolo."

He hissed. "Stop calling me that."

"That's all you care about? The only time I could see you in seven months is when I find you here by accident with some girl you should never be with, a girl you've been stalking, and you're bothered because I'm calling you piccolo?"

"I'm not a child, and I didn't stalk her. I have every right to be with Lina."

"No, you don't," I snarled, losing my composure for a second. I leaned back and blew out a breath. "You were born into royalty, Leo. With that comes responsibility. If you don't want to be treated like a child, then start acting like an adult. Set a date with the Lanzas and leave the poor girl alone."

"Not that again. Dad, please, try to understand me. I can't be with Claudia, not after I…"

"Not after what?"

"Lina is the one, Papà. I'm in love with her."

I swore in all the languages I'd spoken in my head, a volcano of wrath erupting inside me, eating me up, tearing at my sanity. "I'm going to pretend you didn't say that for your sake and hers."

He swallowed. "What does that mean?"

"It means you're Leo Bellomo, my soon-to-be underboss, and she's Angelina Baldi, an outsider, a program kid," I said what he might understand, leaving the real reason out. "You two can never be together." Because she was mine.

"I'm telling you I'm in love with her. I don't care—"

"But she's not in love with you. She's not for you, Leo. Never will be."

"She will. I'm gonna do anything to make her love me back. But first I need to protect her from that asshole."

I'm the asshole? I'm the asshole you fucking spoiled prick? You fucking thief? "Like you can protect an ant."

"By your book, I might be useless, but the truth is I'm not. I can protect her. I'll do whatever it takes."

"No, you won't. All you're going to do is ask *me* for help, like always. *I* will protect her. *I* will save her. Not you. Because you don't want to do whatever it takes."

His jaws clicked as a deep line formed between his brows, his eyes distant as if he was lost in thought.

"Leo, if you really love her and want to protect her, you'll do what's best for her. Leave her be, Son. Isn't it enough what she had to go through all her life, now you want to bring her into yours?"

"My life isn't dangerous. I'm not like you. I don't lead the same life you do."

I snorted. "You're part of the family whether you like it or not. Let's assume she'd forget about today by some miracle, and she'd want to look at your face again when you told her what it meant to be a Bellomo. Have you thought for one second what could happen to the poor girl when the Lanzas know?"

He stared at me as if the thought had just hit him. This boy was going to be the end of me. "Think about it, Son. Don't lie to yourself. You can't protect her. She's better off with someone else."

He nodded slowly, pensively, and I knew I won. Angelina had always been mine. No one would ever take her away from me.

"I've thought about it. You're right. I can't protect her like this," he said.

I donned my scarf and grabbed my sunglasses, rising to my feet. "I'm sorry, Son, but it's the right thing to do."

"That's why I decided I'm ready to become made."

My hands stopped in their tracks. I thought I was too old to be surprised anymore. I was wrong.

"I'm ready for my initiation. I'll take my omertà and be a made man." He looked up at me, his face never been darker. "I'll be your underboss, Papà, like you always wanted."

"You'll do that…for her?"

"Yes. You just have to promise me one thing. Until I do, you keep her safe. You can't let anyone hurt her, not the Lanzas, not that asshole. Keep her safe for me, and I'll be the son you want me to be."

Just like that, the game I thought I'd mastered had turned on me.

Angelina Baldi wasn't a whim to my son. To forsake all his ideals and join the life he'd resented and refused to be a part of for years just for her meant one thing. He was truly in love with her.

He was ready to give me the thing I'd always wanted from him, only if I sacrificed the one thing I wanted more.

No. Not going to happen. He wasn't in love with her. He couldn't be. He didn't mean any of it. I refused to believe he did.

"Would you do that for me?" he begged.

"Do what, Leo? What the fuck do you want me to do?"

His eyes shone with a glint of hope. "Ask her to move in with you, at the mansion. It's the only place she'll be safe. Nobody would dare attack her there. And take her sister, too, so Lina can't say no."

"You're out of your mind. I can't just let strangers into my house."

"Per favore, Papà. I'm begging you. I can't leave her in danger. I have to protect her."

"Let's say I'd agree to this madness. What makes you think she would? To her, I'm not the father of her…whatever you think you are to her. I'm her school owner, and her *stalker's* dad. Do you see the picture? She'd never agree to this, and I can't force her to live at my house." I could. I could do a lot of things. I should've done that a while ago. I should have never waited. I did one fucking good thing, and now I was paying the price.

"Can you, at least, try? She obviously respects you and believes she owes you. She'd listen to you."

"And what should I tell her the reason for your request? I can't tell her the truth."

"Yes, you can." His eyes darted around, and then he stood so he could whisper in my ear. "I think she knows what we do."

"You told her?" I fumed.

"No, of course not, but, like most people, she figured it out on her own. It's not exactly a secret."

I ran out of excuses. If I pushed this further, if I refused without convincing him, he'd never give up, and worse, he could get suspicious. I couldn't let that happen. My son was stubborn as fuck. If I had any chance left to win, I had no choice but to play his game the way he wanted.

"Va bene. I can't promise you anything, but I'll see what I can do."

"Thank you." He threw his arms around me in a tight embrace. "Thank you so much."

I patted his back, flames searing my chest and what was left of my soul. "You really love her? Like you loved Gloria?"

"More than Gloria. More than you think."

Leo stabbed my heart and twisted, his words a serrated blade. He was in love with the one girl I'd been waiting years to have.

My son was in love with my sweet Angel.

CHAPTER 17

Tino

I rang the bell.
Who would have thought I'd have to ring the bell and wait to enter Angel's apartment? And the reason behind this charade? To convince her to move in with me for my boy's sake so that he could *protect* her, so that he could get closer to her, pull her into his trap and make her fall in love with him.

I shook my head violently. This couldn't happen. Not on my watch. Never.

If he ever touched her again, intentionally or by accident, I'd cut his hand off. He could do with one hand. *See what you're doing to me, Angel? You're driving me crazy. I'm thinking about chopping my own son's hand for you. Because of you.*

The door opened, blond hair popping out followed by a yawn. Nicole appeared in pink shorts and patterned, blue shirt, her eyes wide at me and the two bodyguards behind me. "Mr. Bellomo?"

I forced a small smile. "You must be Nicole."

She blinked hard. "Yes, sir."

Waiting for her to let me in was taking forever. She was too stunned to speak or move or do anything except blinking. "May I come in?" I asked.

"Yes! Of course." She jumped out of the way, waving me in with her whole arm. "I'm sorry. It's a little messy." She ran a hand through her hair, picking up scattered clothes and takeout plates with the other. "We weren't expecting visitors."

I left my bodyguards outside and took a seat on the couch. "Don't worry about it." I'd been here so many times before. I'd seen the place in worse conditions. The Baldi sisters weren't the best cleaners. "Is your sister home?"

Her face paled as she nodded. "Is there something wrong? Is Lina in trouble at school?"

"Oh no, not at all. This is a friendly visit."

"Okay. Phew." She wiped her forehead with the back of her busy hand dramatically, allowing herself to breathe. "She's in her room. Lina! You have a visitor!"

A door unlocked as Nicole put away the mess in her grip, footsteps, light and hesitant, in the background. Then my beautiful Angel came out of the hallway, the violin in her hand. Was she about to start practicing?

"Ahhhhh!" She jumped the second she saw me, her hair wild, and the violin flew off her hand.

Quickly, I ran to catch it before it hit the floor. Her gasps landed on my cheek, her sweet scent intoxicating. She, too, was wearing shorts. Cream. Perfect for her beautiful, tanned legs. I straightened, holding the violin between us. My gaze skipped the generous view of her chest in that green tank top—her fucking nipples were showing, and I wanted to do depraved things to them—and locked on her eyes. "Careful now."

"What are you screaming for?" Nicole glared at her. I pretended not to notice the heavy nudge she gave Angel in the ribs. "This is Mr. Bellomo, Lina. Mr. Bellomo himself."

Angel tucked the messy strands behind her ears. "I...I... The men in black at the door scared me."

"Apologies." I smirked. "They're not a threat. Not to you."

She snatched the violin and stepped back as Nicole headed for the door. "Are they coming in?"

I shook my head, so Nicole was about to close the door.

"No! Keep it open!" Angel jumped again.

I inched a brow, laughing under my breath. Then I leaned in for a whisper, but not too close and not too quietly. The things I wanted to do to her were forbidden even for me. Standing too close dissolved my willpower, rendering it almost nonexistent. Even my voice I wouldn't be able to control. I'd sound exactly like I did that night. Struggling. Barely restrained. "I can assure you my men are tougher than your door. They won't let anything or anyone in or out without my permission."

She gulped before she barely whispered back. "Don Bellomo, what are you doing here? Please, my sister doesn't know anything."

"Don?" I leaned back, studying her face.

"I'm…I'm sorry…I…"

"You said nothing wrong. I like it from you. It's honest."

She gulped again.

"Angelina, you don't have to be scared. I just need to talk to you about something. But first, put the violin somewhere safe…and wear something different."

Her hand flew to her chest, and her cheeks turned dark pink. So beautiful. "Yeah. Sure. Sorry."

She hurried away, and I found the couch again, letting out a long, heated breath. *She's still fucking seventeen.*

So it's okay for Leo and not for you? He's over nineteen, and he sure has pictured her seventeen-year-old body doing all kinds of nasty things to him. Have you seen the way he eats her with his stare?

Cazzo! Clenching my fists, I growled.

"Mr. Bellomo, are you okay?" Nicole asked me warily.

I want to punch my own son bloody, kidnap your sister, put her in a place where no one else gets to see her but me and do very bad, unspeakable things to her, but other than that everything is just fine. "Si. I'm great."

"Can I offer you anything? Coffee? Juice? A sandwich?"

Whiskey would have been nice. "Thanks. I'm good."

Angel came back, a bra under her long-sleeved t-shirt, jeans covering her legs. She sat quietly across from me, tugging at the edges of her sleeves, her eyes wary at her sister who was still cleaning up.

"On a second thought, I'd like that coffee, Nicole. Sugar. No cream," I said.

"Sure, Mr. Bellomo." She walked away toward the kitchen, and Angel sighed in relief.

"If this is about Leo, I—"

"Are you in love with my son?" I interrupted. I couldn't bear it. I had to know.

"What?" She shook her head infinitely. "We haven't even dated. He asked me out but I never said yes."

I kept my voice as low as possible so her sister wouldn't hear us. "Do you want to date him? Do you want him to keep chasing you? Fall in love with you?"

"What the… Don Bellomo, are you blaming *me* for what *he* did? You think I wanted him to *stalk* me?"

"That's not what I'm saying. I just need to know if you want him as much as he wants you because he does, very much. And from what I've seen," my jaws clenched, "you don't exactly hate him."

She shrugged, looking down, blushing. "I'd be lying if I said I hadn't thought about it. He seemed...nice, at first. But I knew he was out of my league, even before I knew he was..." she gestured at me, swallowing, "a Bellomo, so I didn't give it much thought." She lifted her gaze to me, the green in them against her olive skin hypnotizing. "However, after our last conversation, I can assure you I want nothing to do with your son, Don Bellomo. Ever. All I want is to live in peace."

The fire in my chest calmed a little. "Allora, knowing my son, he's not going to stop. Do you know he sent me here today to ask you to move into my mansion?"

"What? Why would he do that?"

"Because he cares about you so much he wants to protect you. Well, he wants *me* to protect you from your other *stalker*." I snorted internally.

She looked away, apparently struggling with something. "The only stalker I have is Leo. If I need protection from anyone, it's him."

I loved how she always tried to keep me as her little secret. Her way of protecting me back like I'd protected her. Even if she hated me. My eyes dipped to her lips, the urge to kiss her more prevalent than ever. "I can protect you from him, too."

"You'll protect me from your own son?" she scoffed.

"I'll protect you from anyone. From the whole world if I have to."

She blinked once, her face a deep crimson now, her eyes sparkling at me. "Why would you do that, Don Bellomo?"

Because you're mine. I protect what's mine. "I told you. Your safety is my responsibility. I'll do whatever it takes to keep you safe, even from my own son."

She held my gaze, her face a question mark, until Nicole returned with my coffee. Then she hid her eyes from me again.

"Here you go. Sugar. No cream." Nicole gave me a steamy cup of coffee and sat next to Angel, a grin on her face. "To what do we owe the honor of your visit, Mr. Bellomo?"

My innocent Angel begged me with her eyes not to tell on her. *Don't worry, my sweet girl. Our little secret is safe with me.*

"As hard as it is to say it, there has been a misunderstanding, and I'm afraid my son is to blame," I told Nicole.

Her grin shrank. "What misunderstanding?"

"See, in traditional families like ours, things are a little different. There's a girl that has been promised to my son since she was a baby. Sadly, Leo didn't take that promise seriously."

Angel's brows hooked. "What?"

"Yeah, what?" Nicole repeated. "And what has that got to do with us?"

"Leo has shown interest in your sister, Nicole, without regard to consequences. His behavior is reckless, no doubt about it, but he meant no harm. However, our families don't take matters related to honor lightly."

Nicole's smile vanished completely. A deep frown contorted her face as her stare darted back and forth between Angel and me. "You hooked up with Leo Bellomo?"

"No! He asked me out without saying he was a Bellomo," Angel shifted her stare toward me, "or that he was engaged, and I refused."

"It makes no difference, though," I said.

Nicole's grimace deepened, alarm evident on her face. "What does that mean?"

"The situation can upset the other family either way as it hurts the reputation of their girl."

"But that's not Lina's fault."

"Nobody's saying it is. I'm just explaining the unfortunate situation you've been thrown into."

"Mr. Bellomo, are you saying my sister is in danger?"

"Nothing that can't be avoided. But until the situation is fixed, I prefer to have you both as my guests at my mansion, where I can keep things under control."

They both exchanged glances silently, holding each other's hands, but, strangely, neither of them was afraid. Well, I could have exaggerated it, scared them for real, if I really wanted them to live with me. But I toned it down, and they were smart enough to know even the Mafia wouldn't harm them just because of a few talks. I knew not even a psycho sadist like Enzio Lanza would. This whole thing would disappear if Leo set a fucking date.

"Mr. Bellomo, as much as we appreciate your concern and your offer, I'm afraid we can't accept it," Nicole said.

"Why not?"

"I'm quite capable of protecting my sister, and with all due respect, I don't believe we'll be safer at your mansion. Your son will be there, and that is more dangerous in my opinion."

I couldn't agree more. "But he won't. Leo doesn't live there."

"Still, he can visit. He'll have easy access to Lina. He might even ask you to move in as well. He's your son. You won't kick him out for my sister."

"What about what I've just told you? About the girl's family?"

"Thankfully, you said you could fix it, and the danger is nothing that can't be avoided."

I grunted. "Angelina, is that your decision, too?"

"Yes. I'd like to stay here with my sister," Angel said. "The Bellomos have done so much for us, and we're forever grateful, but I think we should leave it at that. Like I said, we just want to live in peace."

"Understood." I rose, convincing myself that I had done everything in my power to grant my son his wish, even though it didn't work out in his favor. I wasn't even sorry.

The only thing I was sorry for was the night I invited him to the penthouse. I regretted it as much as I regretted his mother's death. My son and my Angel were never meant to cross paths. I should have known he'd get obsessed with her like I was. He was my son after all.

Leo and Angel would stay away from each other until my girl would turn eighteen in a few months. Then nothing could stand between us ever again. Everything was back according to my plan.

"You haven't touched your coffee, Mr. Bellomo," Nicole said, getting off her seat.

"Some other time. At Angelina's scholarship award maybe or your graduation. I hear amazing things about you, Nicole. Keep up the good work."

"Thanks. Let me see you out."

"It's okay, Nicky. I will," Angel said.

"Sure. It's been an honor to meet you in person, Mr. Bellomo." Nicole excused herself while Angel walked me to the door.

"Thank you for not telling her," she whispered. "Is any part of that story you told us true?"

"Every word."

"Wow. I'm such an idiot."

"No, you're not." Leo wasn't playing her. He didn't believe he was engaged. He resented our life, and only for her, he was ready to forsake everything and be a man he never wanted to be. But she didn't need to know that. "I'd like to know as well. Is any of what you told me true?"

"About?"

"The vigilante. Is it true that he's not bothering you anymore?"

Her chin quivered. A haunted look took over her eyes as they glistened. "*He*'s long gone."

I believed Leo when he said she was angry and sad about it because that was what I liked to believe. Now I could see it for myself, and it warmed my heart a thousand times more.

"Answer me this one question. Does he know where you live?"

She nodded, her chin still trembling.

"And you don't want to leave here…in case he comes back?"

Her head jerked up, her eyes wide. A little girl that had just been caught stealing cookies. "No. Of course not."

She lied, but the look in her eyes told the truth. A look I'd never forget my whole life.

The look that changed everything.

CHAPTER 18

Lina

I hadn't seen Leo all week. I must admit, I was relieved, yet the void he'd been filling for me had returned to swallow me.

With Leo's attention, even though I knew it wouldn't last, I thought I was over *him*. The second I was reminded of *his* abandonment, and with nothing to keep my mind off missing *him*, I was lost again, longing for something I should have never desired.

When I wasn't at school, I barely left my room. I buried myself between my books and music, studying and practicing harder than ever. Nicky thought I was working hard to score a Bellomo full ride like she did.

Since we got into Bellomo, we'd been conditioned to believe scoring a scholarship from them was the ultimate goal—the only chance to go to college. The program was the best, and anybody would kill to win one of their scholarships because it covered everything. We, program kids and Bellomo students, were given a head start to secure one.

The only limitation was Bellomo's scholarships were exclusive to the schools in the state. Nicky and I had never thought about leaving Chicago before so that was never a problem. Now, things had become different for me.

I never wanted to stay away from my sister, and if she knew I decided to explore more college options outside of Illinois, she'd freak. But I had more than one reason to leave town.

First, I didn't want to rely on Bellomo anymore. Not after I knew for sure I was living my own version of Great Expectations.

Second, Don Bellomo's assumption was a wakeup call. He read through my mind like an open book. Despite all that had happened, deep inside, I was still waiting for *him* to come back.

If I stayed here, I'd never get over my twisted need to see *him* again. Every place I went to reminded me of *him*. My school, my own room… If I had any chance of forgetting and healing, I needed to get out of here.

Every free second I had, I practiced for the university auditions in the summer and applied for all the scholarships I'd found, which for music majors weren't many, and nothing was a full ride like Bellomo. I didn't mind. I'd work my butt off to make it happen.

Even if it didn't, college wasn't a life goal for me like Nicky. I didn't have to prove to the world that the poor Baldi girl had gone to college and found her place among the elite. I'd be happy to find a job anywhere, playing my violin, making a living on my own, in peace, away from monsters.

That is if no new monster finds their way to the psycho stalker magnet I am in the year and four months I still had left here.

As I walked to my locker, I thought about transferring for my senior year. I couldn't afford an expensive, private academy like mine or a conservatory, but public schools were just fine. None would have a music program like here, though. That could hurt my chances big time, but a year and four months was a long time to stay in this mess.

I went to Mrs. Emmanuelle, the principal's secretary, and, discreetly, asked her about transfer procedures. I didn't want the word to travel to Nicky. She'd be shocked.

Mrs. Emmanuelle was shocked, too. She spent fifteen minutes talking me out of it even though I tried to make her buy I was only asking and wasn't planning on going through with it. I left the office without any useful information, but she set me an appointment with the principal to discuss my options further. I had no doubt he wouldn't help either.

If he didn't, I wouldn't have it in my heart to push it. I owed Bellomo everything, no matter how notorious they'd turned out to be. It'd be ungrateful if I left without their consent. However, Bellomo, all of a sudden, seemed to be a prison rather than a protective luxurious vault. Once you were in, you couldn't get out until you'd served your time.

Well, Sebastiano Bellomo was the Mafia. What did I expect? He treated everything he owned with the same code. Private. Strict. Elite. Exclusive.

Confined.

No one could break free.

My mind drifted to the mystery that was Sebastiano Bellomo. The most beautiful man I'd ever seen. The most powerful and dangerous, too. I used to think *he* was the most dangerous man I'd ever meet. I was wrong. If anyone was *his* match, it was Don Sebastiano. The mobster that had been to all my recitals and was concerned with my safety as if it was his purpose in life. The man with the sharpest blue eyes that pierced right through me with their kindness before their peril.

The perfection of his features, the masculinity of his beard that gave his cheekbones and lips extra hotness. Like he needed more of that. I was never taken by facial hair before until I...

I slapped the memory away and focused on the man with the panty-melting accent and angel tattoos on the back of both his hands; I noticed the other one the day he visited me at home. Why would a man so badass like him choose tattoos so tamed and gentle? Why would he be so kind and caring with me? Why was he willing to protect me from his own son instead of taking his side?

A long list of whys racked up in my head, and the answers would never be mine. Leo and his dad were a brief chapter in my life that wasn't supposed to be there in the first place and would forever remain incomplete.

As curious as I was to find the answers to my questions, I decided Don Sebastiano— God, even his name was hot. Bellomo literally translated into *beautiful man*. Was anything about him not sexy?—was a riddle not meant to be solved or all the appeal would be lost.

It was enough for me to know that someone like him cared about someone like me when he didn't have to.

I texted Nicky to tell her I'd booked the theatre today and would be late at practice. Then I switched off my phone and started Biber's Mystery Sonatas. Dedicated to the mystery man, my Abel Magwitch, Don Sebastiano.

I played until I became one with the chords. No more monsters. No more darkness. No more debts or cages. Just me and the music, shutting the whole world out, losing track of time.

A loud click disrupted my peace, bringing me back to the real world. "Miss Baldi, it's after nine. We have to close."

Lifting a hand to my forehead, I squinted into the spotlight flaring in my eyes. I couldn't make out the voice or the face of who said that, but it must have been the janitor or one of the Drama teachers responsible for the theatre.

"Okay. Sorry. I'm heading out now." I gathered my things, and the lights went out before I even finished.

"Seriously? You couldn't just wait one more minute?" I mumbled as I looked for my phone. When I switched it back on, the battery was at two percent. I rolled my eyes and carried my backpack and violin case, not trying to turn on the flashlight. The phone would be dead in a second, and I wouldn't even have the light from the screen.

As I took the shortcut backstage, the soreness in my fingers, neck and feet from playing and standing all these hours hit me all at once. When I was lost in the music, I couldn't feel any of it. I couldn't feel anything other than the rush of the melody. A psycho stalker magnet like me should have been more aware of her surroundings at all times. I couldn't afford to lose myself like that.

But I was safe now. The word I was never able to believe was finally real. My father was gone. Both my stalkers were gone. I was sa—

My voice was stifled in my throat along with my gasp. For a second, I didn't know what was happening. Then the shock faded a fraction as a heavy hand over my mouth and an arm around my waist dragged me in the dark.

I kicked and screamed in vain. My cries were muffled, and no one was at the theater to hear them anyway. The body pressing my whole front against the cold surface it hit was much stronger than I was, holding me tighter with every resistant move I made.

My phone fell down, rendering the place pitch black. I jerked my body one more time in a feeble attempt to break free from the attacker's grasp, my palms on the coldness I now realized was a wall.

"Shhhh."

My heart stopped along with every other muscle in my body. I even forgot how to breathe. I knew this *shhhh* by heart even though I'd heard it only once before.

"I'm gonna take my hand off your mouth now. You gonna scream?"

I managed to shake my head once.

He did as *he* promised, and so did I, still not breathing, my head dizzy with shock and lack of oxygen.

"Good girl," *he* whispered, *his* breath and beard pricking my skin. "Go ahead. You can breathe now."

As if I had been waiting for *his* permission, I gasped for air. "You're back."

"I've never left, my sweet Angel."

"Yes, you have." I shook with tears.

"No. I've always been here." *His* voice took a harsh turn. "And I've seen what you've done."

"What-t?"

"The boy." *His* hand crept on my collarbone, and another gasp escaped me. *He*'d been watching all long? *He*'d seen me with Leo? Was that why *he* was here? To tell me *he* knew? To warn me? To scare me?

Was *he* jealous?

His fingers glided up to my neck and suddenly tightened around my throat. "Naughty girl. Don't you know you're mine?"

The pressure on my neck was too much. My ears rang as I took a big breath through my nose, inhaling *his* scent that confused the hell out of me. The cologne I'd associated with desire and fear together. The fragrance I'd been missing for months.

"Yours?" I gurgled.

"Yes," *he* hissed. "Only mine."

My tears streamed down my face, and *he* eased off my throat, *his* thumb drawing a line up to my chin, and then brushing over my lower lip. I sucked in successive short breaths, heat squirming through my body.

"I've been waiting for so long…" *He* did it more than once, brushing my lip back and forth with the roughness of *his* thumb, as if *he* had to know the texture of my lips, as if *he* couldn't wait anymore, and with every time, I trembled harder.

"P-please, let me go."

"Why? So you can go back to him?"

"No. I was never with him. I was never with anyone." Panic gripped at my heart as I put as much sincerity in my voice as I could to convince *him*. If *he* was jealous, if *he* got the wrong idea, *he*'d hurt Leo; *he* was a brutal killer. *He*'d punished my father, and *he*'d punish Leo for something he didn't do. Leo might have stalked me, but he didn't deserve to die for it.

"And it stays that way."

"Okay," I sobbed. "Just…please…let me go."

His nose dipped into my hair, inhaling it, and then *he* kissed the tip of my ear. "Never."

My skin should have crawled, but it tingled with comforting warmth. My mind should have feared *his* dark promise, but it only soothed it. As if it was the assurance I'd been waiting to have for months. For years. As if I wanted *his* hand on me. As if I wanted *him* to never let go.

Abruptly, both *his* hands were on my waist, the touch confident and strong, curving around my body as if *he*'d studied it for a while. For years. Then *he* swiveled me, my back now to the wall.

His breathing grew heavier, hotter on my face. I wished I could have seen *him*. I wished we hadn't always met in the dark.

My quivering hands traced *his* breath and found *his* face in the blackness, but even that *he* wouldn't let me have. *He* captured my wrists and crossed them up over my head in *his* tight grip.

Then *his* breath fell on my mouth.

His lips pressed to mine, and my heart careened. All the air left my lungs again, my body turning into goo. As wrong as it was, I'd imagined our kiss countless times before, but I'd never expected it to feel like this.

Like I no longer needed oxygen, only *his* breath.

Like all the pain I'd seen in my life wasn't enough, and I needed the pain only *he*'d prepared for me.

Like my life had meant, would mean, absolutely nothing if it weren't for this moment.

I cried while *his* lips explored and nipped before claiming my mouth. *He* savored me slowly and then passionately. *His* tongue peeked out, parting my lips for *him* to devour. I let *him*, as if I had any other choice, moaning into *his* lips helplessly.

He groaned, *his* tongue dancing around mine. Giddy, I was desperate to kiss *him* back. I shouldn't, believe me, I knew that. I should want anything but. *He* was stealing my first kiss, but I wanted no one else to have it.

I moaned into *his* kiss again, this time licking *his* lips and the corners of *his* mouth, moving my tongue with *his*, drawing from *his* evident expertise that showed my embarrassing lack of it. *His* raw power and dark sensuality sparked flames of desire inside my guts and between my legs.

"I had to be your first." Fingers slid up the side of my thigh, rocking my body with frightened need, sending more heat and shudders as they inched up my skirt. "I have to be your first everything."

He resumed our kiss, *his* hand fondling my thigh, and then *his* fingertips touched the fabric of my panties on my hipbone.

No.

Not like this.

I tore my lips from *his* and writhed against *him*. *His* ironclad grip wouldn't free my wrists. *His* fingers reached the inside of my thigh, tracing little circles ever so lightly. "You're mine, Angel. You've always been. I shouldn't have waited all this time to take what's mine."

I swayed and jerked my body to spare myself the confusion *his* touch always gave me. I needed to fight. I couldn't give up. "Not like this. Not like this!" I repeated hysterically. "Please, not like this!"

He spun me again so that my back would be facing *him*, *his* hand tight around my wrists. Then *he* hiked my skirt up to my waist and grabbed at the side of my panties, *his* fingers scratching my skin.

"No! No! Please, NO!"

The ripping sound of the fabric when *he* snatched it ripped my own heart with it. *He* tore my panties, leaving me exposed and naked for the taking. *His* taking. The man who saved me from the monster who wanted to rape me was going to do it himself.

He was going to rape me.

I sobbed, an unbearable burn inside me. "You can't do this to me. How could you do this to me? How could you ruin everything?"

Ignoring me for the millionth time, *he* inhaled deeply and groaned. "Your smell is heaven."

Oh my God. It wasn't my hair *he* sniffed now. *He*'d smelled the evidence of my shame. *He* realized how much *he* aroused me. How turned on I was for *him*. How wet *he* made me.

Now, *he*'d think I wanted it, too. Now, *he*'d never stop.

More tears squeezed from my eyes. "I hate you. I hate you!"

His fingernails stabbed my butt cheek before a loud smack seared my skin. I moaned, and *he* followed with two more. "My sweet Angel, I didn't know you could be such a naughty girl. You deserve to be punished."

Two more swats, making that a total of five searing spanks. Then *he* did the same with the other cheek, my moans—of pain and arousal—louder with every swat, the uncontrollable and inexplicable wetness between my legs slicker, heavier.

His beard returned to tickle my face. "I don't like to be lied to."

"I never lied to you."

"When you tell me to let you go while all you want is for me to stay isn't lying? When you ask me not to touch you while you're dripping wet for me isn't lying? When you say you hate me while you clearly don't isn't lying?"

I shook my head at how pathetic I was, sobs heavy in my chest.

He spanked me one more time, and I flinched. "Answer me."

"Yes," I cried. "Yes."

One finger glided up the inside of my thigh, tracking the moisture dripping on my tender skin, a fraction away from my vagina. "Now you're being my good girl. My sweet, sweet, Angel."

My whole body tensed, shutting down, shielding me from what was to come. I couldn't fight *him* off. I had to pretend this was another one of the bad dreams that would never end.

His finger went higher and right before where my vagina met my thigh, it stopped. "Remember this. I could have done anything I wanted to you right here right now, and you couldn't have stopped me. But I didn't wait all this time to have you like this, in the fucking dark like a thief. You're mine, Angel. When I take you, you'll be looking at my face in broad daylight."

My lips parted with silent screams of relief, of pain, of torture. "Why are you doing this to me?" I whimpered. "Why are you torturing me like this?" This was another one of *his* controlling mindfucks that were on a mission to ruin my life beyond repair.

"I haven't tortured you yet, my sweet Angel. The spanking is for your lies only. I'll make you pay later for your other mistakes." He kissed my cheek. "The next time I see someone sniffing around you, they don't get to live another day, and you'll force me not to wait anymore. No one touches what's mine. No one will ever take you away from me. Know this, next time you do something that stupid, I won't stop myself from showing you who really owns you, my beautiful Angel."

His thumb brushed my cheek. "Ci vediamo."

CHAPTER 19

Tino

If you were asking why I did it, you hadn't been following. I was the villain of this story. *I am the villain of all my stories. Don't confuse me for anything else.*

But if you already knew that and were still asking, I'd tell you.

My plan had always been to wait for her to turn eighteen and then take her. Yes, my patience had been tested, and I'd thought about changing that plan, more than once, but I'd always managed to bridle myself. For her. Only for her.

After I'd left her apartment that day, after she gave me that look, I'd been at war with myself all week. Guess what? The devil in me had won.

Could you really blame me? I was only a man. A man waiting for years for one girl, obsessing over every detail of hers, waiting for the right time to make her his. A man who found out the girl was waiting for him, too, needing him, only him.

What was I supposed to do? How could I have resisted? How could I deny her what she needed the most?

I couldn't possibly wait anymore. I couldn't bear another moment away from her. I couldn't just stand and watch while she felt so guilty about her need for me that she decided to leave.

The plan had to change.

Angelina Baldi had to live in the same house I did, where I could see and talk to and touch her every day, where she could learn she was wrong about wanting to leave, where she could learn I was her home, the only one she'd ever need, and for that to happen, I had to do what I did.

You'd think it'd have shaken her harder, driven her away, sent her running like she'd intended. But you didn't know her like I did.

I knew my Angel more than anyone. I'd watched her grow. I'd learned how her mind worked. I anticipated all her moves. That was why when Nicole reached out to me to ask me, beg me, to bring her beautiful sister and come live under my protection as I'd offered, I wasn't surprised to the slightest. I was waiting and ready for it.

Underneath all Angel's shyness and innocence lay fury, challenge and a secret affinity for vicious retaliation. Why else would my sweet Angel be so attracted to me after what I did to her fucking father?

As much as I loved that about her, her anger had always irritated me. So infuriatingly passive and always coming in the way. But I knew exactly how to use it. My Angel had been angry with me because she thought I'd abandoned her. She'd been waiting for my return, not only because she'd missed me but also to have her revenge.

With time, she got desperate. Leo and the transfer were nothing but cries for my attention even if they'd seemed to be quite the opposite. Now that she'd got it, she wanted more.

But on her terms.

In her mind, she believed I came and left as I pleased. She believed I could hurt her and she had no power to do the same. And she hated it. She wanted to be in control. She wanted her retaliation.

After she went home and cried her eyes out, squeezing my heart with every tear, she tortured me in her own way. She pleasured herself vigorously. Three times in a row.

I watched. I fucking watched. I took all the sweet torture she dished out until the very end. With her wet panties in my fist and the lingering feeling of her flesh against my palm, I listened to every plea, every moan. I memorized every arch of her body, every contraction of her face when she came over and over and over.

As if that wasn't enough torment, my devious Angel had slept naked all night.

She'd never done that before, as if she'd known I wouldn't have been able to stop myself from going in and touching her when she was. But last night she did. To test me. To bait me. To torture me.

To bring me to my knees for what I'd done.

It'd have worked—fuck, my erection was the size of Texas, and my balls were screaming with the worst case of blue balls ever. I'd been driving all night as far as possible from her building so I wouldn't fuck everything up and fall right into her tempting, destructive, decadent trap.

She'd have been in my arms now after I'd have made love to her all night and this morning some place where no one would have found her ever again.

Her plan would have worked—*Oddio, I so fucking wanted to fall*—if I hadn't had a different plan—as much as I hated to say it, a better plan— that needed to anger her some more so she could do exactly what I anticipated her to do.

What I needed her to do.

The next morning, she caved. She went to Nicole and spilled our little secret; she told her sister everything.

Being the protective older sister, Nicole had no choice but to take me up on my offer. She didn't lie to me or try to convince me it was the fear of Lanzas that changed her mind. She swallowed her pride and told me everything about what truly scared her. About *him* as Angel called me. Even a proud girl like Nicole knew I was the only man who could protect them.

From *the psycho stalker creep*.

I wasn't fond of the nickname, but I wasn't going to complain. Not when Angel was in my house, looking so beautiful, just like each time my eyes devoured her. Not when my arms were wrapped around her to give her the comfort she demanded while she cried in my embrace.

"He kept saying I was his. He was gonna…" she whimpered.

I wasn't gonna… I was only scaring her, making her furious. And she loved our incredible kiss as much as I did. And the spanking… Fuck that was… not the best thought to have while my cock was an inch away from her stomach.

As for the rest of that night, I might have gone too far, but I stopped, didn't I? Believe me, it was one of the hardest things I'd ever had to do. As hard as leaving her alone in bed when she was naked, obviously needing me to thoroughly love her. That must have accounted for something.

"You're safe now. He can't hurt you here." I smoothed her hair away from her face, filling my nostrils with its smell before I gently drew back and cupped her face. "I promise you I'll find him, and he'll get what he deserves."

Alarm crossed her eyes, and she swallowed. "I… I don't want anybody to get hurt. I just want him to leave me alone."

I smirked. "You're so kind…even to your attacker."

"Please, I—"

"You don't have to worry about him anymore. I'll take care of it, Angelina." I dropped my hands and turned to Nicole. "As for your earlier concerns, I assure you Leo isn't going to be here during your stay. I've called him this morning, and he understands. He'll comply for your convenience and for his safety. After all, that scumbag threatened to hurt anyone interested in Angelina, not that he can do anything."

Leo was happy I'd kept my end of the deal, and now it was his turn. He was going to be busy with his initiation, and after that he wouldn't have time to even think about her. I'd make sure of it.

"Thank you, Mr. Bellomo, for everything." Nicole's voice cracked as her chin trembled. Her face was never grayer or more broken than now.

"You've done everything in your power to protect your sister, and you did the right thing, calling me this morning. You should be proud of yourself. As always."

She lifted her chin, her eyes blinking away tears she'd never shed in front of people. She was one of the toughest girls I'd ever known.

I hated that the first time she was about to crack in public was because of me.

"Andiamo. Let me show you to your rooms," I prompted.

"One room is enough, Don Bellomo. We don't wanna take the whole place," Angel said.

That wasn't going to work. At all. She had to have a room all by herself. So I could watch and visit and… I was tired of watching her through a screen. It was time I took our private chances to a new level. "Absolutely not. The mansion is big enough for a hundred people to live in. Each of you would have a room of her own with a private bathroom and a dressing room."

"A dressing room?" Angel squealed, wiping her face, as if she hadn't been weeping in distress a second ago.

"Certo. I think the rooms closest to the pool would suit you best, vero?"

"OMG, yes, *vero*." Angel giggled. I loved the sound of that. I couldn't wait for her to fill my house with her beautiful laughter every day.

And sweet moans.

I'd killed two birds with one stone with my new plan. Finally, my son was on the right path in the family and away from my girl. My sweet Angel was under my roof, trusting me with her life, where I could show her once and for all she did belong to me.

When I'm done with you, my sweet Angel, you'll have no name but mine in your little heart, mind and soul.

Then when you know who I am, you'll learn to forgive me for what I've done.

And what I'll do.

CHAPTER 20

Lina

Awestruck, Nicky wandered around the room Don Sebastiano chose for me on the second floor, where the guest rooms were. He stayed on the top floor. "Can you believe the size of these rooms?"

My gaze traveled to the garden surrounding the indoor pool outside as I stood by the huge stained glass windows. "No." Like I couldn't believe any of the things that had been happening to me all my life.

Hands fell on my shoulders, and I flounced like a fish out of water, a yelp escaping me. My eyes landed on Nicky, her hands in the air.

"Hey, it's me. Just me," she said.

I nodded, shaking. "Yeah. Sorry. I… can you not do that when I can't see you, please?"

"Of course." Tears glistened in her eyes. "You shouldn't say sorry. I'm the one who should apologize…for everything."

"Nicky, it's okay."

"No, it's not okay. You've told me so many times. I should've believed you. I should've done something about it way earlier. I should've protected you before he—"

"There's nothing you could've done. *He* attacked me at school for God's sake. The Bellomo vault like you call it."

"But if I'd done something earlier, he wouldn't have."

"Yes, *he* would've. Stop torturing yourself." She didn't hear the way *he* spoke. She didn't feel *his* possessive hands on her body. She didn't know that nothing would have stopped *him* from finding me. Nothing would. Not even Sebastiano himself.

I didn't agree to come here because the Mafia boss could find *him*. Hadn't *he* been coming to his own school for five years, and no one even knew? *He* was hiding in plain sight. No one could find *him* if *he* didn't want to be found.

The only reason I was here was to provoke *him*. The security at school had been doubled now, I no longer lived in the apartment *he* could easily break into or bug, and I was sleeping in the house of the boy *he* was jealous of, where *he* couldn't break in without being shot on sight.

He was gonna flip and make a mistake. That was the only way *he* would be found even if *he* didn't want to.

The only way to have *him* punished like *he* punished me.

"I haven't tortured you yet, my sweet Angel. The spanking is for your lies only. I'll make you pay later for your other mistakes."

The sting of *his* swats on my butt reminded me of how stupid I'd been. I trusted *he* wouldn't hurt me for fuck's sake. I let *him* kiss me, and I kissed *him* back. My first kiss ever I'd given to a killer who was about to rape me.

I so fucking hated him.

"I don't like to be lied to. When you tell me to let you go while all you want is for me to stay isn't lying? When you ask me not to touch you while you're dripping wet for me isn't lying? When you say you hate me while you clearly don't isn't lying?"

I cringed, my tears falling.

"Hey." Nicky rubbed my arms. "Lina, it's okay. He's never gonna touch you again."

What if that was what terrified me the most? The way *he* said I was *his* sent a chill up my spine, but there was so much need in *his* voice. Possession. It was like *he* couldn't live without me, and I didn't know what to do with that except feeling the same way, too.

Like I was two people all at once. One that cringed at the thought of *him* and the things *he* had done, the things *he* wanted to do to me. The other couldn't help but feeling cherished and loved under *his* extreme passion, couldn't help but want *him* back.

"I need therapy, Nicky. Heavy therapy, not the casual thing they give us at school."

"Anything you need, sweetie."

"I know we can't afford it. Do you think Abel Magwitch will chip in?"

She chuckled, getting the reference instantly. "I don't know about that, but I can ask him."

"How did you know it was him when he came to our place? I didn't know who he was until Leo introduced us. You seemed to have already known how he looked like when we went to that restaurant on my birthday."

"I've seen his picture in the newspaper before. There was this article about a huge funeral in San Francisco. They claimed it was Mafia related, and all the other Dons were at the funeral, including the Bellomos, Sebastiano and Leo. The woman who died was the mother of the Mafia boss there. Her name was Mary or Marta… Oh my God, her last name was Lanza."

"Like Leo's fiancé Lanza? Jeez. He once told me he and his dad went to live in San Francisco for a while, probably with that family. Looks like they're good friends. I can't imagine why Leo would be so stupid to ruin their relationship when it's so strong, get us in the crosshairs of these people."

Nicky's lips pursed. "I don't know how to feel about that."

"What?"

"I mean this whole living under the protection of the Mob when they themselves are a threat."

"It's so confusing." Like every other thing in my life.

"It so doesn't help when they look like that." She chuckled. "You know that movie when that tall, man candy Mafia boss kidnapped that girl and gave her a year to love him or whatever?"

"You mean the soft porno you've rubbed one off to like a million times instead of dating any of the hot college guys you meet every day, yeah, I know it," I sneered.

She made a face. "That's beside the point. I mean if he was a troll, she wouldn't have fallen for him, you know? It's the same with the Bellomos. The way they look makes you, I don't know, wanna trust them even if you know you shouldn't."

Probably true. But in my case, I hadn't even seen my psycho, and I was... "Do you think *he* is a troll?"

"Who cares about that creep right now? Please." Her brows hitched. Then her face lightened when she saw my grimace. "Let's keep our villain interest domestic, shall we?"

She meant it as a joke, but WTF? "Jesus Christ. Don't say you have a crush on Abel Magwitch." I'd be over the moon if she finally decided to give boys a try. Normal, mundane, boring nerds or hot athletes from college or the cute redhead barista with the freckles she worked with, not the dangerous Mafioso with the stalker son and murdered wife.

One fucked up Baldi sister was enough.

"Abel Magwitch was a troll. Tino Bellomo isn't," she countered.

"*Tino?*"

"That's his street name," she said, all smug now.

"How the hell do you know these things?"

"I did some digging, so what?"

I gaped at her. "You know that's what Leo, the boy who stalked me because he had a crush on me, said in his defense."

"When a boy does it, it's creepy. When a girl does it, it's cute."

"Nicky! That's sexist and deranged."

"Whatever, Sis. Have you seen the dude? He makes smart girls do stupid things." She shrugged and sauntered out of the room, giggling.

Great. My sister, too, was a stalker.

I had to agree with the last part of what she said, though. Sebastiano—Tino— Bellomo was so sexy it was confusing and dangerous.

Just like *he* was.

CHAPTER 21

Lina

Thunder vibrated in my bones, plucking my heart out of my chest. Lightning illuminated against the windows, which, despite how beautiful the drawings on them were, looked so spooky now.

A freaking thunderstorm on the first night at a new house that looked like a Gothic church. Great. How the hell was I supposed to sleep in this horror show?

I huffed as I kicked the sheets off me. Then I went over to Nicky's room. Carefully,

I opened her door and peeked in. Her snoring yelled over the thunder. How could she be deep in sleep in that weather?

I hated to wake her up now, so I just wheeled back and decided to wait downstairs until the storm was over.

The halls were silent and dark, and the storm seemed louder outside the vast entrance. Maybe I should just find the kitchen and make myself some chamomile tea. I hoped Don Bellomo wouldn't mind. He did say to feel free to behave as if this place was our home.

He'd shown us around and introduced us to the helping staff, but there was no one up this late, and I was totally lost. I must have taken the wrong turn. No way the kitchen was in this part of the mansion where there was nothing but rooms with closed doors.

"Where the hell am I?" My shoulders slumped as I had no choice but to return to my room, the only place I knew how to go back to, and ask for a freaking map in the morning.

The thunder boomed when I turned around, and I hit something hard in the dark. I gasped, looking up, and blue eyes were staring at me. "Ahhhh!"

"Are you going to scream every time you see me?"

"Shut the f...front door. God, Don Bellomo, you scared the hell out of me. One more of those and my heart is gonna stop for real. Please don't do this again."

"Do what?"

"Sneak up on me like this?"

"I've never snuck up on you, young lady. I heard someone walking in my house in the middle of the night and went down to check. But I understand why you could be so...shaken."

Lightning cracked the sky, and I could see he was, damn, only in his pants. His torso was completely naked, and he had bedroom hair.

I stared, my heart that was about to cease beating a second ago racing. He had more tattoos on his arms. A full sleeve on one, and a big angel on the other arm. There was a phrase on his broad chest, but I couldn't make out the letters in the dark. No ink on his abs. I'd never seen a real eight pack before. Who was I kidding? Not even a real six pack. Was that what I hit when I spun? Sebastiano Bellomo's firm, toned eight pack?

"Angelina?"

I yanked my head up. "Huh?"

"Did you hear what I said?"

No, I'd been busy ogling. "I'm sorry I didn't catch the last thing."

"What are you doing up in the middle of the night?"

My gaze trailed down his pecs and back on those abs. "Yeah, that, I…" I squeezed my eyes shut and jutted a thumb at the windows. "The storm."

"You're afraid of thunderstorms?"

So much. "I just hate the sound." Another boom of thunder made me jump, proving me a liar.

He chuckled. "What do you normally do to get back to sleep when you *just hate the sound?*"

I bit my lip. "I cuddle with Nicky if she's up, but she's fast asleep. A hot drink helps or I just put some music on and play with it. I didn't want to wake anybody up with my music, so I went down to find the kitchen, but I got lost…"

He grabbed my hand. "Come with me."

I stifled a yelp. Uninvited touches, even the simplest as handshakes or friendly hugs from either boys or girls, agitated me, especially after yesterday.

Except with this man.

Every time he held my hand, it didn't bother me at all. It was rather comforting than annoying. The warmth from his grasp soothed me like a balm. So protective. So…daddy like. In the nice, lovely, caring way I'd seen with my friends at school. Not *my* daddy.

He only let go of my hand when he turned on the kitchen lights, and I mourned the loss of his touch.

When he spun around, I saw the gun in the back of his pants. Holy shit. He took it out and put it on the counter before he reached for the upper cabinets, his muscles flexing and stretching. He got out a mug and a glass. "What do you like to drink? Herbal tea? Regular tea?" He asked as he put water in the kettle.

"No, please. I'll do it." I hurried toward him to take the kettle from his hand.

He moved his arm away, smirking at me. "It's not a big deal. Just tell me what you want."

"Don Bellomo—"

"Tino. Nobody calls me Don Bellomo but my staff and soldiers. You're neither."

"So Nicky was right?"

"About?" He put the kettle on the stove.

I didn't realize I said that out loud. I cleared my throat. "Uh…about your street name. She said Tino was your—"

"She's right. It's also short for Sebastiano. That's what you'll call me from now on. Now, about that tea?"

"Just please tell me where the sugar and the tea are." I opened drawers and cabinets nervously, clumsily getting in his way, bumping into his hot, firm body. "I can make my own and will make some for you, too." I almost hit his face, opening the cabinet above him, bumping into him again as I stretched on my toes.

Suddenly, his hands were on my waist, the kettle whistling with the boiling water, and as he lifted me and put me on the counter in front of him, my skin was whistling with heat.

My breath caught in my heaving chest, and my nipples hardened. Shoot. I was wearing a light t-shirt with no bra. If his gaze lowered a tad, he could see.

His gaze held me in place. "When I offer to do something for you, you don't argue, you don't negotiate, you only say thank you."

"Thank you," I said as if in a trance.

"Thank you what?"

"Thank you…Tino?"

"Atta girl. Now, anise or chamomile?"

"Chamomile, thank you."

"That wasn't so hard, was it?"

Giggling, I shook my head.

His hands left my waist, and I could finally breathe. It was like he put me under a spell with his deep blue eyes and mesmerizing voice. Like, in that moment, he could make me do anything he asked and I'd have to obey.

The way his hands felt on my body and the way he commanded me reminded me of the one person that had that effect on me. That controlled and swayed me however he desired.

Him.

I sighed, pushing the dreadful memory aside. It wasn't so hard now when Tino—I loved the sound of that on my tongue— reached up for the cabinet right above me, his chest practically in my face. God he smelled so delicious. Even more delicious than his son. What kind of panty-melting colognes did these guys wear?

I could see the letters of his tattoo clearly here. *Il lupo perde il pelo ma non il vizio.* I couldn't understand it, though. Must be something in Italian.

As if it had a mind of its own, my finger traced the letters on his hard chest. "What's that mean?"

Abruptly, he dropped the tea box on the counter and yanked my finger off his chest, holding it in his fist. "What are you doing?"

"I'm sorry." My heart thrashed. What the hell was I doing? "I…I'm so sorry. I was just curious."

"Curious?"

"About the tattoo meaning." Not about the feeling of his chiseled muscles.

He grunted and let go of my hand. "In English, it's similar to old habits die hard. Literally, it means the wolf could lose his fur," his eyes held me captive again, piercing me with its intensity, a warning, "but not his vice."

"Why…why would you write that on your chest?" I panted.

"Why do you think?"

"A warning." Just like the one in his eyes for me.

"Exactly."

The wild danger seeping from him wrapped around me like a dark cloud, taking my breath away, even after he moved away to place the teabag in the mug.

He added two spoons of sugar without asking me. Luckily, it was how I liked it; I wasn't gonna—couldn't—object if it wasn't. Then he poured hot water. "You're going to be living here for some time. If you wander outside your room, you'll need to start wearing a bra."

My face burned with embarrassment, and I folded my arms over my boobs. He freakin' saw.

"The house isn't empty. There're many people here. Adult men who are used to things little girls like you shouldn't know. I hate to see one of my men lose an eye because you forget to wear a simple piece of undergarment."

I didn't know why that made me angry more than wary or disturbed; it wasn't a figure of speech. A man like him would literally take someone's eye out. *Just for looking at me?* "I thought I was safe here. Like nobody can touch me?"

He kept spinning the spoon in the tea. "Absolutely. If anybody ever laid a hand on you or your sister, they'd be dead." *Again, literally.* "But I can't blindfold my men to stop them from seeing what is not theirs to see or the fantasies that might sprout in their heads if they do." He tossed the spoon in the sink and poured himself a glass of wine.

My lips twisted. "You'll need to start wearing shirts outside your bedroom, too. There are *women* in the house now, who are not used to having half naked men flaunting their muscles around."

He almost spat his wine.

I couldn't believe I'd just said that.

To the man who'd just threatened to take people's eyes out and kill them. What if he got mad and took my eyes out instead? That would be his solution to my *I can't stop myself from ogling* problem.

"Perdona, signorina. Next time when I think there's some intruder in my house, I'll take some time to put a shirt on first before I hurry down to catch them."

With a pinch to my mouth and arms over my chest, I slid off the counter. Then I extended one arm as far as I could to take the mug without moving any closer. "Thank you for the tea."

He just sipped his wine, staring daggers at me.

Another round of thunder burst, and I flinched, spilling some of the hot liquid on the counter and my hand. Perfect.

He mumbled something in Italian including a *cazzo*. Then he dragged me to the sink and opened the faucet. Cold water calmed the burn, but it was his callused, masculine touch that soothed the pain as he made sure the water covered all the redness on my skin.

How could Sebastiano Bellomo be so gentle and caring and kind? I wondered how Leo couldn't get along with him. Who would have a father so protective and loving and not like him?

Tino—it was gonna take me a while to get used to saying his beautiful name without blushing or maybe I wouldn't have to because he'd kick us out in the morning after all the crap I'd done tonight—put his gun back in his pants, cleaned the outside of the mug, grabbed it with one hand and held my own hand in the other. Then he walked.

"What are you doing?" I widened my stride to keep up with his.

"Delivering you and your drink safely to your room."

"I can carry my own drink—"

His warning stare chopped off my words.

"I mean, thank you, Tino."

He chose the stairs, not the elevator, and I welcomed the extra time spent with my hand in his. The silence between us begged to be filled or else my mind and eyes would roam where they shouldn't. I dared anybody to walk side by side with Tino and not do the same. "So, it's not like I don't love the stained glass, but in this weather, which is most of the year in Chicago, don't you think it's a little more spooky in here?"

"No."

I waited for him to elaborate, but that was it. "Oh-kay. Well, it's spooky, like dark, gothic horror—"

"When I painted them, I didn't know a little girl who's afraid of thunder would be living here."

"I'm not a little girl." I didn't know why I had to stress that more often for him. I was two years younger than his own son, so of course I was a little girl to him. It infuriated me, though. "And I wasn't always afraid of thunder."

It started when I was five. When my father began his nightly visits. He didn't use to come to my room every night, but he always did when there was a thunderstorm. He was a truck driver, and whenever the weather was really bad, he stayed at home. For some reason he always chose me to satisfy his sick urges on those nights.

Then the night he was killed, there was also a storm, when I'd waited for the other monster to visit. *He* didn't, and I was all alone, scared shitless, waiting for the pain that didn't come, which was equally painful.

Today I'd come to realize the monsters' absence was as scary as their existence.

Shit. How many memories was I supposed to slap or push away today? "Wait, *you* painted them?"

Tino nodded. "Most of them anyway."

"The details are intricate. So beautiful. How long have you been an artist?"

"It's been a hobby of mine since I was kid. I stopped painting years ago. I've returned to it only recently."

"Is that why you rented the penthouse? To paint again where no one can disturb you?"

"Something like that." He opened my bedroom door with the same hand holding the mug, as if he was afraid if he let go of my hand, I'd do another one of my clumsy, stupid things.

I loved the protectiveness oozing from his every move, but I hated that I showed him I needed it. I wasn't an awkward klutz or a chatterbox or the ogling, touching people without permission kinda girl. At all. I was shy, quiet, fully capable of taking care of myself—except in the kitchen—and had never ever flirted with anyone before.

Not that I was flirting with Tino. That would have been completely inappropriate and weird and wrong and all kinds of taboo.

Right?

He was a Mafia boss. He was Abel Magwitch, and I was Pip. He was the father of the only boy I'd come this close to dating. And above all, he was almost forty, and I was seventeen.

Tino walked me to the bed and placed the mug on the nightstand coaster. "Go ahead. I'm going to stay until you fall asleep. This storm isn't ending soon."

He'd do that? For me? I opened my mouth to ask and object but shut it instantly. I'd learned my lesson. "Thank you, Tino."

I wanted to hear that *Atta girl* again.

"You're welcome, Angelina." He smiled.

Okay. I'd take that. My name in his accent was just…ooof.

I slid under the sheets and held the steamy cup as he found a chair and brought it close to the bed.

"You'll be cold like this. You even left your wine in the kitchen." I felt guilty that he had to leave his warm bed and do all that for a girl he didn't even know.

He tucked me in before he sat. "I'm not cold."

Still, I wanted to make it up to him. "Would you like me to play for you a little?"

"That would be very nice, but I'll take a rain check. Just try to get some sleep."

"Okay." I took a sip after another of the chamomile, our gazes never leaving each other.

Maybe I shouldn't be scared of what the thunder brought anymore. Thunderstorms no longer brought pain and abandonment. They now brought kindness and hot drinks and a fuzzy feeling in my stomach.

CHAPTER 22

Tino

"**W**ould you like me to play for you a little?"

I'd have taken her up on her offer if I hadn't been waiting for her all night to fall asleep. "That would be very nice, but I'll take a rain check. Just try to get some sleep."

"Okay."

I watched as she drank, counting the seconds.

"You're so kind, Tino, you know that?" Her beautiful eyes drooped lazily. The drug

I'd slipped in her tea when she'd been busy ogling must have started to kick in. It was the same kind I'd put in Nicole's dinner. Nothing heavy. Just enough to knock her out for the rest of the night. No interruptions to my time with my Angel allowed tonight.

"Kind is never a word to describe a man like me. Have you already forgotten the warning on my chest?"

"But you are, at least to us." She yawned. "Tino…I think Nicky has a crush on you."

I frowned, not sure if she meant what she'd said or it was the drug speaking. "Your sister is like a daughter to me."

"That's not very assuring for the Baldi sisters, you know?" Her eyes closed as she put away her mug, and she slumped down.

A heavy sigh troubled my chest. "I'll never think of your sister in that way, Angel." I said her name the way I loved it, knowing she wouldn't remember in the morning. I was tired of calling her anything else.

"Can you please tell her that? I don't want her to fall in love with you."

I smirked. Was my little Angel, too, protective of her sister? Or was she jealous? "Why?"

"Even if you ever think of her in that way, even if you love her back," she yawned and rolled on her side, "you'll hurt her. She's been hurt enough."

Pursing my lips, I left my seat, put my gun on the nightstand and lay next to her. "What about you, my sweet Angel? Do you think I'll hurt *you*?"

"Yes," she murmured, her breathing gaining a steady rhythm.

I held her in my arms, taking in her peaceful, innocent face. "But you'll like it, won't you?"

"Mmhm."

"Why, Angel?" I stroked her hair. "Haven't *you* been hurt enough?"

"Don't know. Just want it." She clung to my shoulders, her breath warm and quiet on my chest.

I waited for a minute, making sure she was deep in sleep. Then I traced her lips with my finger, reminding myself of the softness. I thought the years waiting for her were bad. It was nothing compared to now. Knowing the taste of her kiss, the feeling of her skin under my hands, the way she shuddered for me, the sound of her moans, the shape of her naked body…

All that should have happened when she slept in my bed with my ring on her finger, but she had to do what she did, didn't she? So

I'd give her what she wanted. What she needed. Even before time.

Because like me, she couldn't wait any longer.

I inhaled the sweet scent of her hair and groaned. "Why do you have to be so beautiful? So young? So damaged?"

So naughty.

"I can't let your bad, bad behavior last night go unpunished, can I?"

No, Tino. I know I've been bad. I deserve to be punished. So punish me. Please.

I brushed her cheek with the back of my hand. Then I took her lips between mine, inhaling her breath, devouring her in a kiss. She moaned into me, her tongue reaching out to mine. I licked the taste of chamomile and the sweetness of her, and then bit each lip, leaving them swollen, punishing the mouth that spilled our secret.

With my fingertips, I grabbed the hem of her t-shirt and took it off her. Then her shorts. I inhaled them deeply, the smell going straight to my cock. "You were toying with me last night, taunting me, daring me. Well...here I am. Exactly where you wanted me to be, you naughty, naughty girl."

I took a thorough look at her beautiful body, my desire for her excruciating.

"Remember that promise I made you? That when I take you, you'll be looking at my face in broad daylight? You make me wanna break it so bad."

Through a hiss, I dipped my fingers under the edge of her panties. "But I'm the grownup here. I have to keep my promises to you. I have to take care of you. But also, I have to teach you how to behave."

Yes, Tino. I'm so naughty. You have to teach me a lesson. Punish me. Hard.

I pushed down the red lace, careful not to rip it off. No bra, lace underwear. *Who are you wearing lace underwear for, Angel, huh? For him? You thought he'd be coming to your room here and finish what he started?*

Taking the panties off her ankles, I felt the dampness in my hand. Cazzo. She was so wet. CAZZO.

I covered my nose and mouth with them and groaned. "You smell so fucking good, Angel." My tongue darted out for a forbidden taste. "You taste so fucking sweet." I'd take those, too, and put them with the other souvenirs, but she'd be suspicious if she woke up missing them. Soon, I'd make all her panties wet and keep them all for myself.

I needed more of that taste, though, and I needed it now. My hunger for her burned through me as I stared at her pussy. It fucking glistened at me.

Punish me all you want. I want it. I just want it. And I want you. Take me, Tino. I'm yours. I've always been yours.

I wiped a palm across my face, huffing and hissing. "I want you, too, Angel. All of you. Every broken piece of you. Every shred of your soul. Every fragment of your heart. I want all of you." I parted her legs and knelt between them. Then I pulled my cock out, my teeth spearing my lip. "But you said not like this, and I made you a promise I intend to keep."

Stare on her wetness, fist filled with her panties, I stroked myself. The sound of her moans along with the face she made when she came and the feeling of her ass on my palm all flashed in my head. "My cock will fill your virgin pussy very soon, my sweet Angel. I'm keeping all my promises to you. Tonight, I'll only mark you for what you did." My breath snagged in my chest as I groaned again, my cum dripping on top of her pussy. "So you'll never forget what you've done or who owns you."

CHAPTER 23

Lina

"**W**anna go see the new Mike Gennaro movie? You know, cheer you up a little?" Nicky said over lunch. We both had slept in and skipped our Sunday brunch for the first time in months. It was really weird how I'd slept like that during the storm. It never happened before. Must have been the incredible softness and comfort of the bed that made me sleep like a baby.

"I'm not in the mood." Not because of the *incident* like she must have believed. Last night,

I had the weirdest dream that confused me more than I'd ever been.

"C'mon, isn't the Italian Heartthrob your favorite?"

I did have a thing for hot Italian bad boys. Obviously. The ridiculous wet dream I had last night…was killing me. My panties were drenched with the stickiest cum ever. I didn't know girls could produce that amount of juice in an orgasm. Unless it wasn't just one orgasm? Damn. "Don't you have to go to work?"

"I'm taking the week off."

"The whole week? Since when do you take any time off? Nicky, you don't have to do stuff like that. This is not what I need from you. Not anymore. Yes, I had a terrible experience, but I'm no longer a child. You don't need to babysit me."

"I'm not babysitting you, sweetie. I'm being here for you."

"What about all that money you need to save up for when you don't have time to work?"

"I figured since we're not paying the rent for some time—"

"Why aren't we paying the rent?" I dropped my fork. "Did you give up the condo?"

"Of course not. Sooner or later, we're going back there. Guess what, though?"

My eyes tightened at her. "No way. Don't tell me he's paying our rent, too."

"Uh…not technically. He's giving us a grace period until we go back."

"How can he do that? It's not his building."

"Apparently, it is. Well, it belongs to one of his corps." She made air quotes in the end.

"Unbelievable. Did you know that when you signed the lease?"

"Nope. But what if I did? It wouldn't have made any difference. He didn't give us a special discount or anything. We pay like everybody else." She took a bite of her sandwich. "Why are you so upset about Mr. Bellomo's help all of a sudden? We've accepted his help all our lives and till last night you were fine with it. Aren't you the one who wants me to ask him if he could pitch in for your therapy?"

"I don't want you to ask him for anything anymore."

She quirked a brow at me, her eyes scrutinizing. "Lina, what the hell happened last night?"

I had a wet dream about Tino. Well, it was half Tino, half *him*. It was *him* with Tino's face and body, which was even more confusing. As if I pasted Tino's face and torso on *him* because I never saw *his*. Because I fucking wanted to and *he* denied me. Because I needed to materialize *him* somehow, and I took the features of the first man with *his* build, the first man I'd ever seen half naked, and gave them to *him*.

As if my fucking mind could only have a sex dream about *him*.

I wouldn't have been half upset if the dream had been about Tino himself. It'd have been sick and inappropriate but therapeutic of sorts, like I could desire someone else, even if it was wrong.

But even in my dreams, I was under *his* mercy. *He* had held me captive, and as *he* promised, *he* would never let me go.

And, against all logic, against my own will, I fucking liked it.

"Lina? Did Mr. Bellomo do anything to you?"

"No, Nicky. Nothing happened. If anything, he was even more generous, and I was the weirdo." I glanced at the empty chair at the head of the humongous table, where I imagined he'd sit to eat his meals. "Do you know if he's here?" I needed to apologize for my behavior last night. I fucking touched the guy, and fuck me, I probably told him Nicky had a crush on him. She was gonna kill me if she found out.

Fuck, I said more fucks today than I'd said my whole life.

"That bodyguard said Mr. Bellomo had gone to work, and if we needed anything or wanted to go somewhere we asked him. What's his name again? Like Michael but not Michael.

"Michele."

"Yeah. He was assigned to us." She chuckled. "We're VIP now."

I snorted.

"Doesn't he look familiar?"

"Who?"

"Michele, our designated bodyguard."

"Maybe. Who cares?"

"I feel like I've seen him before, but I can't remember where."

"What? Do you have a crush on him, too?"

She giggled. "Nope." Then all the humor left her eyes. "I don't have a crush on Bellomo either...or anyone else for that matter. I was only trying to make you laugh yesterday."

Shoot. "Did you talk to him today?"

"No. Why do you ask?"

"No reason! You know what? Let's go see that movie. Mike Gennaro is the best."

"Awesome." She got off her chair, her gaze alight again. "It's one of his wife's directions, not the cheesy shit he used to star in."

"Ugh, really?" My shoulders slumped.

"Oh, I remember you hate Maggie Dawson. You blubbered ugly when they got back together."

"She's such a bitch."

She laughed, taking my arm. "Why, 'cause she makes the Sexiest Man Alive an ugly villain in all her movies?"

"Well, there's that. I don't mind the villain part, but why the hideous makeup?"

Another giggle fled her throat. I rolled my eyes. "Beside that, I still think she doesn't deserve him."

"What are you talking about? Your precious man candy lied to her about something horrible. If I were in her shoes, I wouldn't have forgiven him like she did. *He* doesn't deserve *her*."

"What?! He's done everything to give her all she's ever wanted. When he lied to her, he was protecting her."

"That makes it okay because?"

"Because he loves her more than anything. He's crazy for her."

"Still, she had the right to choose, and he robbed her of it. If he loved her that much, he should've told her and let her choose."

We grabbed our bags on our way out, Michele in tow. Strangely, it didn't weird me out, the feeling of having someone watching my every move. After five years of being stalked, I was so fucked up that I'd gotten used to it. It was the norm. At least, with the bodyguard, I could see that he was following.

He walked us to a black Escalade and said he'd drive us to the movies. On the way, Mike and Maggie's story occupied my mind. I wondered if Mike was just scared of telling her the truth because then she wouldn't have wanted to be with him. He was afraid of her choice, so he made it for her.

To have her. Simply because she belonged to him, and he couldn't live without her. He was obsessed with her.

Look at me, making excuses for the bad guys again, justifying twisted, dark love that might not be love at all.

Obsession, possession, need but not love.

Definitely not love.

Michele got our tickets and ushered us in himself. We sat in the back, the whole row to ourselves, with him sitting one row behind us. Now, that was weird. I wasn't complaining, though. Security, even if it was an illusion, was a good feeling; I was certain if *he* wanted to find me, *he* would, despite the fort for a mansion and the seven-foot personal bodyguard.

I pitied the Bellomos. They had everything but couldn't enjoy the simple freedoms of life, like enjoying a night out or going to the movies without an elaborate military strategy. I bet they booked the whole place to themselves and had it under siege when they went anywhere.

But I never saw any bodyguards with Leo, and he roamed free everywhere. He was the only son of a Mafia boss. Didn't that put him in danger all the time? Especially if that thing with his mother was true.

As the commercials started, my mind wondered about the Bellomo family and all the hidden secrets that lay with them. The family tragedy Leo talked about must have been his mother's death. He went to San Francisco with Tino to live with the fiancé's family, I assumed. For Tino to unite forces against whoever attacked the mother? To avoid danger or provide extra protection for his son? To grieve?

Leo must have been thirteen or fourteen back then. He must have been so sad. I lost

Mom when I was five, and my whole world shattered. To lose a parent, good or bad, changed you. It took away from you. It changed a child to an old soul even if they didn't realize it at the time. Leo must have changed, too, after his mother died.

At the one time I saw them together, I could easily tell Leo didn't like his dad. Did he blame Tino for his mother's death? Was that why he rebelled against the lifestyle? Went to college to study something that had nothing to do with the Mafia, had no bodyguards and wanted to date an outsider?

Was that what I was to him? An act of rebellion to piss off his dad?

But why me? Anybody else would have served the same purpose. Why all the stalking? Why the protective act?

He couldn't have been that obsessed with me or he wouldn't have stopped that easily. Being the object of a psycho murderer's obsession taught you that much.

I might have exaggerated what Leo had done. He might have been a little intense and gone a little overboard, so what? It wasn't always a bad thing, and he did nothing to hurt me.

My reaction was a displacement for all the twisted fuckery *he* put me through.

A huge shadow fell over Nicky next to me followed by a chorus of Italian curses from Michele. I looked at him over my shoulder, and he was racing out. "What's going on?"

"Nothing. Sit tight." He hurried down the steps.

Nicky, suddenly, jumped to her feet. "What do you mean sit tight? Is that piece of shit here?"

My eyes widened, and my heart thrashed. Was *he*?

No way. *He* would never just show up like this. Even if *he* did, how would they know it was *him*?

"Back off, Michele. You can't stop me from watching a movie." A male voice boomed in the entrance, and Michele said something in Italian. Damn, I should start learning the language.

People started to turn their heads toward the heated argument, mumbling their protests. Nicky stepped forward, hissing, but I grabbed her wrist. "Don't go anywhere. It's not *him*." *He* wouldn't call the bodyguard by his first name.

If *he* was really here, *he*'d be among the people already in. My heart leapt at the thought. What if *he* was in here, watching as always?

My eyes searched the faces that were now looking my way, my chest heaving. *Where are you?* Tears burned my eyes, and I hated the emotional turmoil *he* triggered in me just by the mention of *him*. "Show yourself."

"Fuck. It's Leo," Nicky said.

I jerked my gaze toward the figure Michele accompanied up to our row. The dancing lights from the commercials exposed Leo's face to me.

Nicky took a protective step in front of me. "Stay away from my sister."

I shook my head as I got off my seat. "It's okay, Nicky." I took back what I said about exaggerating what Leo did—he was still stalking me after I'd made it clear he needed to stay away—but he wasn't the real danger here. Leo himself was in danger by being here.

"I just want to talk," he said.

"There's nothing to talk about." Nicky fumed.

"Nicky, please, just sit." I held her arm. She looked like she was about to lunge at him. "And Leo, please go. Everybody is looking our way. I just want to watch a movie in peace."

"You heard la signorina. Now, let's go. Your dad is gonna fucking kill me for this," Michele mumbled, pulling Leo away.

Leo yanked his arm out of Michele's grip. "Lina, you have to hear me out. Sooner or later, we have to talk."

"Not here." My sweaty hands twisted together as I searched the staring faces again. "Please."

"Where then?"

"I don't know. Just get out of here." I willed him to understand. It didn't matter if he was Tino Bellomo's son. His life was in danger.

Because of me.

What had I done? What was I thinking going out to the movies like everything was normal? What was I thinking when I agreed to live with the Bellomos to provoke *him* when I knew this could put Leo's life at risk?

How could I have been so selfish? Was this how I repaid Tino for all the good things he'd done for us? Put his son's life in danger? Putting his own life in danger, too?

If anything happened to either of them, I wouldn't be able to live with myself. I should've just left like I'd planned.

What had I done?

CHAPTER 24

Tino

Angel burst into my office. The bodyguards, including Michele yelled at her for barging in, nobody touching her as I'd ordered.

I nodded at them to shut the fuck up, and the room shrank in silence.

"I'm sorry." She sniffled. She'd been crying again. Her red eyes glanced over the other guards standing in front of me, Leo's guards. "I didn't know you weren't free. I just really need to talk to you. I'm sorry. I'll come back later."

"You can come in any time you want, Angelina." I smiled at her as I stood, and then I glared at the guards. "Out."

The second we had the room to ourselves, she burst into tears. I couldn't stand it anymore. I went over to her, and my arms folded around her.

She embraced me back, her head pressed to my chest, her tears wetting my shirt. I cradled the back of her head and kissed her hair, her scent and the feeling of her body on mine intoxicating. Wary she might recognize it, I only shushed her in my head like I did whenever she was scared in my presence, the sound that silenced her fears even if she thought it worsened them. "Get it all out. I'm right here."

"Can you ever forgive me?" she whimpered.

I lifted her chin so she could see me. "There's nothing I can't forgive you for." I might get mad at her. I would punish her. But I'd always forgive her.

She teared up some more. "Even for putting your son in danger?"

"It's not your fault that Leo is a fool. He wouldn't stick to the rules. He's the one who needs forgiveness, not you." That devious fuck thought he could manipulate me like that. He didn't pull that stunt because he couldn't stay away from her anymore. He was putting himself in danger on purpose, so I'd rush to protect him by bringing him here to my mansion, where he'd be safe as well.

Not too shabby. If only…

"When I came here, I was only thinking about myself. But when I saw Leo in the movie house, the same place where *he* might have been lurking… I didn't know if *he* was there, but *he* could have been… *He* could have hurt Leo."

"No, he couldn't have." Not when it was my only son. If he'd been anyone else, I'd have wiped them out without a second thought. But it had to be him.

"Yes, *he* could. Tino, that man is dangerous. *He*'s a killer."

"And you think I'm a tomato seller?"

Her gaze dropped. "I know what you do, Tino. But what if—"

"Don't even think about saying it. If you believe he's a threat to me, I'll take great offense."

"I…I don't…"

"Enough with this silly talk then. In a matter of weeks, your attacker would no longer exist."

"Weeks?"

"If not less." I enjoyed the way she paled now. She didn't want me to get hurt. She didn't want me dead. "And don't worry about Leo. He's safe."

"Okay." She sighed. "But he won't stop trying to talk to me. I'd like to get this over with. I think it's best if he just comes here and we talk it through once and for all. It's the safest place where we can meet."

My eyes twitched. The idea of them together, alone, talking... one thing might lead to another, and the next thing I knew they would be fucking dating. "I don't know how to respond to that." I did. A big fat no. I had no valid excuse to say it, though.

"Why not?"

I wiped under her eyes, biding my time. Then I just said it. "I don't like it. I don't want him alone with you."

She tilted her head back, her eyes narrowed at me. "If you're worried I'll steal him away from his fiancé—"

"That's not what I'm worried about. It's pretty much the other way around."

The corners of her eyes crinkled some more. "What do you mean?"

If I told her now, I'd come too strong. She'd freak out. She wouldn't understand. "I'm worried he'll make you forgive him. I'm worried he'll make you fall in love with him. Leo will steal *you* away, only to break your heart, Angelina." She was too fragile now to see it on her own. She needed the care, the love. She'd throw herself into the first arms that promised her those. He already thought he was in fucking love with her, and he was her age, and he looked like me. The only man she'd ever been attracted to.

She'd fall right into his trap if I didn't stop it.

Her lashes cast a shadow down her cheeks, and then her sparkling green eyes held my gaze. "Then don't leave us alone together."

The way she looked at me, vulnerable, innocent, a little kitten in need of shelter, stretched a smile on my face. I loved it when she needed me, when she hid in my embrace, when she asked for my help. "Bene. I won't."

She smiled back. "Thank you, Tino."

My smile turned into a grin. The things I'd give to kiss her right now.

Dark pink painted her cheeks. God, she was killing me. Her gaze dipped to my lips. She, too, wanted to kiss me. All she had to do was ask.

She cleared her throat and ripped her gaze off my mouth, but she wouldn't leave my arms. That she couldn't bring herself to do. "I feel like I need to apologize for last night. I was being…" She laughed nervously.

Naughty? Lovely? Breathtaking? "You were being what?"

"Inappropriate. Whatever that was, I think it's because of the incident. I…I'm dealing with it all wrong. I mean, my whole feelings about *him* are wrong."

Do tell. "What kind of feelings do you have for *him*?"

Tears fell off her eyes again. "I never told anyone about this, but I feel like I can tell you. I want to tell *you*."

I took her hand in mine and kissed her forehead. "You can tell me anything."

"He plays with my head, Tino. He makes me…want him." Her voice shook. "I hate it. He's the last person I should feel that way for, and I'm so angry and confused." She stopped crying all of a sudden and stared at me. "I want to be with him so much."

The heat in her words went straight to my cock. Fuck. I raked her from head to toe, my jaws clenched, the devil in me snarling.

Plunge your fist in her hair and show her how much you want to be with her, too.

Press her to your cock and let her feel what you have for her. Bend her over your desk and give her what she's always wanted.

Take what's yours.
NOW.

"But I won't do it. I will never let him have me. I'll never be with him. Ever," she added.

I wanted to choke her. I should bend her over and spank the fuck out of her while choking her pretty neck. Let's see if she'd say that shit again. If she'd be able to say anything at all.

"I…might have been looking for a replacement to get him out of my head, and my behavior yesterday was…that," she said.

"You're replacing *him* by *me*? Your desire and need for *him*? You think I can give that to you?"

Her blush deepened, and she flustered in my arms. "That's why I need to apologize. It's inappropriate but completely not real. I don't want things to be weird between us. I respect you so much. I owe you everything, and I don't want you to think that I'm ungrateful or don't know my place, Don Bellomo."

Not real? Not fucking real? You don't know shit, Angel. What you feel for me is the most real thing you'll ever have. The only real thing she'd ever have. "Tino. I'm still Tino."

"Sure. Do you forgive me, Tino?"

"No."

"Oh my God. Please. I'll do anything."

Don't say things you don't mean, Angel. "I said no because there's nothing to forgive."

She sighed in relief. "Oh God. Thank you." She hugged me tight.

I shifted a little so she wouldn't feel my erection. I didn't want to be *inappropriate.* I'd show her what was inappropriate tonight and every night to come.

"Can you please forget what I said about Nicky, too? It was a joke, and I was being weird," she said.

"Already forgotten."

"Yay, you're the best." She drew back. "Thank you. For everything."

"Anything for you, Angelina."

A big smile brightened her face. "Um...about Leo?" she asked on her way out.

"I'll arrange for a meeting after his initiation."

"Initiation?"

"It's a family thing."

"Oh, I get it. So is he...um...gonna become like you one day?"

"That's the plan."

"I thought he was studying Economics." She chuckled.

"He changed his mind."

"I see." She waved awkwardly and opened the door to leave.

"Angelina."

"Yes?"

"If Leo hadn't been engaged and hadn't been stalking you, would you have dated him? Would you date a made man? The heir to the Bellomo kingdom, knowing what it is now?"

Her throat bobbed with a swallow. "That's a tough question to answer."

I grunted. Not what I expected. Not what I hoped for. *I'll have to make her find the right answer, the only answer, at that fucking meeting.*

CHAPTER 25

Lina

I t'd been three weeks since I'd lived here and I hadn't tried the pool once. Nicky used it and the gym on the roof almost every day. She worked so hard on her body, just like she worked so hard for everything, and she had no problem showing it. I, on the other hand, had become more self-conscious. I was surrounded by perfect bodies all day. Nicky's, the bodyguards', Tino's...

The man of the house was rippling with muscles. If I thought he was hot the day I saw him without his shirt, well, watching him coming out of the pool, water dripping from his dark, sexy curls onto his tall, broad, sculpted body, while his swim trunks stretched over his…package was a whole different story.

Wrong and fucked up as it might have been, I'd touched myself that day, thinking of Tino for the first time, not *him*.

The star of my continuous wet dreams had morphed into my new protector. The dangerous almighty Mafia boss who had kept the monster away.

For now.

The man I saw in my dreams had Tino's face, body, scent and now accent. He no longer spoke or behaved like *him*. He was all Tino with his sweet touch and warm embraces, always looking at me with his deep blue eyes that promised care and protection.

Except that he called me his sweet Angel.

A troubled sigh blew out of my chest as I sat in the greenhouse, my favorite place in the mansion where I could be by myself and practice without disturbing anyone. Tino kept saying he'd find *him*, but I'd lost hope. I thought I'd provoked *him* enough to show up. To make a fucking move. To stop abandoning me. To pay for what *he* had done to me. But again, *he* proved to me I was nothing but a toy *he* played with only when *he* wanted whenever *he* desired however *he* pleased.

He didn't snap or lose it for not being able to watch or see me. *He* wasn't going to go crazy and make that mistake I thought passion and obsession would drive *him* to make. *He* wasn't coming. Why risk anything for me? I meant absolutely nothing to *him*.

I'd come to terms that I didn't need *him* to come back so I could heal. The void in my chest because I fucking missed *him* so much had shrunk. Even the need to see *him* punished had faded or just been smothered under the beautiful distraction named Tino Bellomo.

When *he* stopped calling me my sweet Angel in my dreams, I'd know I was healed. Only then I could move on and put *him* behind me. Only then I could live *my* life, not the one *he* painted for me. Whether Tino kept his promise and found *him* soon or not.

Then I'd have to deal with the super inappropriate, unhealthy, temporary crush I had on Tino Bellomo. Abel Magwitch who had now turned into Jervis Pendelton from Daddy Long Legs. A very dangerous, villainous and oh-so-fucking-hot Daddy Long Legs.

"You and I are having dinner at Leo's tonight."

The bow fell off my hand and on the fake grass as I jumped. Tino picked it up for me and sat beside me on the greenhouse bench so relaxed as if he hadn't just startled me to death.

How couldn't I hear him come in? The guy was a freaking ninja.

"I know this is your house, but please stop startling me like this." I grabbed my bow back.

"You shouldn't be so startled all the time. You need to work on your reflexes."

I cocked a brow. "Well, not everybody is you, Don Bellomo."

He glared at me for calling him that. I was crazy to love to tease him. He treated me with kindness, but he was a scary guy who always carried a gun. I saw him punch one of his guards the other day, knocking him down, tooth flying, blood splattering and everything. And that was a man he trusted for years.

"The next time you're going to disobey me I'm going to bend you on my knees and spank you."

My eyes widened in shock, an immediate burn to my cheeks, an inexplicable gush of arousal between my legs. "Tino!"

"That's what brats get in my house, young lady."

I jumped to my feet, my hands on my hips. "I'm not a brat, and I'm not a little girl."

His eyes dropped to my chest. "Is that why you're missing your bra again? To show me and every other fuck in here that you're not a little girl?"

My jaw dropped. "What the hell? I'm not showing anybody anything. I'm wearing a freaking parka. Nothing is showing."

He crossed his legs. "I can perfectly see your nipples. Again."

I glanced down, my nipples pebbling harder with every inappropriate word he was saying. Fuck. He was right, and I hated that he was. With my angry stance the parka moved back and my nipples were pointing out for him to see. Shoot.

My arms jerked to shield my chest, but then instead of pulling the parka to cover myself, I pushed it further back. "It's my body. I'll do what I want with it. If I want to show any part of it, that's my business. You and your men should look away if you don't like or approve of what you see."

Face made of steel, he didn't take his eyes off my chest. Of my boobs with the nipples he made hard. His tongue darted out of his mouth and licked his lip, and a new gush wet my panties. Jesus. Why the fuck wasn't he looking away?

"Stop staring." *Or don't.* "It's…"

"Inappropriate?"

"Yes."

"You said to look away if I didn't like what I saw." He got up, towering over me. "What if I do?"

My eyes couldn't grow any wider. "Tino, what the hell are you doing?"

"Teaching you a lesson." He stepped forward, and I stumbled back. He kept moving toward me, and I retreated until my back hit the glass. He placed his palms on either side of me, caging me in, his eyes piercing me.

"Why are you scaring me? I don't like this. I don't like this at all."

My chest rose and fell with every gasp. He stared again. "I think you do. Very much."

Damn you, nipples.

"Stop it. Whatever this is, stop it."

"Are you sure that's what you want me to do, Angelina? You don't want me to stare at your tits? You don't want my hands on them? You don't want my mouth you're staring at now to worship them?"

My pussy throbbed. Fuck him. Fuck the sinful, depraved images he was planting in my head. Fuck what he was doing to me. Fuck my goddamn body that didn't understand it should never react like that to bad guys who wanted to have me without permission. "Why are you being such a—"

"Dick?"

"Yes. Fuck yes."

"Because I warned you and you didn't listen." His breath, sweet and hot, fanned my face. He grabbed the lower edge of the parka and pulled me closer, ripping a gasp out of my chest. Then he pinned his stare to my mouth. My lips parted in response. Fuck, piss and shit. "What if it was someone else here right now? What if I found someone else here, like this, with you right now?"

Words eluded me. I could only gasp.

"You know what I'd have done. Is that what you want, Angelina? You want me to maim and kill for you?"

I shook my head rapidly, vigorously. "No. No one here could have done what you're doing right now. Isn't that what you told me?"

"Maybe not one of my men unless he had a death wish, but what if it was Leo? He's a sneaky bastard and knows this house better than any of my men. He could've broken in and found you here all alone with your hard nipples in his face. You know he has a thing for you. He wants you so bad. What if he thought with his cock and took advantage of you?"

"I wouldn't let him."

"What would you do to stop him, little girl?"

A surge of anger ran through me. My knee lifted to smack his balls, but it met his palm. How could he move it so fast off the glass, as if he'd anticipated my move?

"Not bad. What else?"

I tried the other knee, but he blocked that as well. Both his fists gripped my knees and spread my legs with one swift move. His weight pressed me to the glass, his hips less than an inch away from my crotch. "How about now? What if he went crazy and cornered you like this? What if it wasn't Leo at all? What if it was *him*?"

Pain seared my chest, seeping into my soul, and tears blurred my vision. "Please stop."

"That's what you're going to do? Cry and beg him to stop like the little girl you are? Would you even try to stop him at all?"

"You're an asshole."

"An asshole that doesn't want any sick fuck around you taking what's not his. An asshole that will kill to protect you because you have no skill whatsoever to protect yourself."

I wanted to smash my violin over his head, but it was too precious to waste on Tino fucking Bellomo. I pushed it against him. I fucking pushed against the wool of his coat, one hand holding the violin and bow, the other a fist, over and over, but he wouldn't budge. He was a freaking wall.

He let go of my knees only to grab my parka again. His tongue did that darting thing and dragged a quivering long breath out of my lips. "You're a beautiful girl. You drive men crazy. If you're not careful, you're going to pay a terrible price." Abruptly, he zipped up my parka and stepped back with a warning stare.

My lips and chin trembled with the tears I pushed back. No more crying in front of him. I spun to storm out, but he grabbed my wrist. I darted an angry gaze at him over my shoulder, but he grabbed me to his embrace.

When his arms wrapped around me and he printed his soft kiss on my forehead, I couldn't fight back the tears.

He waited it out, as always, and then his gaze, now fatherly kind as it used to be, smiled at me. "Did you hear what I said when I first came in?"

I blinked, remembering. I heard it, yes. It only registered in my head now, though. "We're having dinner at Leo's?"

"Yes. It's Valentine's Day."

My mind stopped working for a moment, and my heart did that fluttering move it always did for the wrong people.

"I want you to play at Leo's as a part of the restaurant celebration," he added.

"Oh." Of course that was why he'd ask me to dinner on Valentine's Day. "Wow."

"Is that okay?"

"I…I'd love to. My first gig outside school…and a free meal at Leo's. The food is excellent there. I… The Halloween special you have there is… Wow. Thank you, Tino."

"Prego. Eight O'clock sharp. I'll be in charge of your wardrobe, undergarments included."

My jaw twisted. As much as I was dying to protest and *disobey*, I'd learned my lesson. He knew how to give one. "Fine."

"Also Leo will be there for that meeting you asked for."

"Oh. Okay." I nodded, pensively. *So that's what this is all about?*

"Are you going to be prepared?"

"For the gig? Yeah, sure. Anything in particular you want me to play?"

"I meant for Leo."

Was I? *I guess we'll see tonight if I am.*

CHAPTER 26

Lina

A burgundy red dress cascaded along the bedspread, awaiting me in my room as I got out of the shower.

I got it out of the bag, the feeling of the pleated shimmer satin elegant and luxurious. This must have been the softest thing I'd ever touched in my life. My glance fell on the tag, and I swore. *Valentino*.

I put it down so carefully and stepped away. Then I put my hands together, as if praying to the divine dress.

"Oh my God!" Nicky's squeal pierced my eardrum as she came running to me.

"Exactly."

"It's so beautiful!"

"It's so expensive."

She saw the tag and screamed.

"I can't wear this."

"You can't not wear this. You're so wearing the—" She screamed again. "Matching shoes."

I followed the path her eyes just took and got blinded by the sparkling beauty of the red pumps by the foot of the bed.

"Uh…Lina? Has Mr. Bellomo just bought you underwear?"

I looked up, guilty and flushed. She was holding a new, red, padded bra and panty set and dangling it down my face.

I snatched it and held it behind my back. "He did, yeah. For the dress. I didn't know what kind of dress he was going to get so I didn't know what set of underwear would match it. It's totally normal."

"Yeah. Not even a Valentino could conquer a bad bra day." She pursed her lips. "I bet you were as red as a tomato when he asked you about your cup and panty size. I know I would."

He never asked me, and I forgot to tell him, my mind preoccupied with what I was gonna say to Leo. "Yeah. You should've seen my face. Hope he got it right." I tucked my hair behind my ear and held the dress by the hanger only. "I'ma go try everything on."

In the dressing room, I checked the size of the dress and underwear. They were accurate. Too accurate for a guy to just guess. He got me a thirty-eight B and a half bra. The only cup size that fit me right but so rare to find. I mostly got a C or a B because that was all I could find. How many guys knew the difference between a B and a half and a C cup in the first place?

Tino must be quite a ladies' man, who had bought a lot of women's underwear before, and, well, he'd been doing a lot of staring at my boobs so…

My face matched the dress at the fresh memory of that moment in time that was awkward, scary and embarrassingly arousing. Tino's expression of overprotectiveness could be dark and angry and disturbing but somehow it played the strings of my soul, hitting all the right notes, singing to the dark corners of my heart, dancing around the wounds that wouldn't heal. His dark melody spoke to me in ways I didn't understand before.

Ways he knew and taught by heart.

I looked at myself in the mirror. The dress was so beautiful and classy and—of course—covered me from neck to toe. Except for my arms, nothing was showing. I was glad he chose a sleeveless dress so I could move my arms with ease when I played. I wondered if he thought of that when he made his choice. I knew he did. He paid attention to everything, even the simplest detail of the minor comfort a sleeveless dress could give a violinist.

And the perfection of a B and a half rather than a C cup on her boobs.

I chuckled as I twirled, watching the amazing flow of the design over my body. I was wearing a Valentino dress to play at the most expensive restaurant in the city, having dinner with the owner himself on Valentine's Day.

My first gig.

My first Valentine's date—it wasn't a date at all, but that was how I was gonna remember it for the rest of my life.

I admired the dress one more time, doing one more twirl, another memory burst in my head.

The dress *he* put in my closet.

A bleak cloud darkened my mood as I remembered how similarly happy I was that day, only to have gotten my heart shredded later. Would that happen today, too?

"Stop ruining my life. I'm done letting you toy with me. I won't let you ruin tonight for me." The situation was similar but way different. A man who knew exactly my size without asking bought me a beautiful, expensive dress and left it in my room.

He figured my size and the dress I was dying to wear by stalking me and going through my own closet without permission. Tino figured it out because he was here, with me, out in the open, staring at my body so bluntly. Uncomfortable yet clear. No hiding. No stealing.

He thought *he* could buy me with the dress. Tino had no ulterior motive other than overprotecting me from unwanted eyes.

He was fucking up my world. Tino was giving me the world.

I took a deep breath, determined I wouldn't let *him* steal from me again, neither from my time nor my happiness. Enough was enough.

"Mr. Bellomo, you're here." Nicky's faint voice streamed into the dressing room.

I hurried out. Was I late? Shoot. I hadn't done my hair and makeup yet.

"Nicole, per favore, mia figlia, call me Tino. You're family now," he said as I stepped out into the bedroom.

"If I'm late, I'm so sorry. I thought it was still seven. I'll be ready in—"

"You're not late." His eyes fixed on me, sparkling, and he swallowed.

"Thank God. And thank you," I gestured at my body, "for this. It's perfect."

"It is." There was a slight shake to his voice that wasn't like him. His gaze on me was different than the one I was used to from him. It was more manly than fatherly.

Or that was what I hoped for.

Butterflies in my stomach, I went to grab the shoes. "I'm gonna go finish now."

He grunted, not looking away. "Nicole, have you tried your dress yet?"

"My dress?" she exclaimed. "You got me a dress, too?"

"Certo. It's in your room."

"Wow. Thank you. I didn't even know I was invited."

"That goes without saying. Unless you have something more important to do."

"Not at all. You didn't have to get me anything, though, Tino. It's extremely generous of you."

"Oh, don't be silly. What did I say? We're family. Go try it on."

Nicky gave me a quirky, surprised smile behind Tino before she left. I grinned back and then looked at him, pointing at the dressing room. "I'll be in there."

"I'm coming with you," he said.

My brows shot up. "To the dressing room?"

"Yes. I'm doing your makeup."

"Excuse me?"

He just walked toward me, grabbed my hand and practically sat me in the dresser seat. "What did I say about—"

"Thank you, Tino, but what the hell?"

He went through the few brushes and scattered products I had, choosing some with meticulous care. "Language. I let it go earlier because you were only speaking the truth. I was being a dick and an asshole on purpose. But now I won't be so tolerating if you don't watch your mouth."

"So what? You'll spank me?"

"Swear again and see for yourself."

Fuck. Fuckfuckfuckfuck FUCK! But I wouldn't say it because I believed his threat.

He wouldn't shy away, and I'd end up with his strong slaps on my butt. I stared at his big, tattooed hands, thinking that might not be such a terrible thing.

He chuckled and then bent, his beard almost touching my cheek. "Go ahead or are you afraid you'll enjoy it so much?"

I didn't blush this time. I looked him straight in the eye. "Yes, Tino. I soaked my panties when *he* did it. I know I'll enjoy it when *you* spank me, too."

I thought that would make him uncomfortable, but he didn't even blink. "Because I'll remind you of *him*? Or because you want *me* to do it?"

"Both." Who injected me with truth serum?

The acceleration in his breath and the way his eyes changed again with the flicker of lust I saw a few minutes ago lasted only a second, but I noticed.

"Except that your desire for me isn't real," he said.

"Mmhm. Not real," I mumbled, my gaze zeroing in on his lips. "For argument sake, what if it was real? What would you do about it?"

His fingertips brushed my forehead, smoothing my hair off my face, a simple touch yet made of flames that zigzagged their way to my core. "I would…spank you harder until it stopped feeling good."

"To punish me?" My whole body throbbed at the thought. Apparently, I was a sucker for it.

"To expel that silly feeling out of you for good." He picked up a brush. "Close your eyes, Angelina."

Seriously? "Are you really doing my makeup?"

"Si, si. Are you doubting my skills, young lady?"

Again with that enraging crap. "Are you trying to make me swear on purpose so you'll have an excuse to spank me?"

"Who said I need an excuse?" He winked, and my ovaries exploded. "Close your eyes, Angelina. I'm going to start with them until you stop blushing."

I giggled—only with him—and did as I was told, trusting him against all odds, praying he'd betray that trust and do something else entirely with me other than doing my makeup.

For the next twenty minutes, his strokes and breaths on my skin set me ablaze, and when he touched my lips, I could have simultaneously combusted. My breathing was out of control, and the sleeves of his suit jacket grazed my heaving boobs more than once. Thank God for the padded bra. The new panties, though, were no good. I needed a new pair.

When he stopped painting my face—that was how I imagined it. He wasn't doing my makeup. He was painting, and my face was his canvas—his fingers massaged my scalp.

"You're gonna do my hair, too?" I asked, no resistance left in me. I still had my eyes closed, and his fingers were doing wonders relaxing my muscles.

"Yes. It'll look better up."

"What if I like it down?"

"You'll still wear it up."

"Because you say so?"

"Yes."

"You're a possessive control freak, you know that?"

"Absolutely. Thank you for the precious insight."

I snorted. "Do you think you have the right to control me because you're paying for everything?"

"No."

"Then why?"

"I want what's best for you, and you trust me to give you that." His fingers left my hair and found my hand. He lifted it and printed a soft kiss on it. I trembled in response. "You can open your eyes now."

Taking a deep breath, I looked in the mirror. I froze for a second or ten. The woman—definitely woman, not girl—looked like me, but I almost didn't recognize myself. So elegant, so confident, like I was going to play at La Scala, like I belonged with the kind of people that dined at Leo's every day, like I was fit to be Tino Bellomo's date.

I rose and headed to the full length mirror. Then I checked myself back and front, feeling the exposition of the back of my neck that somehow gave me extra height and a better posture. "You were right. You *are* giving me the best."

He grabbed the pumps and bent on one knee, asking me to extend my foot. In awe, I did as he asked. His big hand cradled my foot as he put the shoe on it, and I indulged in this Cinderella moment that might never happen again.

When he got to his feet, he took a step back, looking over my body. Then he asked me to twirl for him. Giggling, I did, checking the amazing flow of the dress for the millionth time.

"One more thing," he said.

"It's perfect the way it is, Tino. I've never looked better."

He reached inside the pocket of his suit jacket and got out a big velvet box. "Put it on, but don't get too excited. It's a rental."

Dazed, I stared at him. "You rented jewelry for me?"

He opened the box, and the bling of the diamonds and rubies in the bracelet and ring set bedazzled me. "Something to take away from your beauty. I want people to look at them instead of you."

Why did he keep saying that? I was nothing to look at. A wallflower. The only attention I'd ever got was from sick stalkers. Well, maybe that justified his concerns. He was the one protecting me and didn't need more creeps attracted to the psycho stalker magnet.

Impatient, he put them on my hand when I didn't do it myself and cocked a brow at me.

"Thank you, Tino."

"Atta girl."

CHAPTER 27

Lina

"Ladies and gentlemen, I have a special guest for you tonight. Please welcome, our very own Bellomo prodigy, signorina Angelina Baldi," Tino introduced me himself, looking absolutely dashing in his black suit, standing next to a slick piano under the spotlight. Everything about him shone with masculine formidability that took my breath away.

He stretched a hand in my direction. My heels clicked toward him, growing confident as I focused only on his eyes. Our hands met, my cold fingers absorbing his heat. Then he kissed the back of my hand, never failing to induce a shiver through me.

"In bocca al lupo," he said.

"What?"

He smiled. "Break a leg."

I laughed nervously as he eased away. The restaurant was fully packed, so many eyes on me. I thought I wouldn't be nervous; I never suffered from stage fright. But I was. There were so many strangers and a sophisticated audience I'd never played for before. Inhaling, I reminded myself that I wasn't Lina, the school girl, today. I was Tino Bellomo's special guest, the entertainment at the most expensive venue in the city. I was dressed for the occasion, and if there was one thing I was confident about, it was my music.

Nicky was sitting in the center closest to the stage, and Tino joined her shortly. I concentrated on them, as if I was going to play only for them. "Good evening, I'm Angelina Baldi, your entertainment for the next thirty minutes. It's an honor to be here tonight. If you have any special requests, please pass them to your server, and I'll do my best to accommodate them all. Happy Valentine's."

People wished me a happy Valentine's Day as well, lifting their glasses. Nicky cheered for me, and Tino gave me an approving nod.

I pressed my chin on the violin and started an international favorite. *Beauty and the Beast.*

To my beast with the sexy beard that was giving me the best. Tino Il Lupo. The wolf that wouldn't lose his vice but remained my good luck charm.

People started to dance, and I was no longer nervous. I was happy. The happiest I'd been in a very long time. Nothing clouded the joy swirling inside me. What Tino had done this morning long forgotten. The anxiety of meeting Leo buried deep. Even the fear that *he* might show up tonight nonexistent. I wanted *him* to come. To see. To fuck up.

I wanted *him* over.

I wanted my freedom so I could live my life. The one Tino was showing me I deserved.

It was only when he asked Nicky to dance with him that a pang set in my chest. I'd have loved to dance with him, except I was here, playing the music they danced to.

I knew he didn't think of her as a woman. Even if he did, he'd never be with either of us. But if this was a different world, and we weren't the Baldi sisters, the charity cases, if

Tino was to choose one of us, it'd be Nicky. The smart, beautiful, strong woman who wasn't afraid of taking what she deserved or fitting in a world like his, who wasn't a psycho stalker magnet that let sickos take advantage of her. The woman he wouldn't have to protect and take care of all the freaking time.

He twirled her, and she flowed with him as if they'd danced together a million times before. They held their eye contact during the whole dance. Only when the song was ending had he bend her back and lifted his gaze. His smirk hit me as he winked at me.

I looked away as I wrapped up the song. A quick smile landed on my lips as I received a round of applause. A server brought me the requests, and I sifted through them. Almost all of them were hardcore classics. Were they testing me?

I chose the hardest of them all. Caprice No. 24 by Paganini. It was fast and crazy, and Paganini himself couldn't master it at first.

Challenge accepted.

Starting the melody, I took my time looking at my audience one by one, meeting their scrutinizing stares with equal examination. I never needed to prove myself to the society elite, but the fire of jealousy in my chest forced me to show them all, to show Tino I belonged here like anybody else.

My eyes wandered among the busy tables and the swirling dance floor. People weren't listening while they ate now. They stopped their scrumptious meals to listen with full attention to the music.

To me.

Tino and Nicky were back to their table, listening too, as if they could no longer keep up with my rhythm, yet admiration and pride etched all over their faces.

I tore my gaze away from them. Right now, I didn't need their support. I demanded their attention along with everyone else's in the place, and I was getting it.

With the angry notes, I closed my eyes and let it all out. Then I found myself in the melody, gaining back my balance. When I opened my eyes, Leo's face was there.

He just stood there, watching me with the yearning of a lover that had just found their soulmate.

I should have averted my gaze, but I smiled at him, pretending to be playing for him. Didn't Tino call me a brat? Well, I'd live up to it. Let's see if he'd keep his promise.

You'll dance with my sister. I'll dance with your son. My way.

CHAPTER 28

Tino

*Y*ou *can't give what's not yours, Angel. Not even your smile. It belongs to me.*

Not him. Never him.

I tilted my head at Leo, nodding for him to sit. He sauntered to our table, his eyes glued to my Angel, a fucking grin on his face. "She's amazing, isn't she?"

"Wipe that smile off your face or I'll punch it off for you," I gritted.

"What? Why?"

Because she's mine. I nodded at Nicole instead. She was fuming, staring daggers at Leo.

He shifted his smile toward her, taking a hint. "Buonasera, Nicky. Happy Valentine's Day."

Her fists clenched, and I held the one on the table, patting it, reminding her of what we were here for. She breathed out. "It's Nicole to you." Her stare, and his, returned to the stage.

To my Angel, whose eyes twitched when they found my hand on her sister's. Quickly, she looked back at Leo, giving him another smile.

Don't do it, Angel. Don't play the jealousy game with me. You'll lose. We'll all lose.

Leo took the request card and scribbled something down. Then he gestured for a waitress to give it to Angel.

"What are you doing? Do you even know why you're here?" I asked him.

"I'm passing down a request, and yes, I know exactly why I'm here."

I leaned back in my chair, gripping on the sliver of patience I had left to tolerate this charade till the end. My gaze followed Angel, even if she was no longer looking at me like she should have been.

What did I expect from a brat? *You're asking for it, Angel.*

She finished the piece perfectly. Applause filled the air. Leo was on his feet, clapping with everybody else, his stupid grin pasted on his face.

The waitress handed her his request. When Angel opened it, she flashed her teeth at Leo and nodded. "This song is for Leo Bellomo."

Nicole glared at her, and Angel winked as she lifted her bow. "Back to December."

I didn't know the fucking song, but the title was enough to simmer my blood. Back to December when they hadn't had their fight yet, when she still liked him. I pulled out my phone and checked the lyrics. This was a fucking second chance song. An *I'm sorry please take me back* song.

Che Cazzo?

I leaned into him. "What the fuck do you think you're doing?"

"Dad, please, save it until after the song." He gazed at her as if he was enchanted. "She's playing for me."

I growled, the sting of his shitty words searing. "Stronzo una volta, stronzo sempre. Va bene, Leo. Have it your way. But mark my words. She will *never* be yours." *She's mine. Her body. Her heart. Her mind. Her soul. Her smile. Her music. All mine.*

She finished the fucking song and played two more before she took her bow and joined us at the table. Leo sprang to his feet and kissed her hand in a greeting. I'd bend them both over my knees and spank the fuck out of them.

"You were amazing up there." He gave her the once-over. "You look…"

"Perfect, as always," I said, stepping in between them. "You did amazing, Angelina. The customers are very pleased."

"What about you? I saw you dancing with my sister. I guess you were pleased, too." She glanced over Nicole. "Nicky?"

"You were fabulous. I loved it. The best you've ever played," Nicole said, oblivious to what was really happening.

My little Angel was jealous.

As much as it warmed my heart and brought me one step closer to owning hers, it was about to backfire.

"My private booth is ready for our dinner." I linked arms with Angel, marking my territory, and gestured for Leo and Nicole to move ahead.

Leo kept glancing at Angel over his shoulder all the way up to the booth. I wanted to kick his ass. "Eyes front. Don't fall."

Angel snickered, and I glared at her. She looked down, her lips still twitching with laughter.

"Everything you do has consequences, Angelina. So laugh all you want now."

"Is that supposed to scare me, Don Bellomo?"

"It's supposed to knock some sense into you, but it looks like words don't work with you." I let go of her arm and spanked her little ass. A loud gasp fled her throat as her body jerked, almost tripping. I held her arm to stop the fall. "I'm done talking."

Nicole and Leo glanced over us simultaneously. "You okay?" she asked Angel.

"Yeah," Angel mumbled, her face as red as her dress. "I was gonna fall, but Tino caught me. Thank you, Tino."

"My pleasure. Always." I led her into my booth while Leo was waiting for her to sit next to him. Hand on the small of her back, I ushered her to her side of the leather couch—beside me. Then I blocked her end of the table, securing the place, staring at Leo. "Sit beside Nicole."

"At the very far end," Nicole added, sliding into the booth.

"Okay." He chuckled as we all took the right seats, right where we fucking belonged. "Obviously, there's a lot of air to clear here."

"Not really," Nicole said. "There isn't much to do here, Leo. You stalk my sister, creep your way into making her like you, while you're fucking engaged? The only thing we expect from you is an apology and a goodbye. Then we'll say congratulations and wish you all the best with your new position and the wedding."

I poured myself some wine, a smirk on my lips. I loved this girl. We always saw eye to eye.

"Lina, is that your opinion, too?" he asked.

My ears perked up.

She opened her mouth, but the servers interrupted her, bringing our plates and bread before she spoke.

"We should eat first," Angel said. "It's my first Valentine's Day…event. I'd like to enjoy it to the max," her eyes traveled among the three of us, "if that's okay with you."

"Sure." Leo smiled, while Nicole apologized. Angel glanced at me, waiting for me to say something, too. I only took a sip of the wine and placed a napkin on her lap for her.

The little jerk of her thighs as I touched her amused me. Would she jerk the same way when my hand was on her pussy? I bet she'd come all over my hand in less than ten seconds.

T-minus eight and a half months.

If I could wait that long.

"Happy Valentine's Day," Leo said, pushing a narrow rectangular leather box in her direction. "I hope you like it."

Angel laughed under her breath as she opened it. He got her a fucking necklace. "Leo, it's beautiful. I...I don't know what to say."

"Just put it on. I'd help if you weren't guarded like an army secret."

She giggled. Since when did she giggle for anyone but me?

"She can't accept it." Nicky intervened before I'd rip the fucking thing off Angel's neck if she decided to wear it and kick Leo's stinky ass out. Thank fuck.

"Why not?" *Stronzo* exclaimed.

"You can't buy your way into an apology with your expensive gift."

"I'm not trying to say sorry with this. It's a Valentine's gift."

"Only couples exchange gifts on V-Day. You're not a couple."

Lina dropped a fork. "Enough, Nicky. I'm right here. You don't have to speak for me." She directed her gaze toward Leo. "Thank you for your gift. It's a beautiful gesture. Whether I can accept it or not is up to me and only me to decide." She snapped the box closed and placed it next to her on the table. "Now, can you guys promise not to talk about anything until we finish dinner? I'd like to eat in peace, if that's not too much to ask."

I patted her thigh, and she jerked again. "You got it. No more talking. For now."

When the food arrived, and she saw I ordered salmon pasta for her, she blinked. "How did you know that's what I was gonna order?"

"I didn't. It's the best pasta dish in the house, that and the pineapple ravioli, but I know you're not a fan. You don't want the salmon pasta?"

"I do. It's my favorite. Thank you, Tino."

"No need to thank me." I dipped a fork in the truffle gnocchi and moved it to her mouth. "You should try this, too."

"Oh, okay." Her lips wrapped around the fork, and I pictured them on something else entirely. Her tongue licked the creamy sauce off her lip, sending a big twitch in my cock. "It's so delicious."

Yes. That's what you're gonna say. "More?"

"Yes, please."

That too.

As promised, we finished the meal without bringing anything up—except my territorial cock. I exercised self-control around her more than I ever did around anything or anyone else. When there was another male dying to sniff her, to snatch her away from me, that was a different story.

"Can we talk alone, please?" Leo asked.

"Not happening," I uttered. "Angelina only agreed to this meeting if I *chaperoned*. She doesn't trust you alone with her. Neither do I."

"It's okay, Tino. You shouldn't waste the rest of the evening for me. I can take care of myself. The live band has started. You should take Nicky and continue your dance."

I shifted on the couch, my knee brushing hers, but I didn't move it away. I pressed it further so that the sides of our thighs touched, too. "Not. Happening."

"Fine. I don't mind saying what I came here to say in front of you. I don't mind saying it in front of the whole world," he said. "Lina, I'm sorry if I scared you before.

Everything I did was because I really like you and wanted to get to know you. I should've asked you out earlier to find out about all the things I wanted to know instead of…finding them out on my own. I also should've given you the choice whether to see me or not instead of following you around, forcing myself in your way like this.

"I admit I was, still am, obsessed with you, not like your actual stalker, but in the way any boy feels about the girl he likes this much. I think there's nothing wrong with that."

Nicole was about to say something, but Angel lifted a finger, silencing her. "You're right. My reaction was a little exaggerated because of my…situation."

Fury rumbled inside of me. Che cazzo?

"That doesn't change the facts that I can't be with you or anyone until *he* is caught and you're engaged, Leo," she added.

"I'm not afraid of *him*, and I'm not engaged."

"What the fuck? Of course you are," I spat.

"A girl was promised to me when we were kids. I never had a say in it or agreed to that engagement. Not once. I'm not a kid anymore. I have the right to choose the person I'm gonna spend the rest of my life with."

"The only reason you didn't want to marry Claudia was because you didn't want anything to do with the family business. That has changed. You're made. What's your problem now?"

"I don't love Claudia." Il cazzone pinned his gaze to my Angel. "I'm in love with someone else."

Her chest heaved, her eyes wide. "W-what?"

"It's hard to believe because we don't know each other, and I know it makes me sound fucking crazy, but I don't care. I stopped caring a long time ago. Believe me, I tried when I was away, but fighting it is pointless and only makes me more edgy. I can't run from the truth."

"What truth?"

"I'm in love with you, Lina." He swallowed. "And with your permission, I'd be honored if you'll let me spend the rest of my life getting to know you."

"Oh for fuck's sake," Nicole grumbled. "Are you out of your mind?"

My fists clenched so hard my knuckles turned white. All my attention went to Angel. I needed to see how she'd react to this bullshit. *Tell him to fuck off, Angel. Tell him you*

can never love him back. Tell him you can never be
his. Tell him like you told me, you belong to me.

Her silence and quivering breath insulted me. If she wouldn't speak, I would. I'd do a lot more than speaking. "You'd better shut that mouth of yours right now."

"No. I did everything you asked of me. Now, let me choose the one thing in my life I still can choose." Leo stood and then got down on one knee, a small box open in his hands, a fucking ring inside it. "Angelina Maria Baldi, you're the love of my life. I promise I'll always protect, love and take care of you. Will you—"

Blood filled his mouth instead of the outrageous shit he was saying.

Yeah, I punched the motherfucker silent.

CHAPTER 29

Tino

She hadn't said a word all the way home, and once we arrived, she stalked away with her violin case into the gardens.

"Where are you going?" I yelled after her.

"The greenhouse! Don't follow me!"

I rolled my eyes and waved for Michele to go after her. After I'd left Leo with a bloody face at the restaurant with the useless bodyguards who had failed to stop him from following Angel to the movies before, he might show up uninvited to cause more damage.

A fucking proposal. *Ma a che cazzo sta pensando, Leo?*

"Tino, can I have a word?" Nicole asked.

"Not now, Nicole. Go to bed. We'll talk tomorrow."

"I'll have to wait for Lina."

"No." *I'll be waiting for her.* "Don't talk to her tonight. Tomorrow the three of us will sit together and say everything that needs to be said."

She sighed and nodded reluctantly. "I don't mean to interfere between you and your son, but punching him like that in front of Lina…"

What the fuck was I supposed to do? Give him my fucking blessing or wait for her to say yes? "You shouldn't interfere," I warned.

She blinked, startled for a second. I never spoke to her harshly. "I'm sorry," she said. "Just for the record, she wouldn't have said yes."

"She didn't exactly say no, did she? She accepted his gift, his love declaration. She stood there, tears in her eyes, gasping and emotional while he got down on one knee." Fire gnashed through my whole body. "She did absolutely nothing to stop him. She fucking led him on."

"Tino—"

"Buonanotte, Nicole."

I made sure she went to her room before I let myself in Angel's. I thought about drugging Nicole like that night with the thunderstorm, but that was a one-time thing so that Angel couldn't have slept with her. Tonight was different. I wasn't going to watch Angel in her sleep while I lay in her bed.

I was staying the night. Under the bed.

Wasn't that where I was supposed to be? I was the monster under her bed.

When I reached her bedside, I took off my shoes and hid them under the bed. Then I sat, filling my nostrils with her lingering scent in the sheets, and cursed my cock for wanting her so badly.

After the death of my wife, whenever I felt the need to fuck, I'd go through a long list of women who had no problem throwing themselves at the most eligible bachelor in town hoping and trying for something that would never happen.

But now... The thought of being inside any woman other than Angel was hideous. Useless.

Yes, she was fucking seventeen. Yes, I shouldn't think of her that way. Not yet. But I did. And so did Leo. He fucking proposed to her. If she'd said yes, he could have been her husband in a week, sinking his cock in her virgin pussy that was mine.

The thought alone made me want to flay someone alive. Angel was mine, and she'd continue to be mine. I'd make her mine in every way humanly possible.

Me. Not Leo. There was only room for one monster in her world.

Footsteps echoed outside the room. Hers. Quickly, I dropped to the floor and managed to slide myself under the bed. Facing the mattress, once I made sure I was invisible to anyone who entered the room, I relaxed. She'd stopped looking under her bed for months now. She wouldn't look for me. And with being her free self without knowing I was watching, with her right where I heard her every move, her every tear and breath, I could close my eyes and sleep forever.

Click!

She locked the door? She never locked the door.

Light streamed into the room, and angry heels came toward the bed. The mattress sank around the edge, and her shoes went flying one by one.

"Fuck you. FUCK YOU!"

Was that for me or my asshole son?

"Don't swear. Don't call me Don Bellomo," she mocked. "Well, fuck you, Don Bellomo."

Gladly, Angel.

The springs gave a tiny squeak, and her toes landed in my vision. "Wear a fucking bra. I can perfectly see your nipples again. Here's your goddamn bra."

Zip! Burgundy red pooled over her feet. Then her bra dropped next to them. I suppressed a moan, picturing her standing topless a few inches away from me.

"Do you like what you see now? Or you need the full view?" Her panties fell to her ankles. I narrowed my eyes to see if they were wet, but I couldn't tell from here. Later, I'd have my fun with the whole outfit.

"Want your hands on my tits and your mouth worshiping them?"

Yes.

"Want to bend me over your knee and spank my naked ass?"

Fuck yes.

"Here I am." She kicked the dress and panties off her ankles and stepped out of them. Then the mattress sank again. "But you'll never come and do it. You'll go dance with my sister and punch your son in the face for loving me, for wanting to marry me.

Because I'm not good enough for any fucking Bellomo."

You're good enough for one Bellomo. The only Bellomo you'll ever have. The only man you'll ever have.

"I'll always be the program kid. The nobody with the psycho stalker threat, the outsider that could break Mafia allies and screw family friendships. The little girl."

Was she mad at me for stopping Leo from being with her or for seeing her as a little girl? Who did she want? Me or him?

The bed squeaked again as she settled her back on it, her feet still in my view. "I'm not a little girl, Tino. In my dreams, I'm never a little girl to you."

I looked up at the mattress, a silly grin on my face. *You're not a little girl, Angel. I wish I could still see you as one. I wish I could still protect you from myself. But that ship has sailed.*

"I know I can please you in real life as much as I do in my dreams." Her feet pulled up, and her body slid back and sprawled over the mattress. "Even if I can't at first, you can teach me…"

I bit my lip and closed my eyes. *Soon, my sweet Angel. Soon, you'll learn everything you need to know from me. Only me.* Not that she needed to learn anything. One look at her sweet body, at her beautiful pussy, and I became undone.

"Tino, what have you done to me? I hate you for making me want you so bad. I hate you for making me think about you when I should be thinking about Leo, the boy who wants me, who loves me, who thinks I'm worthy of anything, who has the balls to defy you, almighty Tino, and fucking propose to me."

What Leo had for her was nothing compared to what I had. She thought he had balls to defy me for her sake, and I didn't? *I'll defy the whole world for you, Angel.*

I was waiting for your sake, not mine. Did you want me to just kidnap you? Force you to marry me? Use your young body for my pleasure against your will?

I'm not an angel like you. Did you know how many times I'd fought to prevent myself from doing just that?

Then you had to bring Leo between us. My own son. I wish it was someone else so I could put us all out of our misery. I'd have killed the fucker and taken you away as you wished. But now, I can't.

I just couldn't lose my son, too.

"I hate you as much as I hate *him*. I want you as much as I want *him*." Her voice grew softer, and then she moaned.

My heart thundered in my ears as she fidgeted, whispering my name. She was masturbating…to me. Tino, not *him*.

Cazzo. My now rock-hard cock and swelling balls begged me for some freedom.

"Mmmm." She squirmed.

I unbuckled my belt with her next moan so she wouldn't hear. I should have taken it off with my shoes earlier, but I didn't expect she'd be masturbating naked above me. Soon, she wouldn't have to. I'd give her every orgasm she never knew she wanted as her naked body squirmed beneath mine.

"I want you all over me. I want you inside me." The smell of her wetness clung to me, and my fist wrapped around my throbbing erection.

"Were you hard when you stared at my nipples, when your cock was an inch away from my pussy? Did your cock ache for me like I ached for you when you were breathing all over me, doing my makeup? Did you stare at my tits again when my eyes were closed? Did you get hard when you spanked me, Tino?"

Yeah. Yes, Angel. The bed rattled as the speed of her movements picked up, a slurping sound in the background. I stroked my cock harder, faster, yet careful not make a sound.

"I bet you're so big you'll split me in half." She moaned through the slurping. "I see the huge outline under your swimsuit. God, tonight I was so close to drop some food on your pants so I could clean it up and feel how big your cock is."

I wished it'd been my cock inside of her right now. I bit back a groan, jealous of her own fingers, but the burning of my jealousy cooled down when she whined my name.

"Oh, God, yes," she choked out. Her breathing grew ragged, and a chorus of successive moans flew out of her chest. With every one of those, I was going to moan, too, and expose myself. "Look at how wet you make me. Wanna come have a taste? A big bite. Fuck me, Tino. Fuck my pussy with your big cock."

Merda. I lowered my pants and pushed the elastic of my underwear, making room for the mess I was about to make.

"Tino!" She came so hard. Her sweet moans and the smell of her orgasm milked my own. A little groan I couldn't contain almost gave me away as my cum jetted all over my underwear.

Her breathing was hard, but she was still. After a moment, she sighed. "I might hate you, but you just gave me the best orgasm of my life so far. Thank you, Tino."

Then the lights were out and the room fell silent.

Patiently, I counted the seconds, the long minutes that turned into hours until her breath was deep and even. Then I slipped out from under the bed. When I stood, casting a shadow over her body, I pulled away the sheets and watched.

If anyone could live up to their name so accurately, it was her. She looked angelic in the moonlight as she slept. So delicate and perfect. Fragile even. And so very naked. The thought of anyone laying a hand on her precious body had my hands itchy for sweet, slow torture.

I ached to suck another orgasm from her. But I settled for one of the things I'd long denied myself yet she offered tonight. I allowed myself a simple taste.

My finger dipped in the wetness that still filled her and smeared it all over my mouth. She tasted fucking delicious, and I couldn't wait until I could tongue her essence straight from her pussy myself. Soon enough, I'd have my mouth buried between her legs and devour her perfect pussy whenever I wished.

She'd beg for it. I'd give her everything because she deserved it.

God, she smelled forbidden. Debauched, depraved and sweet sin. I grew harder with the need to push inside her gorgeous body. I slowly licked my bottom lip and inhaled the devilicious scent. Then I sat next to her, collected her scattered clothes and hugged them, letting her fragrance wrap all over me.

My cock begged me to be where it belonged. Inside of her. But I wouldn't listen. Not now. After I kissed her panties, I scattered the clothes back and lay next to her for a minute. A smile tugged at my lips as she rolled, still sleeping, and clutched onto me like a lifeline.

Every night together will be like this, Angel, and you'll want this as much as I do.

I kissed her forehead and slipped out of her grip and off the bed. Then I covered her body with the sheets. She rolled over again, now her back to me. I was just about to get back under the bed—I was sleeping here tonight in case Leo decided to show up—when she stirred and grumbled.

I froze when she kicked off the sheets and bolted upright. I was standing there, staring, my cock hard, her cum on my finger and my mouth, my own cum staining my underwear, as she got out of the bed and shuffled toward the bathroom.

Instantly, I dropped to my belly and hid back under the bed. *Tinkle.* She was peeing in the bathroom, and I got harder just imagining another scene that belonged in the future. One day, I was gonna fuck her mouth first thing in the morning before she even peed.

One day, I'd fill her with my seed until she carried my children. She'd be the mother of Leo's siblings, and she'd never think about him ever again.

That day couldn't come soon enough.

CHAPTER 30

Lina

Tino didn't have breakfast with us. Good. I was still mad at him. I didn't want to see him.

That was a lie. I wanted to see him, but I needed to stay mad at him. If I looked him in the eye after last night's orgasm show, I'd crumble to my feet in shame or worse, throw myself at him in need. There was a good chance today would be our last day here. I wanted to leave with my pride and dignity, at least, intact.

He summoned Nicky and me to his office. Time for my verbal spanking. Would Leo be there, too, to get his share of the punishment? Or the little, greedy gold digger Tino must have thought I was now was the only one to blame?

Nicky had told me that Tino was angry I didn't say no. He didn't believe I'd have refused. What he said earlier about how he was afraid *Leo* would do something bad, not me, was all a lie. It was me all along. He was worried *I* would steal his son away.

"Do you think he's gonna kick us out?" I asked my sister as we walked down the hall to his office. She—even if she was being a dick last night to Leo and with Tino—I couldn't stay mad at for more than a few hours.

"I hope so."

Her response shocked me. "Why would you say that?"

"As crazy as it sounds, I think you're safer with a psycho stalking you than you are here, stuck between the Bellomo wolves."

"What's that supposed to mean?"

"I have a bad feeling about you staying here, Lina. I feel like I'm gonna…lose you one way or another."

"What? Why? Did something happen you didn't tell me about?"

"What else do you need to happen? Leo is fixated on you. He's a Mafia prince, a made man who's gonna have soldiers of his own," she whispered. "What if he decides to defy his dad some more and kidnap you or worse?"

I came to a halt. "Worse? What could be worse than that?"

"His father," she continued whispering. "What do you think a man like him would do to stop his defiant prince from running away with a girl he doesn't approve of?"

My heart sank to a deep hollow in my stomach. "No. No, he said he'd protect me. He can't…" Could he do this to me? Could he kill me?

"Look, I know he likes you, and I don't mean to scare you. But I'm scared, Lina. No matter how much he cares about us, he cares about his son and his work more."

The bodyguards at the office door waved for us to move quicker. I dragged my feet toward them, trying hard not to cry, and walked inside.

I chanced a glance at Tino. He was sitting on the couch, not behind his desk, crossing his legs, frowning, dark circles under his eyes as if he hadn't slept at all.

The guards snapped the doors shut, and I flinched. There was no one here but us. And his gun.

"Before you start, I'd like to say that we want to go back home," Nicky suddenly said.

"Just like that? You think you can come and go whenever you like? Waste my time and resources and then just go? What about the fucking stalker? You don't give a shit about your sister's safety anymore?"

"I care about my sister more than I care about anything in this world. That's why I want out of here, Mr. Bellomo. I've protected her my whole life. I will find a way to protect her from—"

"Silenzio!" He jolted to his feet. "Both of you are under my protection until we find the prick. No one is leaving here until I say so."

"Oh my God, you're really gonna kill me," I whimpered.

"What?" He leaned forward, his hands on his hips, his gun peeking out. "Che cazzo dici?"

"You want to get me out of Leo's way so he'd marry the girl you chose for him. If Leo won't stop chasing me, it's the only way."

He pinched the bridge of his nose, and then he cocked a brow at Nicky. "You filled her head with this shit, vero?"

"Mr. Bellomo—"

"You're lucky I like you, Nicole." He blew out a breath. "Is that what you think La Famiglia is all about? Killing little girls to get them out of the way? Girls I swore to protect?"

"My sister is all I have. Your son is all you have. You can't blame me for—"

"This family is about honor!" he roared, and we both jumped. He was so scary I wanted to run away from him, into him. I wanted to hide in his arms, as if he was the only one that could protect me from himself.

How could I feel that way?

"Get out, Nicole. I want to talk to Angelina alone."

"But I—"

"One more word and my men will escort you back to your condo…alone. I can easily protect you from there."

My jaw fell. I couldn't live without my sister. *Please stop talking, Nicky.*

Nicky stared at him, her eyes hard, not an ounce of fear in them, only fury. My superhero wasn't afraid of the Mafia wolf. "I stay where my sister stays…Tino."

"Then take my advice." He waved at the door.

Nicky lifted her chin and flipped her hair as she marched out, proud as always.

As Tino and I became alone, he grabbed my arm and gave a hard tug. I slammed right into his firm body, unable to be angry at him like I'd planned, the throwing myself at him in need so close.

"Do you think I'm going to kill you?" he asked.

I shook my head.

"Why not?"

"I trust you."

"That's stupid and naive."

"I know, but I do." Especially when I was in his protective embrace. My mind started working better now that Nicky wasn't saying scary things and I was in the safest place I'd ever been. "Besides, if you wanted to kill me, you'd have done it by now. Ever since the first day we met when you knew about how Leo felt for me. Why go through all that trouble to protect me? Why wouldn't you let the Lanzas kill me or *him* kidnap me and get it over with?"

"Finally, someone says something that's not total bullshit. What about Leo?"

"What about him?"

His jaw flexed, his lips puckering. "Do you love him?"

"I...I don't hate him."

"Straight answers, Angelina," he warned, the blue in his eyes almost black.

"I honestly don't know. I've never been in love before, and my feelings are always weird. I don't...trust them."

"Let me make it easier for you. If he weren't my son, would you want to marry him?"

I shrugged, groping for an answer. It wasn't that simple, but I opted for the simplest answer. "Yes."

Dangerous sparks as if made in hell flamed in his gaze.

"Would you let me talk without getting mad?" I asked.

"Spit it out."

"I've never led a normal life, with my father and *him*... Leo is a saint compared to them, even as a mobster. And he's kind and handsome and he says he loves me. I believe him. I believe he'd do anything, even defying *you*, so we can be together...because he loves me for real."

"He doesn't. He just wants you, and he wants to piss me off."

"He's never tried to touch me before, and he proposed to me, Tino. He treats me with the same manners he'd treat any Mafia princess. He doesn't see me as an outsider or some quick lay he might get."

"So you'd have said yes?" he grated.

"No."

"Don't play me!"

I shuddered. "Please don't yell at me."

He closed his eyes for a second and breathed out. "Fine. Continue."

I tugged at the lapels of his suit jacket. "What I said is just logic speaking. It's the answer in my mind, not my heart."

"And what does your heart say, young lady?"

"That I really hate it when you call me that."

"Don't change the subject."

"Can I ask you a question first?"

He rolled his eyes, impatient. Then he nodded, a muscle ticking in his jaw.

"Why did you really punch Leo?" When I looked in his eyes now, I had a feeling it was because of something bigger than the obvious. "Is it really because of Claudia and me being a charity case outsider—"

"You're not a charity case, and nobody here treats you like an outsider, Angelina. The second I opened my doors for you, you've become family."

"Then why?"

His hands cradled my face, and he did that thing when he held me captive with his intense, piercing gaze. "Because he wants to take what's not his."

He kept saying that, but he never acted upon it. *It's time you speak, Don Bellomo.* "But I'm not anybody's, Tino," I said, and his eyes flamed again. My heart thudded hard against my ribs. "Or am I?"

His right hand moved to the back of my head and plunged into my hair. His stare dropped to my mouth, and I fell to pieces. My lips parted with a quivering breath that clashed with the closeness of his. My heart did one backflip after another as he kept leaning forward. My eyes fluttered closed as I wet my lips, getting them ready for a moment I didn't know I'd been waiting for all my—

"Scusi, Don Bellomo," someone said, bursting into the office, brutally disrupting my life-changing moment.

Tino's breath became distant, and his hands abandoned me completely. "Che cazzo, Michele?"

"Perdona, but you need to see this. It's about Leo."

CHAPTER 31

Lina

"What do you mean he's missing?" I sobbed. I couldn't wrap my head around what Tino and the bodyguards were saying now.

After Michele came barging in earlier, he and Tino spoke alone for about fifteen minutes, and then Tino gathered me, Nicole and all his personal bodyguards to tell us the awful news.

"Leo eluded his bodyguards this morning, and he's nowhere to be found at his regular spots," Tino explained again.

"Maybe he went out of town?" I hoped.

"His car is still parked. He didn't take the plane either," Michele said.

"This is all my fault. *He* must have found him. *He* must have been at the restaurant and saw. Oh my God, Tino. I'm so sorry. *He* must have him."

"Let's not jump to conclusions. If *he* or anyone had tried to take my boy in broad daylight, the guards would have caught them."

"Broad daylight," I mumbled, a pang in my chest. The way Tino said it reminded me of how *he* said it. Why *he* said it. "That's when *he* said *he* would..." *He* would find me in the dark, but *he* would take me in broad daylight. "Oh my God."

"Calma, Angelina. I'm sure Leo is just doing something even stupider than what he did yesterday somewhere. That's why he eluded the bodyguards." Tino directed his stare at Michele. "Have you tracked his phone?"

"It's still switched off."

"Check the airports. San Francisco flights in particular."

"You think he's going to the Lanzas?" Nicky asked.

"Yeah. Like I said, to do something more stupid," Tino grumbled.

"Like breaking off the engagement." Nicky massaged her temples, swearing.

My hand flew to my mouth, stifling a gasp. I didn't know what was more dangerous. Leo being kidnapped by *him* or going to the Lanzas to break off the engagement with the Mafia princess.

Either way, we were screwed. All of us.

Tino stretched a hand toward me. "Angelina, give me your phone."

I reached inside my pocket without thinking and handed my phone to him. He gave it to Michele, and the bodyguard exited rapidly.

"Wait, what are you gonna do with it?" I asked.

"Tapping it. He's going to call or text you. We'll find him when he does." Tino brought out his own phone. "Now if you'll excuse me, I have a phone call to make."

My eyes narrowed at him. "How can you be so sure? And so freaking calm? Why are you eliminating the possibility that he's actually been kidnapped? By a psycho killer?"

He rolled his eyes. "Go to your room, Angelina. Rest or play some music. Maybe chill by the pool. Enjoy your winter break while I handle my business. I'll find my son by the end of the day."

I was about to give him another piece of my mind, but Nicky grabbed my arm and practically dragged me out of the office.

"Let go, Nicky. Why are you taking his side now all of a sudden? Didn't you think he was gonna off me earlier?"

"I still think he would, especially if you interfere with Mafia business," Nicky said.

I shook my head in disbelief. "Nicky, I'm so scared. If something happens to Leo because of me, I'll never forgive myself. I have to do something to help him. Anything."

"What can you do?"

"I don't know. There must be something."

"All we can do is wait, pray and let the Mob does what the Mob does. C'mon, put on your bathing suit and let's go for a swim. It'll take the edge off while we wait. Maybe get the violin, too. It'll help us all relax."

My shoulders slumped in resignation. How helpless I was agitated and saddened me. *Why did you have to like me, Leo? Why didn't you stick to your fiancé, to your world where people like me didn't belong or fit?* "How did we get into this mess, Nicky?"

She puckered her lips and rubbed my back. "It doesn't matter how we got in. It's how we get out that matters the most."

CHAPTER 32

Lina

Tchaikovsky's Violin Concerto, second movement. One of the saddest pieces ever made. I'd been playing it for the past two hours.

"Can you please change this goddamn song?" Nicky wiped her wet face, glaring at me in the pool.

"Fine." I switched to Schindler's List Theme by John Williams.

She slapped the water. "Oh for fuck's sake. Something not so dark. Please."

"Well, I don't exactly feel peppy at the moment." I was scared shitless. For Leo. For myself. If *he* took him, *he* would finish the rest of *his* threat and come for me. To take me too. To rape me. If Leo just went to the Lanzas, who knew what they'd do for payback? They'd hurt me. *They* would kill me to get me out of Leo's way.

"Then stop making it worse by playing sad songs."

I took a deep breath, shaking my head and checking my phone for the millionth time. I couldn't believe I'd ever say that. "Please, call me, Leo."

Staring at the phone, willing it to ring, didn't work. I put my bow back in position. Music was the only thing keeping me from going insane.

Back to December.

Maybe he'd listen.

I started the melody and Nicky still protested. I ignored her and focused only on the music and the flashes of Leo's smiles from yesterday.

How could every good occasion in my life turn into a terrible trauma?

The day I thought life took away the monster that ruined my life for twelve years was the day a worse monster took over my life to continue ruining it forever.

The night I attended Nicky's ceremony, happy for her, wearing a gorgeous dress I'd always wanted was the night I'd first met *him* and learned I was nothing but a body for sale with a target on my back ticking like a bomb.

The first time I went out on Valentine's Day and had my first real gig, the first time a boy told me he loved me, proposed to me, turned into a miserable night when he got punched in the face and went missing the next morning.

And now I waited like a prisoner for the rest of my miserable destiny, my punishment for sins I'd never committed, with zero power to stop it from coming.

I finished the song for the third time, and my phone remained as silent as death.

Tears came out of my eyes without an invitation. Of fear? Of sadness? Of helplessness? I didn't care. What good were they now? They couldn't save him. They couldn't save me.

I set down the violin. "I wish *he* could have just taken me that day."

"Lina!" Nicky jumped out of the pool and covered her body with a towel. Then she rushed to my side and wrapped her arms around me. "Don't say stuff like that, Sis."

"Why not? It's gonna happen sooner or later. Why would someone else have to suffer for it?"

"We don't know what happened. Tino said it couldn't be *him*."

"Stop trying to sedate me, Nicky. We both know that's not true."

She rubbed my arms gently. "It's awful of me to say what I'm about to say, but I really hope it's *him* who took Leo."

"Why would you say such a terrible thing?"

"Because if *he* did, Tino would find and kill *him*, and it'd all be over."

"At what expense? You don't care if Leo died?"

"Of course I do. But if Leo had to die so you could live, so you could be safe, I can live with that."

A lump clogged my throat, and more tears fell down my face. "I can't. I can't, Nicky." My whole body trembled, and I sobbed in her arms, feeling like I was on the verge of having a nervous breakdown.

"Angelina! Nicole!" Tino's voice boomed as he entered the swimming pool area.

I jerked up, bracing for the worst.

He marched in our direction, his phone in his hand. "I found him."

"Where? Is he okay?" I panted, my heart thundering.

"My men stopped him in San Francisco before he met the Lanzas. They're bringing him back," he said.

I fell to my knees, my face in my hands, a long sigh of relief wheezing out of me. "Thank God."

"So he was going to break off the engagement?" Nicky exclaimed. "I thought this whole thing with my sister was a fling. I never thought it'd be so serious…"

"Fling or no fling, it needs to stop. We honor our words, and we've given our word to the Lanzas." He gave me his phone as I wiped my face. "Call him."

"And say what?"

"Fucking move on, for starters."

I rose and nodded. Tino was right. I should push Leo away. I was no good for him. For anybody. He had to stay away from me for his safety. It was the least I could do to repay a fraction of my debt to Tino.

I tapped the green icon and put the phone on my ear. One ring. Two rings. Three…
"Papà, I told you—"

"It's me, Leo. Lina."

"Oh amore, I'm so sorry I didn't try to reach you earlier. You must have been scared."

Amore? I wished I could have been loved by anyone without signing their death certificate. I wished I could have enjoyed hearing it from him, from anyone. I wished I'd been allowed to ever say it back. "I was. Very much."

"I'm fine, Lina. Don't worry about me. How are you doing, bella?"

"Leo, listen. You need to stop. We can't be together. I can't…marry you."

"I know you still have school. We'll wait until graduation—"

"Leo, you're not listening!" I glanced heavenward. "You can't break off your engagement for me. I can't marry you *ever*. I can't be with you in any way."

There was a long pause. "Did Dad tell you to say this?"

"Yes, but I'm saying it, too. I'd have never said yes, Leo. I just can't and you know why."

Another pause. "You're right. I shouldn't have proposed last night. I did it all wrong."

"Yes." I nodded, assuring Tino. "Thank you for understanding. Now, you need to get back to your fiancé and honor your word. It's the right thing to do. I'm sure she's amazing, and unlike me, she can actually make you happy."

"Lina…can you tell Dad I'm not coming home?"

I blinked. "Okay. So you're going back to San Francisco? To Claudia?"

Tino narrowed his eyes at me and mouthed for me to open the speaker. I did as he asked, anticipating the answer.

"No," Leo said. "There's something I have to do, had to do before I proposed to you. I'm not coming home until I do it. It's the only way you'll give me a chance."

My heart dropped on the floor. "Leo, what the hell are you saying?"

"I won't rest until I find *him* and bring *his* fucking head to you."

CHAPTER 33

Tino

" **H**ow could you not stop him?"
I stopped counting how
many times Angel had asked
me that question. She'd been killing herself
with worry for no reason at all.

There was no way for me to put her out of
her misery other than telling her the truth.
Leo was chasing a ghost.

The only person who should worry was
me. The only danger here was Leo finding out
the truth and telling Lina.

I was the one who killed her father.

I was the psycho stalker creep.

I was the monster that terrified her.

"You don't care about the safety of my son more than I do, Angelina." I gave her the same reply every time.

"It's been months. I'm dying every minute since this shit started. Every time my phone rings, my heart stops. Every call Leo makes to tell me he hasn't found *him* yet but won't come home until he does drives me crazy. You don't understand how I feel. I'm losing my mind."

I hated to see her like this, but any intervention on my side could make me lose her forever. I couldn't lose her. I couldn't lose Leo either. *I* was losing my mind.

My arms opened for her. I hadn't touched her while she was awake since that moment I almost kissed her. She'd been so distant. She barely talked to me about anything but Leo. He'd taken up all her mind with his conniving move.

She stepped back, rejecting me. She never rejected me before. It stung like a slap on the face. "Why haven't you found *him*? Didn't you say you'd find *him* in weeks? It's been months."

I sighed and dropped my arms. "You want to know why I'm not concerned about Leo chasing that piece of shit? Why I haven't found *him*?"

"Yes," she hissed.

"Leo isn't really in danger because he can't really find *him*, Angelina. Neither can I."

"What the fuck does that mean?" She jabbed the air with her index finger. "And don't even think about lecturing me for swearing."

I slapped her finger and grabbed her whole hand in my fist, pulling her to me. She yelped, staring at me with angry yet scared eyes until she dropped her stare. "You don't tell me what or what not to do, understood?"

She gulped. "Why can't either of you find *him*?"

Disappointed I couldn't make her drop it, I had to lie. "Because I know *his* fucking kind. Patience is *his* game. *He* can wait as long as it takes for you to become vulnerable again before *he* makes a move. *He* won't show up unless I use you as bait."

"Bait?" Her head whipped up, her beautiful hair flowing off her face and down her back. "How?"

"It doesn't matter. I'll never do it."

"You have to do it. I'm not scared of *him*. Not anymore. You have to do it, Tino." Now she clung to me. "Please."

"You'd put your life at risk for my boy?"

"I'd do anything to keep him safe."

I'd counted each day Leo was away from her as a blessing, but I was wrong. His absence hurt more than his hovering around her. It was a silent curse that could cost me everything.

This wasn't about my secret that was in danger of getting exposed. There were thousands of ways to keep Leo in the dark. It was this look in her eyes that I'd never thought I'd see.

The distance didn't take him off her mind. It only made her care for him more than she'd ever have if he'd been here.

"Please, Tino. He can't get hurt because of me. I need him safe," she pleaded.

I closed my eyes and nodded. "I'll think about it. I'll let you know when I have a plan."

"Thank you. Thank you so much." She gave me a small hug and left.

My Angel was slipping away from me.

I already had a plan to bring her back, though. One I didn't want to execute until later. Until Leo was fucking married so he wouldn't put her under his spell again.

I had no choice but to expedite things and go ahead with it. Now.

CHAPTER 34

Tino

A scapegoat.

A man my height with a beard, who spoke Italian but had no accent. Pepper his place with Angel's pictures and stalking gear. Pay his greedy ass double to kidnap Angel when I set the trap. Go kill him and be her hero.

I found him already. Marciano Andretti. A bastard that earned his button a couple of years after me. Used to be in my crew but split twelve years ago. Still ran for me sometimes, but mostly he worked solo. I kept him on my payroll so he wouldn't sell me out. Most of my men didn't know him, and importantly, Leo never met him.

I gave Andretti the job. As far as he was concerned, it was a real kidnap. Some girl to take to teach someone a lesson. He didn't have to know anything else.

Angel agreed to all my instructions without question. Nicole and she went back to their apartment. I loosened the security around them at home and at the academy, pretending they were no longer under my protection, but kept Michele on their duty. I'd agreed with Angel to stay late at practice every day all week until *he* showed up. I resided at the penthouse for a few days while I waited for Andretti to make his move as planned. I couldn't rush it or it'd look too suspicious.

All these days I did nothing but watch and paint her. Not having her in my house where I talked to her every day and stayed in her room every night was driving me out of my fucking mind.

Friday was the day it all ended, and I'd have her back in my arms.

Andretti was all set to take her from school. I lurked in the dark backstage, where I used to listen to her beautiful music without her knowing, where I watched for years without being seen, where I waited and daydreamed.

Angel wasn't going to take the shortcut backstage. It'd be too convenient and suspicious if the situation was real. I even told her music teacher to stay with her in the theatre until she finished. The teacher would get hurt a little in the way when Andretti arrived, but she'd be heavily compensated. Andretti would drag Angel backstage, and that was when I did my part. He wouldn't even see it coming.

The music stopped just in time for his arrival. I had my gun ready. Time to be her savior. She was a sucker for that. She'd fall for me and never look back.

"Excuse me, the theatre is closed," the teacher said.

Thud.

Scream.

Heels coming…not my way. The sound was rolling away, fading. Che cazzo?

I strode to the stage, careful not to blow my cover in case—

Another man's voice shouted, and curses flew.

Bang!

More screams. Angel's.

I ran to the theatre, my heart roaring in my temples. What the fuck was going on? I'd torture the son of a bitch if he hurt her. *Bang!*

I leapt off the stage, the teacher passed out in the middle of it, and reached Angel in two strides. She was standing her back to the wall, blood on her face and clothes, her mouth hanging open but she wasn't breathing, two men bleeding on the floor one by each foot of hers.

I put a bullet in Andretti's head when I saw his face. Then I pointed the gun at the other bleeding body balled next to her left foot, kicking the gun beside him out of reach. "One move and you're dead."

As he groaned and turned his head toward me, all the blood in my body rushed out and then was pumped back in all at once.

"Don't shoot. It's Leo," Angel sobbed.

"Hey, Dad," he mumbled in pain.

I put my gun down and squatted next to him, applying pressure on his wound. "You motherfucker."

CHAPTER 35

Lina

This couldn't be *him*.

I barely saw *his* face as he came from backstage and knocked down my teacher. *He* held me from behind as always, but it didn't feel the same. It was rough, violent, fast. *He* had a gun pressed to my head for God's sake, and *he* didn't utter a single word.

This couldn't be *him*.

When *he* dragged me to the entrance unlike where Tino and I had anticipated *he* would, I kicked and screamed, almost yelling Tino's name. Something was wrong. This couldn't be *him*.

Then someone slammed the entrance door and swore. *He* swiveled us, and I saw Leo's face, a gun in his hand. *His* gun left my head and pointed at Leo. What the hell was going on? Why was Leo here? Tino promised me he'd take care of it, not Leo. Leo had to stay away. To be safe.

They yelled at each other in Italian, like they'd known each other. This couldn't be *him*. This wasn't the voice that rendered me speechless and wreaked havoc on my body. Something was wrong. Leo shouldn't be here.

Bang!

Leo dropped on the floor. His blood had splattered on my face and streamed out of his stomach, pooling out fast and reaching my shoes. This couldn't be happening. It was a bad dream. I'd just close my eyes, and it'd be all gone.

Bang!

Something else dropped on the floor, and no hands were on my body, no cold metal pressed to my skull. More thick, wet splatter on me. My back slammed against the wall so I wouldn't collapse. As I opened my eyes, Tino was running my way, a bleeding body on either side of my legs. *He* was gonna die. Leo was gonna die.

Bang!

He was dead. This couldn't be *him*.

I was still shaking, the taste of blood, *his* or Leo's I didn't know, sickening in my mouth. More blood trickled down *his* face and stained *his* beard. *He* looked so…dead. This couldn't be *him*.

"Don't shoot. It's Leo," I sobbed.

"Hey, Dad," Leo mumbled in pain.

Tino put his gun down and squatted next to Leo, applying pressure on his wound. "You motherfucker." He glanced up at me, getting his phone out. "Are you hurt?"

I didn't know. I wasn't feeling anything, so I just shook my head.

Tino's men streamed in and took Leo. Strong hands carried me up, cradled me gently. I stared into the dark blue eyes and held on to Tino like my life depended on it. "*He* is dead."

"Yes," he said as he walked us out of the theatre.

That couldn't be *him*. "*He* looked nothing like I imagined."

"It doesn't matter. What matters is that he's gone."

"What if it's not *him*?"

He gave me one of his intense, piercing looks. "It is *him*. You're just in shock. Your mind is playing you like it always has when it comes to *him*. You don't want to believe *he* was finally gone. But *he* is. Long gone."

He was probably right, but my mind wouldn't stop saying it. That couldn't be *him*.

CHAPTER 36

Tino

As we arrived at the mansion, Angel asked to see Leo. He was already with the doctors, trying hard to stabilize him.

"Why don't you go take a bath and rest? I'll let you know what the doctors say as soon as they finish," I said.

Angel wouldn't move, but Nicole held her arm gently and convinced her staying outside Leo's door wouldn't help. As Angel dragged her feet away, Nicole glanced at me, mouthing her thanks.

I nodded, and as soon as they disappeared upstairs, I sank in the chair outside the room Leo was in, my face in my hands, going through what happened, trying to figure out when and why it'd gone wrong.

Why was that fucker Andretti taking her outside instead of backstage as we agreed?

How did Leo find out the right place and time of the trap? I didn't tell him anything.

Why did Andretti shoot Leo? To be exact, why would Leo let Andretti shoot him? I taught my son how to shoot, how to easily incapacitate a captor. They were face to face, their heights the same, and Angel was short in comparison. Leo had a clear shot of Andretti.

"Brutto. Stronzo."

If he hadn't been shot already, I'd have done it myself. In the dick. I'd fuck my only chance to have grandchildren without an ounce of care. I didn't want them if he thought he was gonna make them with my Angel. I'd have more children with her, and they'd have my grandchildren, not that punk.

Could I really blame him, though? For loving her? For doing what he'd done?

I growled at the ceiling. "Like father like son."

Michele came to tell me about Andretti. He'd taken care of the body and the police, and the fucker's apartment—it wasn't really his, but I'd chosen one close to hers and made it look like it was Marciano's—was all set with the evidence Angel needed to believe.

The doubt in her eyes would be long gone when she saw for herself the details of the monster tale she'd been living in her whole life etched over every corner of that place.

The only one standing between me and her now was Leo. After the little game he played, it'd be a lot harder to get him out of the way than I thought.

Hours later, the doctors assured me they got out the bullet and stopped the hemorrhage. No vital organs were affected—of course.

I stayed all night in the room downstairs where he was, rewinding his whole life in my head since he was still in his mother's belly. The first time I'd felt his kick. The tears in my eyes when I held him in my arms after he was born. The lullaby I sang for him when he was too stubborn to sleep. His first birthday party that was the talk of the city for weeks. His first bike and the nasty knee scrape he got on his first ride without the training wheels that left a visible scar until now. His first day at school. The first time I caught him smoking. The smile on his face on his play dates with

Claudia. The first time I taught him to shoot. The first time he stole my car and my cologne. The first time he drank my whiskey.

The look on his face when he found out about his mother's death.

"I love you, Leo, more than anything. I've done everything that I can to protect you, and I've always wanted you to be happy even if you don't believe it." Not knowing if he could hear me, I kissed his forehead, his skin warmer than usual. "I didn't believe you the first time, refused to believe it until today. You really love her, don't you?"

I didn't need him to say it. I knew. "You must be to go behind my back and have your own deal with Andretti. To make him betray me and play for you. To make it look like you were saving her, taking a bullet for her." I took a long breath and let it out slowly. "Now you'd be stuck at home where I can't kick you out with a gunshot wound, where you can be with her, a hero in her eyes, her savior. She'd take care of you to repay you for saving her life, and you'd dazzle her, charm your way to her heart."

The only way to ruin his plan was to tell her it was all staged, but he knew I couldn't without outing myself, too. The fucker Marciano must have told him everything about the fake kidnapping. Leo must have thought I was doing it to make him stop chasing the stalker, prevent him from becoming her hero, but he turned the tables on me.

Well played, Leo. Well played.

In the morning, he opened his eyes and slurred her name. I cradled his hand between my palms and kissed his forehead, his temperature normal now.

"Papà? Were you here all night?"

"Certo. Where else would I be? Meno male."

"Thanks. Where's Lina?"

I sighed. "I'll send for her. She was so worried about you."

One of the nurses that had been checking on him all night came in and told me everything was normal. I waved for her to bring Angel and Nicole.

Angel's gaze as she saw Leo put a sword through my chest. That look would have been for me, was meant for me, not him.

But it was too late now.

I lost my Angel.

CHAPTER 37

Lina

Marciano Andretti. That was *his* name. My pictures, the pink tank top I'd been missing for months, the night binoculars, everything that was in the apartment two blocks away from my condo proved *he* was Marciano.

Tino said Marciano had been renting that apartment since I'd moved to the condo. He had easy access to the academy because he'd worked for Tino before.

So many secrets had unraveled since Marciano died. Like the fact that my father had done a few jobs for Tino, too, and that Marciano was my father's friend.

It was all hard to believe. How Marciano died. Why Tino hid that fact that he knew my father. How everything always went back to the Bellomos. It wasn't a miracle that got us into their program. It wasn't Marciano either.

It was fate.

My father had to be the sicko he'd been. He had to work for the Mob. He had to be friends with Marciano. All so that Marciano would find out what his friend did to his daughters and kill him. So that Tino would feel obligated to take care of his daughters and send them to his school. So that I'd grow up with my father's killer growing an obsession for me. So that he'd threaten and attack me, and I'd find my way back to the Bellomos. To Tino. To Leo.

"How was your exam?" Leo asked as we strolled together in the mansion garden under June's sunny sky. That had been my routine now for the past week. Study, practice, sit for the exam, take a slow walk with Leo as his health improved— not chaperoned, which worried me about Tino. It wasn't like him at all.

"Easy." I smiled.

"Awesome. I want you to finish school as fast as possible."

I rolled my eyes. "And we're back to that."

"Yes, we are. And don't even start about Claudia. The second the doctors clear me to travel, I'm going back to San Francisco."

"God, Leo."

"You said the two things that were standing between us were that piece of shit and the engagement. I took care of the first obstacle. I'll take care of the other, too."

"You took a bullet in the stomach when you handled Marciano. When you break off the engagement the bullet will be in your head."

"You think the Lanzas will kill me?"

"Or me. The way Tino speaks about Enzio Lanza, how he deals with anything that touches the honor of his family… How Tino Bellomo himself deals with anything that touches the honor of his family… You don't wanna piss him off."

He touched my chin to make me look at him, at his smile. I shook my head. "What are you smiling for?"

"I'm smiling because you're considering it."

"Considering what?"

"Marrying me. The only thing that's stopping you from saying yes is the families, nothing else." He brushed my cheek with the back of his hand, the gesture reminding me a lot of Marciano's touch in my dreams with Tino's tattooed hand. A touch I loved so much from the wrong people and now I could receive from a good man. "I love you, Lina."

My face warmed, and I remembered how much he loved to make me blush. I swallowed. I couldn't say it back. I'd probably never be able to say it back. "It's not only the families, Leo."

His hand dropped, and his face darkened. "Don't tell me you're still attached to that Marciano asshole."

It was complicated. Too complicated.

Marciano was the first man I had ever desired. After his death, I realized it was only an illusion, and everything that attracted me to him wasn't real. He did save me from my father, but he wasn't watching after me like I thought. He only killed my father so he'd have me for himself. It was sick and disgusting, and I regretted it with all my heart.

It wasn't Marciano that confused me now, though. It was the man I'd never be able to understand or speak of my feelings for with Leo.

Tino. His father.

At first, I believed I was displacing my feelings to get over Marciano. All the dreams, too. Yes, he never stopped calling me his Angel in them, and that was enough proof none of it was real. Then that moment at Tino's office happened.

That was real.

Not just on my side.

I'd be a fool to chase that feeling or pursue anything further because of it. It was a stolen, interrupted moment that would never be complete.

With Leo and Marciano, Tino had long forgotten it ever happened like he should. Like I should. I should have never wanted it. Not even in my dreams.

It was wrong and taboo and forbidden. Everything I'd felt in that moment must be locked in the darkest corner of my heart.

"It's not Marciano. It's Tino. I don't know why you and your dad don't get together very well, and it's none of my business, but I'm in debt to him. I can't be that ungrateful bitch."

"Because of school?"

"Yeah, among other things. He took me in. He went through a lot of trouble to protect me."

"Because of me."

"I'm aware you're the one who asked him to bring me here for protection in the beginning, but—"

"He never wanted to do it."

"What?"

"He was never gonna do it until I traded my future for it. He only agreed when I promised to go through with my initiation and become his underboss soon."

That fell on my head like a sledgehammer. Everything Tino and I had was never about me? That entire caring and overprotective act was to get his son to do his bidding?

Of course, why else? Who was I for the almighty Bellomo to take in or protect? He would gain absolutely nothing from taking care of an orphaned little girl and her sister. The daughters of a piece of shit, expendable employee he never bothered with.

He'd only do it to get his prodigal son to return. The sole heir to his kingdom.

Tino used me, like my father, like Marciano.

For how long would I remain that naive? For how long would I let people take advantage of me?

I stared at Leo through the tears. "Are you using me, too?"

"What? Of course not. What would I use you for?"

"To get back at your dad, for whatever beef you have with him."

"No, amore," he said, his voice thick with emotion. "I love you. You stole my heart with your little violin before I even saw you, and the second I laid my eyes on you, you ruined me for any other girl. What I feel for you has nothing to do with Dad or anything else. Ti amo tanto, Lina bella."

His sweetness and sexy Italian numbed me for a minute. I was indeed a naive, inexperienced, traumatized girl that was desperate for love, and he was having his way with me. I shook my head, as if shaking the trance he was putting me in. Why would I believe him? Everything I'd believed before turned out to be a big fat lie.

"What more can I do to prove it to you?" he asked.

"I don't know. I mean, you gave up your education, the future you've ever dreamed of. You even risked your life to save me from my stalker. And now you want to leave your wealthy, well connected fiancé to marry me. There's nothing else to do."

"I'd do it again in a heartbeat. I'd do anything to make you mine, Lina."

When he said stuff like that, I could melt and surrender without a fight. He was so romantic and beautiful and hot. My mind pictured us growing older when he'd be even hotter. As hot as Tino.

Shoot. That was not cool on my side. Totally inappropriate.

"What about your father? He might not have helped me with Marciano for my sake, but he still gave me and my sister a home and an education when we were all alone and helpless. That alone is enough for me to respect his wishes. I owe him a lot."

"Stop making excuses, Lina. If you want me as much as I want you, nothing is gonna stop us from being together. The Lanzas can't hurt you as long as I'm alive. I'll protect you like I protected you from Marciano. As for Tino, you don't have to worry about him. No matter how much you owe him, he owes me more."

"Is this about the Mob thing you had to become?"

"It's called a made man, but no, not just that."

This must have something to do with his mother. "Are you ever gonna tell me what happened? Your family tragedy, I mean. It's only fair that you tell me, now that you already know everything about me."

He resumed our stroll, and I'd realized we'd been standing for so long. "We should sit. You're still on the mend. We don't want you to rip a stitch or pull a muscle."

He gave me a small smile and pointed at the greenhouse. "Let's sit there. A little birdie told me it's your favorite place here."

"Uh…maybe not." The memory of that one frightening yet inappropriately sexy encounter with Tino got me hot and bothered every time.

He smirked. "Are you scared of me?"

"Not really. I don't think you'll try anything with your gunshot wound."

He laughed. "That's the only thing you think will stop me?"

"That and having Tino's bodyguards on the lookout everywhere. Tino will kill us both if we're busted."

His hand touched his stomach as he laughed harder.

"Easy." I helped him to the nearest bench and sat beside him. "Now, about your mother?"

The laughter died, and his eyes drifted to afternoon sun. "I was thirteen when I lost her.

She…uh… She was so beautiful and kind and… She didn't belong in our world."

My heart squeezed for him. "What happened?"

"Don Bellomo happened. Before Dad became the boss, there was a feud and bad blood between him and another Capo who wanted the position. That other man was pure evil. He threatened Dad if he accepted to be the boss, he'd ruin his family in return.

"Mamma was scared. She begged Dad to refuse the position, but Don Bellomo doesn't take no for an answer. He always gets what he wants. If he thinks something is his, nothing else matters. Nothing stops him from having it. Not even his own family."

"So when he accepted to be the boss…"

"Seppi killed my mom…and my baby sister."

"What?" I gasped.

"Mamma was six months pregnant when he…" He burst into tears.

"I'm so sorry." I rubbed his back and wrapped my arms around his shoulders, but he cried harder. "Leo, please, take it easy."

"He raped her, Lina. He sat there and watched her bleed out my baby sister, and then he slit her throat."

My tears fell with his, my heart in shreds. Why would anybody do something this horrid for a seat? "I'm so sorry. So sorry. Where were you and Tino when it happened?"

"I was sick that day and couldn't go to school. It got worse by the afternoon. The doctor was too busy to come to the house so he asked her to drop by the clinic. Dad was home and said he'd take me so she'd rest. Her pregnancy wasn't a very easy one.

"Seppi came to the house around three p.m. with his men, murdered all the bodyguards and tortured my mom to death."

"That's terrible. If you and Tino were there, too, you'd have been murdered as well."

"But if Mamma and I had been at the doctor's, Tino would have died, and she and my sister would have lived. Away from this fucking mess."

"You don't know that. Maybe Seppi would have found you all. You can't blame Tino for what happened. He was taking care of you. You should be glad you and your dad survived."

"Glad?" He chuckled bitterly. "None of that would have happened if he hadn't become the fucking boss."

"You can't think that way, Leo. Tino is a good father."

"Why are you taking his side?"

"I'm not taking sides. But when you have a father like him, you don't take it for granted. What happened is a terrible tragedy, but it's happened to both of you."

He rested his forehead on his palm and shook his head, a troubled sigh escaping him. "Anyway, what's done is done." He looked at me, trying to smile. "Can we stop talking about Tino now? You're making me jealous."

"Jealous?" I tucked my hair behind my ear nervously. "W-why would you be jealous?"

"Because he's hot, and you look at him like he's something to eat."

Heat came off my face in waves. "I…I don't—"

His smirk taunted me. "It's okay. I'm the spitting image of him. It's normal that you find him attractive, too. I'm also aware that girls like you dig older guys."

"Girls like me?"

"Beautiful, innocent, blushing, amazing girls like you who swoon over beards and tats."

"Oh my God, Leo. You are…"

"I can grow a beard if you want. And," he leaned in, "I have tattoos of my own."

I bit my lip, imagining where on his body they could be. "Do you?"

"Yeah. Wanna see?"

Yes, please. I jerked up, leaving him alone on the bench. "You're trouble."

He wrapped his fist around my wrist and gazed up at me. "Marry me, Lina. Make an honest man out of me."

I laughed. A wholehearted laugh. I didn't think I'd ever had one of those before.

"What do you say, Lina bella? Will you give me the chance to make you as happy as you make me? Will you share this life with me that without you will mean absolutely nothing? Will you do me the honors and be mine for as long as we both shall live?"

CHAPTER 38

Lina

Tino's stare at my hand in Leo's curdled the blood in my veins. As I stood in his office, I was shaking like a kitten in the rain, while Leo was snickering. How could he not be scared of his dad when it was Tino Bellomo and he looked like he was gonna stab someone?

"With your permission, we'd like the wedding to be on Lina's eighteenth birthday," Leo said.

Tino didn't reply. He seemed to be frozen in place, a deep line between his brows, two fingers rested on his temple, his thumb under his beard, the rest of his fingers covering half of his mouth but not the pinch to it. His legs crossed as he sat on the leather couch. He didn't take his eyes off our clasped hands.

I tried to free my hand from Leo's grasp, but he squeezed it, holding to it tighter. "I know it's less than five months away but it's—"

"Angelina," he interrupted Leo, and I almost pissed myself.

"Y-yes, Tino?"

"Come sit beside me."

Shoot. This was about the hand. Why did Leo have to provoke him all the time? I tugged my hand out of Leo's tight grip. He wouldn't let go easily, but I managed to break free. Then, my heart in my throat, I sank in the couch beside Tino.

"What do you say, Papà?"

"You know what I'm going to say."

"I'll take care of the Lanzas."

"How?"

"I'll tell them the truth. I can't make their daughter happy."

"And you expect them to just say congratulations?"

"They should."

"In what world do you live in, Leo?"

"The same world that you do. The same world you dragged me into. If that world, with all its power, doesn't make it possible for me to live with the one person my heart wants, then maybe I don't belong there at all."

Oh. My. God. I must admit, Leo was the bravest person I'd ever seen. To challenge and threaten Don Bellomo himself…

Or maybe Leo wasn't brave at all and was just stupid.

Either way we were screwed. When I said yes, I knew it was a long shot. I didn't expect Tino to approve of our marriage. He'd never give us his blessing. Heck, I didn't expect Leo to go through with it and tell Tino.

Part of me only said yes to give Leo what he wanted so his fixation would fade, and maybe I'd find out it was nothing but an obsession, a need to have something he couldn't have. After all, things like having a boy like Leo fall in love with a girl like me didn't happen, not to people like me anyway.

I was wrong. Leo was going through with it with more determination than ever, and the other part of me that hoped he would was dancing with happiness.

However, happy fairytales didn't belong in my world. Tino would never let this marriage happen, and I'd never want to come between a father and his son.

Tino's leg dropped. The sound of his shoe hitting the floor made me flinch. He leaned forward, his hands clasped under his beard. "Give me a minute with Angelina."

I gulped, glancing over at Leo. *Don't leave me alone with your scary father right now.*

Leo smiled at me, but nothing would reassure me at the moment. "I'll be right outside."

My chest heaved as the door closed behind him. I scampered to my feet, trying to stay as far away as possible from Tino, but he grabbed my wrist before I took a single step.

"Where do you think you're going?" he asked.

"Nowhere," I barely said.

He pulled me back down on the couch. "That's right."

I tried to swallow again, but my mouth was as dry as a rock. I bent my head down with guilt.

"Look at me," he ordered.

I did as he said. As always. I might tease him sometimes, but I always obeyed him in the end.

"I'll ask you the same question I've been asking you since I knew about you and Leo. Do you love him?"

I'd been asking myself the same question, but the answer had never been a yes or a no.

"Do you love him?!" he roared.

Trembling hard, I just leaned back, tears threatening to spill from my eyes.

"Answer me, goddamn it!"

"He loves me! That's what matters."

"That's not my question."

"Then yes. Leo is the only person that *truly* thinks I'm worthy of having any man I want. He believes I'm good enough for him. Yes, I've started to love him, and I know with time I'll love him with all my heart."

The fury in his expression turned into something morbid, something that made me feel like the worst of traitors; I betrayed Tino's trust. I stole his son away from him.

"I warned you he'd make you fall for him," he mumbled.

"You shouldn't have left us alone then." I regretted the words as soon as they fell off my mouth. Why the hell would I say that?

I knew why. I was angry at him even if I had no right to be. I was angry he used me. I was angry he pretended to care. And above all, I was furious that he ignored that moment we had together.

But he was doing the right thing, and so should I.

"If the wedding is too soon, we can wait after my graduation. Either way, I won't marry him without your approval. You have my word," I said quickly in a feeble attempt to fix what I'd just done.

"Well, here's *my* word, Angelina," he whispered, but his voice thundered through me, bringing up a feeling I'd only experienced with…Marciano. Why would Tino's whisper remind me of Marciano's? Why did they sound so alike?

Why did my mind play those tricks on me? In this moment when I'd never needed clarity more?

My breath quivered as I exhaled, blinking away the tears and the confusion. "I'm all ears."

"Congratulations."

"Wha—"

He jutted up, leaving the whole office, leaving me behind in a pool of sweat and shock and disbelief.

Don Bellomo had just agreed to the wedding.

I was gonna marry Leo Bellomo, the Mafia boss's son.

CHAPTER 39

Tino

Halloween Eve. The night before she turned eighteen. The night I'd been waiting for for years. The night I'd imagined a thousand times but not once had I pictured it to become this agony. To become the night before she married my own son. The last night I'd be able to sit in this chair and watch her in her sleep.

Tomorrow, my sweet Angel would never be mine again.

She'd belong to Leo. My son was going to taste her lips, touch her beautiful body, watch her bend under his hands, savor her moans while he made love to her.

There were no words to describe the blazing pain corroding me. The thought of another hand on her was enough to bring out the demons to play.

"Why did you do this to me, Angel?" I whispered. "I did everything for you. How could you betray me like this?"

I tiptoed to her side of the bed and felt the softness of her hair one last time, moving it off her peaceful face. "How could you sleep like that, tonight of all nights?"

The back of my hand brushed her cheek and feathered on her lips, her breath kissing my skin like a whisper. "How could you let me go?"

How could I ever let her go?

A wet drop smeared my hand and another plopped down on her face. My...own tears? I never cried. For the past twenty years I didn't remember a time I cried except when my wife died. "Look what you've done to me, Angel. Look at how much you've hurt me. Look at how weak you've made me."

I wiped my eyes fast and yanked the sheets off her body. "I'll have you right now and ruin this fucking wedding before it starts."

She'd broken all her spoken and unspoken promises to me. Why should I keep mine? I stripped her with the patient speed I used every time and knelt naked between her legs, my cock ready to take what had always been mine.

I put my knees on either side of her parted thighs and braced on my palms.

Do it. She belongs to you. You didn't wait all this time for someone else to sink his cock in her virgin pussy.

She's ready for the taking. Your taking. Do it.

Why should you be the one sacrificing her? Why shouldn't Leo? You had your eyes on her long before he did. He's the one who should step down. You're not stealing her from him now. You can't steal what's yours. He's the one who should have never stolen her from you.

It's time for him to pay. For both of them to pay.

Do it. You know she'll love it. You know she'll beg for it.

Do it.

DO IT!

Her innocent face stared at me in the dark, oblivious to my presence, yet begging me to shelter her from all evil, tugging at my heart like it always did. Then my son's face flashed in my head, slicing me open with a blunt blade.

Do it.

Do it.

DO IT!

I squeezed my eyes shut and let out a silent scream at the ceiling. "I can't do it."

Not to him. Not to her.

I got off her and put my clothes back on. Then I took my gun, felt its weight in my hands as if for the first time. Then I took a pillow and pointed it with the gun at her head.

"You leave me no choice, Angel." If I couldn't have her, no one else could. Not even him.

She stirred in her sleep, and the moonlight hit her stark naked body. I'd forgotten to put her clothes back on. I couldn't kill her while she was naked and leave her for everyone to see her body. Not even in death.

I set the pillow back in place and waited for her breath to gain its steady beat. Then I fully dressed her. She moaned, blinking as I fixed her shorts in place. Swiftly, I straightened and grabbed the gun.

Her eyes opened, and my heart thundered in my ears. "Tino? Is that you?" she asked, her hands quick with the lights.

As she sat up and saw the gun pointed at her, her gaze widened. "What are you doing?"

Yeah, what the fuck was I doing? What the fuck was I doing to my sweet, little Angel? My shoulders slumped as I put the gun down. "I...I thought I heard something. I came straight to your room. You know, with the wedding tomorrow, and the Lanzas not pleased..."

Her eyes darted around in panic. "Is someone here?"

"No. False alarm."

She jumped out of bed and threw her arms around me. "Thank you, Tino."

Startled, I didn't dare hug her back. I pulled away and put the gun in the back of my pants. "For what?"

"For watching over me. Even if it wasn't for my sake."

"What do you mean not for your sake? Who else's?"

She drew back. "Leo, of course. Who else? It's okay. I know all you've been doing for me since the attack has been for him, but I'm still grateful. I mean, look at you, even now, you wake up in the middle of the night, always coming to the rescue."

I scratched my temple. "Did Leo tell you that?"

"That you only accepted to protect me so he'd be your underboss? Yeah, he did. I hope you don't mind him telling me. I don't want you two to fight again because of me."

"Nobody is fighting, Angelina. Not anymore. When did he tell you?"

She shrugged. "Around four or five months ago."

"On the day you agreed to marry him?"

"I think so."

Of course. "I see. Now, go back to your beauty sleep." It was time I left her be for a bit.

She chuckled. "Thanks."

I spun and headed for the door, the acid corroding my soul searing harder.

"And Tino?"

I stopped in my tracks, my fist crushing the knob. "Si?"

"Thank you for giving me away tomorrow. It means a lot to me."

"Anything for you." *My sweet Angel.*

CHAPTER 40

Tino

She looked at me with her big green eyes after she twirled in her wedding dress. "How do I look?"

A vision.

That was meant to be for me.

"Like an angel." I held her hands in mine and squeezed gently. "Leo is one fucking lucky bastard."

A natural, more beautiful blush overpowered her makeup. "Did you see him? Is he…nervous?"

I wished. "He's waiting for you with the warmest feet ever."

Her grin lit her face and darkened my heart. I removed my hands from hers so I wouldn't squeeze too hard.

"Are the Lanzas anywhere in sight?" she asked.

"Didn't Leo say he took care of them?"

"Yes. He said Claudia wasn't upset at all, and that she, too, wanted to marry someone else, but you know... What if she was lying to save face?"

"Probably. That's why I've compensated the Lanzas heavily for my son's indiscretion. They'd be very stupid to back down on the business agreement we've made. Besides, I doubled the hotel security inside and out. You have nothing to worry about."

"Thank you, Tino. I don't know what we'd do without you."

I gave her my arm. "Shall we?" My voice came out thick.

With a nod, she linked arms with mine. I swallowed the pain and rage about to burst in everyone's face and painted the world red, buried it under years and years of expertise.

The security team surrounded us until we reached the ballroom of my hotel designated for the wedding. The second ballroom had a

Halloween party. Some of its guests were scattered outside, ridiculous masks on their faces.

When the bodyguards opened our doors, I didn't pay attention to the five hundred guests and the camera flashes of the peppered press down the aisle.

I had to silence the demons. One word only could shut them up.

Piccolo.

Leo was grinning from ear to ear as I walked on fire, delivering my Angel to him myself.

He was fucking happy, and so was she. Wasn't that what I wanted? To see them happy? To give them the best?

Why did it hurt so badly? Why did I feel like I was about to explode and destroy everyone in the way?

At the last step, I took my time, looking at her through the veil. Then I lifted it and leaned forward to inhale her smell for the last time, to kiss her goodbye.

"I love you, Angel," I murmured too low for her to hear as my lips touched her cheek. I confessed it for the first time to her, to myself.

With a heated breath, I drew back and switched my gaze to Leo.

"Grazie, Papà." He grinned.

I nodded once and squeezed his shoulder. My legs barely carried me, so I took my seat.

The ceremony started. With closed eyes, I listened to the priest mumbling the clichés.

"Do you take Angelina Maria Baldi as your wedded wife?"

I do.

"Do you promise to love her, comfort her, honor and keep her for better or worse, for richer or poorer, in sickness and health, and forsaking all others, be faithful only to her, for as long as you both shall live?"

I do.

I put a hand over my squeezing heart to silence the persistent ache. A noise outside the ballroom as Leo finished his vows distracted me for a second. I glanced at the entrance doors. They were closed, and the bodyguards were at their places. It must have been coming from the other party.

Shifting back in my seat, I listened to Angel saying her vows as she looked into my son's eyes with everything a groom may ever want to see in his bride's gaze.

More noise.

The men began to fluster, pressing their ear buds, mumbling to each other.

"I now pronounce you husband and—"

The rapid, successive *bangs* of a machine gun boomed from outside and into the ballroom. Screams filled the air as dresses and suits tumbled on the floor. I dashed through the panicked crowd, my arms stretched with a gun in each hand, and threw myself at the altar, knocking down anybody in the way.

I swiveled and, along with my bodyguards, I shot at the fuckers with the machine guns. They were in suits, their faces covered with Halloween masks.

When my men sheltered my body with theirs, I saw Leo was on the floor, his shoulder bleeding, Michele covering him with his body.

"I got him, but she's down! Take her and go!" Michele yelled over the bullets.

I glanced to my right. At my Angel. At the redness smearing the center of her dress in a growing circle. At her silent face. At her screaming sister.

"NOOOOO!"

CHAPTER 41

Lina

Blackness. An infinite ocean of blackness.

"Wake up, my sweet Angel."

"Marciano? Are you here? Am I dead?"

"No, Angel. You're here. With me."

"But you're dead. Marciano?"

Dark blue eyes taunted me in the dark. *"Tino. My name is Tino."*

"Tino?" A gasp snagged in my chest as I opened my eyes, a pounding headache and queasy stomach hitting me hard. Was I dreaming? No, I was awake. The dull pain resonating through my body told me so. It was still dark, though; I couldn't see a thing.

For a second, I couldn't remember what day it was or where I was. Then the fog enveloping my head cleared a bit. I was at…my wedding. My fucking red wedding. The horrible events rushed in. There was a shooting. Leo! Nicky! Oh my God.

What happened to them? What happened to me?

I was lying on something comfortable. As comfortable as my bed at the mansion, but it was different. The air was humid and the smell of the room, sea breeze and lemon, confirmed I wasn't at the mansion at all. I attempted to get up, but I could barely lift my head, let alone my body. There was so much pain in my lower abdomen. What the fuck?

I checked my body. A blanket covered me, but I was naked underneath. Panic took over me. I reached a hand to check between my legs. Something was inside me. A…tube of sorts. I felt the extended length and found a plastic bag attached to it. That must be a catheter? To my huge relief, I felt nothing there other than the mild discomfort caused by the catheter. No pain or sticky wetness. No signs I'd been violated. For now.

My hand moved to the source of pain and found a lump on my stomach that felt like a bandage or a dressing. Had I been shot?

Tears burned my eyes, but I fought them. I had to be strong for whatever was going on. To face whoever took me—it wasn't so hard to guess it was the Lanzas—and find a way out.

Were they planning to kill me? Of course not. Not now. They wouldn't patch me up if that was the plan. Torture me? Rape me? Rape me and then kill me like Seppi did to Leo's Mom?

Every horrifying story I'd heard from people or seen on the news or in a movie ran through my mind. My life was the biggest horror show I was forced to experience live. What did I expect? I was the girl born on Halloween. Horrifying me had been the entertainment of others since I could remember. For some reason, despite my luck and long history of unfortunate events, I was convinced having my wedding on that fucking day was okay.

Like it'd have mattered. The Lanzas would have come on any day the wedding would have been. What was I thinking?

I thought of Nicky and her protective embrace. I thought of Leo and his smile. I thought of Tino and all the trouble I'd caused him. I thought of my wedding that went from a fairytale to a nightmare. I thought of all my plans to finish high school and get a scholarship to become a distinguished violinist.

Would I ever see any of those again?

Anger kicked in and held back the panic. I bit back a scream as I forced myself up, the pain unbearable.

Carefully, I felt my way out of the bed, securing the blanket tightly around me. My bare feet touched the floor. Smooth and cold. Not hardwood. Porcelain.

I adjusted the blanket around my body so that it covered my back and I could hold it from the front. Then I stood, stifling a groan. A faint squeaking of a door opening boomed in the silence. Light drifted in and blinded me for a second. I blinked a few times, my heartbeat throbbing in my skull. Then my eyes adjusted, and I could see the figure standing in the doorway.

"Tino!" Grateful tears of relief rushed out of my eyes. "Oh thank God. I thought I was kidnapped."

He rushed toward me. "What are you doing up? You need to rest."

"I was… It doesn't matter. Where's Nicky and Leo? And where are we?"

Brightness flared in the room as he flipped a switch. There was a window where the sea and sand stretched behind the curtains. It was a moonless night, though. No wonder I couldn't see anything. The room itself was big yet simple with the décor and furniture. A king size bed. A wardrobe. Two small chairs and a small table. There was a door to my left, which I assumed was the bathroom door.

"Let's get you back to bed first. You must rest until your wound is closed. You were shot. You had surgery." Tino's strong arms were on my back, and he carried me with one effortless move.

Startled and embarrassed to be in his arms naked, even with the blanket around my body, I flinched. "I can walk."

He smirked as he placed me on the mattress and adjusted the pillows behind my head as if I'd said nothing. His eyes traveled to the blanket I was holding onto like my life depended on it. "The weather here isn't like Chicago. It's hot and humid. Nurse Arancia thought it'd be better to keep you naked so no infection would happen and to be easier for her to clean you and change your dressing. Are you cold?"

And terribly worried. "A little, but that's the least of my concerns. Please answer my questions."

He grabbed a chair and sat by my side. "Nicole is fine. Not a scratch. Leo took a bullet in the shoulder. Nothing serious, though. He's already on his feet."

"Thank God. And what is this place?"

"Italy. A private island of mine."

I shook my head in confusion. "O-kay. What are we doing here? And where are Nicky and Leo? They should be the ones taking care of me, not you."

"Nicole and Leo aren't here. It's only you and me…and Arancia, the nurse and housekeeper that has been taking care of you…and the bodyguards, of course."

"What? Why aren't they here? Where are they?"

"What's the last thing you remember?"

It was all fuzzy. "The shooting…and then Leo wasn't standing next to me… There were screams… Nicky was running toward me, but then someone or something knocked me down on the floor. Everything went black afterwards. It's the Lanzas who did it, right?"

He stared at me pensively for a few moments, as if he was saying, "I told you so."

"Right. They'd managed to hide among the guests of the Halloween party."

I pursed my lips. "So where's my sister and my…husband?" The word felt strange. Off. Were we even married? Did the priest get to finish the ceremony?

Something flickered in his eyes at the word, too. He, too, felt its weirdness, or maybe it angered him. It sure did. Marrying Leo turned a family ally into an enemy and got his son shot. "Nicole is safe back home. Guarded around the clock. Leo is making sure she stays safe."

That alarmed me, not assured me. "How?"

"However he sees fit. He's a man now, and he needs to take care of his family."

My heart raced. "Is he gonna retaliate? Is that what it is?"

"I don't mean to rub salt on your wounds, but any actions have consequences, especially in our world. You're both adults. You knew what you were getting yourselves into and still went through with it. It's time to deal with those consequences."

"Can't he just drop it? He hurt them, and they hurt him back. Can't it end that way?"

He leaned forward, a dark frown on his expression. "It never ends that way."

A horrible chill ran down my spine. "What did you do when Leo's Mom was killed?" The situation was pretty similar. The Lanzas almost killed me. I needed to know how far Leo would go.

"You don't want to know."

My lips trembled. "Tino, you have to help him. You can't just leave him to them like that. He's not as powerful as you are."

He left his chair angrily. "Ever since his mother, I've gone easy on that boy for years, fixing every mistake he makes for him, and look what happened."

Now was not the time for tough love. Leo could die out there. "Please, Tino."

"You don't have to beg for him. I am still helping even though I shouldn't."

"How are you helping him?"

"I left everything behind and got you here where no one can ever touch you again."

My heart banged harder. I swallowed, the taste of my mouth awful. "Thank you, Tino, but that's not gonna help him with the Lanzas."

"He caused that mess with them. He needs to take care of it on his own."

"Tino, you can't—"

"Get some rest, Angelina." He raised his voice in warning. "I'll make sure Nicole and

Leo know you're awake. See you in the morning."

CHAPTER 42

Lina

Early dawn was peeking in through the windows. As I let out a yawn, the door opened and a woman came in. She was holding a tray with one hand, the other carrying a dress bag by the hanger.

A big smile stretched her lips. "Buongiorno. You're up already or did I wake you?"

I stared at her. She was...so pretty. Early thirties. Long red hair. Tall. Manicured nails. Red summer dress. Sexy Italian accent. She looked like one of those James Bond's women, not a nurse slash housekeeper on a secluded island.

And I was naked, my hair all messed up, bloody gauze covering my body and a bag of piss coming out of my vagina. "I just woke up. You must be Arancia."

"Si, si." She placed the tray on the small table and the dress on the chair next to it. "And you're Angel."

I blinked. "What did you just call me?"

"Don Bellomo said your name is Angelina. Isn't Angel short for it?"

"Please don't call me that again. My name is Lina."

Her smile widened. "Mi dispiace, Lina. Can I change your dressing, per favore?"

I nodded, and she picked some things off the tray. "Do you think I can remove the catheter today or would you like to keep it for another day until you can walk easily?"

"Yes, please, take it out."

"Va bene." She removed the blanket. Reflexively, I hid my boobs with my arms, and then I bent one knee up and tilted my thigh to cover my vagina. When she started with the dressing, I stared at her arm. She had a small tattoo. A heart with wings. Like she needed to be even hotter. "Do you live here?"

"Only when Don Bellomo needs me to."

"Oh." Was she his...mistress? Wow. I'd never seen Tino with any woman during my stay at his mansion. I'd always wondered how a man like him would live all these months without a woman. I felt guilty that our stay at his place could have been the reason he wouldn't bring any women home. Obviously, he'd been getting his needs taken care of on the privacy of his island and who knew where else, too.

Why did the idea of Tino having sex with incredibly hot women get on my nerves? "Does anyone else live here when he needs them to?"

"Not that I know of." The burn from whatever she applied on the wound distracted me for a minute. "You're healing very well. Two more days and you won't need any help to go by your everyday routine." She finished patching me up, and her hand moved between my legs. "Take a deep breath."

I held my breath and squeezed my eyes as she pulled the goddamn thing out. It was fine at the beginning, but with time I was convinced whoever invented it with a sadist.

"Allora, do you care for a sponge bath?"

I was desperate for one, but having her hands on my...everything, when she looked like this, and I looked like that, was...ugh.

"I'm sure you wish it weren't *me* giving you that bath." She winked.

"W-what? What do y-ou…" I stammered.

"I meant Leo." She laughed. "You must miss him. I'm so sorry about your wedding. You must be devastated."

My lashes fluttered. "Yeah. I am." Right?

In all honesty, I was more scared than devastated. I didn't care about the wedding or the marriage as much as I cared about Leo's life. And mine and Nicky's.

I was so foolish and naive to care before, but after what happened, after I saw it with my own eyes and felt the pain and the damage we'd caused to ourselves and others…

Guilt buzzed through me. I had to apologize to Tino. I'd put him through a lot. He didn't deserve that, especially not from me.

Arancia got a basin and sponge and did the awkward job. Then she helped me brush my teeth and put on the cotton dress she'd brought earlier. I wasn't allowed underwear yet. Only when she was sure I could go to the bathroom all by myself and the swelling on my body was gone that I'd be allowed panties and bras.

I stared at my reflection in the wardrobe mirror. "What about my nipples?"

She chuckled. "Scusi?"

"This is a cotton dress. My nipples will show. Tino doesn't like it when..." I bit my lip, embarrassed to share something like that with a stranger. A stranger sleeping with him. "Never mind. He probably wouldn't notice." Not when she was here.

As I spun, the door was slowly pushed open, and Tino appeared, fully dressed in a white dress shirt and black slacks. As if on cue, my treacherous nipples hardened. Those attention sluts.

I crossed my arms over my chest, but I noticed his smirk. He did see. As always. "Buongiorno," he said.

"Buongiorno," I said in a terrible accent.

"You look nice. How are you doing today?"

"A little better. Catheter free."

"That's always a blessing." He looked at Arancia and said something in Italian. When she replied, he extended his arm toward me. "Have breakfast with me on the beach."

I dropped my arm and took his hand without a thought. So what if he saw? I was like a daughter to him now. And he was a good father.

As we left the house and walked to the breakfast table already set on the beach, I realized the house was a two-story beach villa, and my room was downstairs. The place was beautiful, sunny, calm. Being rich did have its perks. Arancia didn't sit or eat with us. There was no one else but Tino and I as far as I could see.

I drank some orange juice and glanced at the chocolate crepes and biscuits. "Who prepped this meal if it wasn't the housekeeper?" She was with me all the time before he came down to the room.

He drank his coffee. "I did."

"Wow. Thank you, Tino."

"Anything for you, Angelina."

Mocking and blame dripped off his voice. He was here, taking care of me, protecting me, unwillingly. Last time he was getting something out of it. This time, he was just stuck with me. "Leo told you to bring me here, didn't he?"

"You mean like he told me to bring you to the mansion?"

"Yes." Because I'd always be that girl. The fragile, little girl that always needed a babysitter. Someone to take care of her. To save her.

He downed his coffee and stood, his jaws tight.

"Did I say something wrong?"

He spun fast and leaned in over me with more aggression than I'd ever seen from him. I jumped, leaning back as he blocked the sun, squeezing the edges of the back of my seat. "Everything you've been saying since he got into your head is wrong."

His face was scary dark yet hurt. It terrified me, but I felt so guilty that I'd hurt him this much.

"You think Leo or anyone tells me what or what not to do?" he fumed.

Great. I'd offended him, too.

"*I* have protected you all your life in ways you don't even know. *I* darted to the altar to cover you when he didn't even shoot back at them. *I* got you here, where no one can find or hurt you, while he was busy getting shot like a helpless victim."

"I…" Was speechless? Was clueless? Was a fucking idiot? "I'm sorry, Tino." I put as much sincerity in my apology as I could. I was sorry from the bottom of my heart.

"For what?"

"Everything."

He straightened his back. "Good for you."

He left me at the beach and strode fast back to the house. A couple of bodyguards in black suits appeared out of nowhere and helped me back to my room.

Tino's words replayed in my head all morning. What did he mean he'd protected me all my life in ways I didn't know? In the afternoon, Arancia came with lunch and some pills. She ate with me and made sure I took all the medicine. Then she told me Tino was leaving the island.

Fear jolted through me. I only felt safe in the middle of nowhere because he was here. "What? Where is he going?"

"Non lo so. I don't ask."

I shuffled out of the bed to see him, but she stopped me. "You need to rest, Lina."

I frowned at her. "I need to see him before he leaves. Excuse me."

Loud noise boomed from a distance. A plane taking off noise. "He left already?"

"That's what I was trying to tell you."

"Why didn't you tell me earlier? I could've caught him before he took off."

"I do what he tells me to do. I'm sure you know how it is."

I sighed. "Do you know when he's coming back?"

"No."

"Fine. Do you know where my phone is?"

She shrugged. "I don't think you came with one. There's no reception here anyway."

"How do you make phone calls here then or use the internet or even shop for supplies?"

"We don't." She chuckled. "Don Bellomo gets everything we need on the plane with him whenever he visits, and there's one satellite phone on the island, but only Don Bellomo has access to it."

"Ugh... How can I reach my sister and Leo? I need to call them."

"Don Bellomo mentioned nothing about that. You can ask him when he returns." She lifted the lunch tray and headed for the door before I could say anything else.

Awesome. Just like the academy and the mansion, this little piece of paradise was nothing but another Bellomo prison in disguise.

CHAPTER 43

Lina

If the bullet didn't kill me, boredom would. I hadn't left the room in three days. There was nothing for me to do but eat and sleep. I couldn't exactly drink cocktails and go for a swim like Arancia did every day, flaunting her gorgeous, tanned body in a red bikini. I didn't have my violin or my phone or my books. I couldn't believe I'd say this, but I missed homework.

"Buongiorno." Arancia's early morning grin had started to annoy me.

"It's just another boring morning. Nothing is good about it."

"Someone is cranky," she said playfully as she placed the breakfast tray on the nightstand. "Would you like to eat on the beach instead?"

The one time I ate at the beach didn't end up so pleasantly. "No, and I'm not hungry."

"You have to eat to take your meds."

"I said I'm not hungry."

"Don't you want to get better, Lina?"

What I wanted was to turn back the time. "And then what? Will I go home?"

"That's up to Don Bellomo."

"I know Tino well enough to figure he won't take me home until it's over with the Lanzas. And I'm so scared of *how* it'll be over with them that I don't want it to happen."

"I'm sure Leo and Don Bellomo will take care of things like they always do. Why don't you let them do what they do best and try to enjoy your time here away from the world and its problems? Consider it a vacation."

"Alone. Away from my sister and the husband I haven't had the chance to marry. Even Tino left."

She smiled. "I see."

I heard something in her tone I didn't like. "See what exactly?"

Her shit-eating grin grew. "It's okay to miss him. He has that effect on people. But he'll be back before you know it."

"What the hell are you talking about?"

She shook her head, her infuriating grin intact, and reached for the toast and butter. "Nothing. I'll make you a sandwich."

I knocked the whole tray off the nightstand. The contents bellowed, spilled and smashed into pieces everywhere.

Arancia got to her feet, the fucking grin finally wiped off her face. She inched a brow at me. "When Don Bellomo said you were a brat, I thought he was exaggerating."

He told his bitch what?

"I don't think he'll be pleased when he knows." She puckered her lips at me as if she was sorry for me. That bitch. "I'll go clean this up."

When she exited, I went to the bathroom and cleaned my dress as best as I could, blood pounding in my skull. That woman got on my nerves more than she should have. She was gonna tell on me and make things worse between Tino and me when I was trying to apologize. And what was that shit she said that got me angry in the first place? *It's okay to miss him. He has that effect on people.*

I didn't miss him. Why would I miss him? I was only agitated that he left me here for days with nothing to do or a means to call and only his mistress for company.

I used more force than I needed to open the bathroom door. She was hunching on the floor, cleaning up my mess when the sound of a plane approaching had my heart leaping.

A feeling I couldn't find a name for washed over me. Despite how angry I was and how worried about his reaction when Arancia told on me, that feeling soothed me.

Arancia finished cleaning the floor and then she changed the sheets. I heard the plane land and his footsteps in the house, but he went directly upstairs. I'd been waiting for his return for days, and when he did come back, he wouldn't even acknowledge me with a simple greeting?

I decided not to go outside to greet him either. I stayed in my room for hours, listening to the waves and the quiet chatter in Italian and the occasional laughter between Tino and the mistress. *She he talks to and laughs with. Me...*

It wasn't until lunchtime that he was standing in the doorway, watching me as I pretended to be sleeping. He turned his back, about to leave, but I cleared my throat. I was so mad at him for ignoring me, but I didn't want him to go.

When he didn't turn back, I called out his name.

Finally, he entered the room, dressed in all black, his hands in his pockets. "Go back to sleep."

"I wasn't sleeping."

"Lunch is ready. You must be hungry."

Shoot. She already told him.

"You're free to join us if you like."

"Us?"

He left without another word.

Great.

I splashed some water on my face and headed outside. My room was down the hall from everything. The whole floor was an open area where the kitchen, dining table and lounge mingled together.

Arancia was serving lunch in a fucking couture dress, Tino already at the table. I walked to his right side and reached to pull out a chair. His hands were faster, pulling it out for me.

"Thank you, Tino," I said.

Arancia set a plate for me and served us all soup before she sat across from me. I grabbed a spoon and started. As much as I hated to admit it, the soup was delicious like all her cooking.

Tino said something to her in Italian, probably complementing the food, and squeezed her hand. A lump rose to my throat. I barely managed to push the spoonful in my mouth down.

"Did you talk to Nicky or Leo while you were gone?" I asked, mostly to interrupt, the pitch of my voice higher than I intended it to be.

"Yes. They're fine. Happy that you are, too."

"Can I talk to them?"

He took his time savoring another spoon of the soup he liked so much. "No."

"Why not? You have a phone we can use to call them."

"For your safety, nobody knows where we are, not even Leo or Nicole. The Lanzas don't even know you're alive, and it has to stay that way until it's all sorted out. They want you dead, Angelina. Calling now might risk everything."

"So what? I'll just stay here indefinitely without even talking to them?"

"It's better than being dead, isn't it?"

The lump in my throat grew to block even the air in. I dropped my spoon and excused myself to cry alone in my room.

Was I doomed to live in fear my whole life? Fear of my father, fear of my stalker, fear of the Mafia? When would it ever stop? When would I ever start living?

His footsteps came up behind me as I was lying down, sniffling in bed. "You need to eat. Isn't it enough what you've done at breakfast?"

"Sorry about this morning, and I'll apologize to your mistress later, but right now I've lost my appetite."

"My mistress?"

I rolled my eyes as I shifted up and met his gaze. "*Si, si.* I'm not stupid."

He chuckled, and I noticed the tray in his hand. He sat beside me and set it down. Then he placed a napkin on my lap, filled a spoon with soup and moved it to my mouth. "Open up."

"Thank you, Tino, but I seriously don't—"

He pushed the spoon into my mouth. "What did I say before?"

I almost choked on the food, but I managed to swallow. He cleaned up my mouth and scooped another spoonful of soup. I ate. I finished the whole thing. I'd be lying if I said I didn't like that he was here with me instead of eating with her. I'd be lying some more if I said that deep down I didn't like that he was feeding me himself.

He wiped my mouth again and stood. "Arancia will be back for the tray and to give you your meds." Just like that, he was leaving again.

"How does Leo feel about having your mistress taking care of your daughter-in-law?" I was playing with fire, but I didn't care. I was tired of being ignored. I was tired of everything. "He's very fond of his mother. He won't like it."

He stopped in his tracks. Then he wheeled back to me and bent so that our eyes leveled. He didn't say anything for a few seconds, but he got me shaking when his gaze penetrated me and our breath clashed against each other. At least, I got his attention, and he was still here.

"I only gave you a good spanking once. I didn't know you'd miss it so much," he said.

I blinked hard. "Jokes on you. You can't bend me over your knee with the wound and all."

"Who said that was the only position I could use to give you the hard spanking you deserve?"

My teeth stabbed my lower lip. A feeling I thought I'd buried months ago hit the surface. An old need I'd convinced myself wasn't real screamed inside me louder than any other reality.

"Leo is my son and one of my men. He doesn't get to like or dislike what I do or say. He obeys, one way or another. Like everybody else, understood?"

I pressed my lips together and just nodded.

"Good. One more thing, you're not my daughter-in-law, Angelina."

"I-I understand the ceremony was ruined before the priest did his thing, but I'm still Leo's fiancé."

A sound part chuckle part snort burst out of his mouth. Then his thumb brushed my cheek. "No." My heart thudded in my chest. The feeling of his thumb on my skin felt so…terribly familiar. He smirked. "You were never his."

CHAPTER 44

Lina

They'd been swimming together for an hour while I was in bed to *rest*. I was supposed to be on my honeymoon with the younger version of this infuriating man, having hot sex until my *husband* and I both couldn't walk. Instead, my wedding was painted red, I wasn't married, I almost died, and I ended up stuck on this God forsaken island for God knew how long. The last thing I wanted to do was fucking lie down and do nothing all day while everybody else had fun. Or was out to kill someone.

I'd be more than happy to do either.

I ambled to the beach, the sun hot on my skin, and slowly helped myself to one of their beach recliners, moaning a little with the tight stretch of the skin around the wound.

When he saw me, Tino got out of the water, looking hotter than Mike Gennaro in his beach movie. Wet curls. The most beautiful blue yet dangerous eyes. Water droplets on tanned, sculpted to perfection, tattooed muscles. Wet swim shorts attached to his junk like a second skin.

I stole a glance. I wanted to know if he was hard for her. He was a guy, and she was...*that* in a red bikini. Why wouldn't he be hard for her?

My eyes narrowed at his crotch. It was difficult to tell, though. I had zero experience, and he'd probably adjusted it before he got out. All I could tell was the incredible size of that man. He was definitely bigger than Mike Gennaro. And Leo. At least, that was what I gathered from the outline of their dicks.

I couldn't believe I was gonna die without seeing a real dick. Without having sex.

Tino cleared his throat louder than normal. Shoot. I was still staring. I looked up at him, my face hot.

"It's too hot for you to hang out here. Get inside."

Too hot indeed. "You guys are doing fine. Why can't I?"

"I don't want you to get sunstroke. Your body is still healing."

"I'm fine. I think we're good to remove the stitches. I'm also ready for *underwear*. I'm sure you're tired of seeing my nipples all the time."

"I'm never tired of seeing nipples." He bent over, casting a huge shadow over me. Then he leaned in for a whisper. "Just like you're never tired of ogling *my* cock."

Shit, piss and fuck.

He leaned back. "Get up."

"No."

He scooped me up in his arms without warning. I yelped and wrapped my arms around his neck, his body so hot and wet and hard. Then when his palm smacked my butt, I yelped again.

"When I tell you something, you do it." He smacked my other butt cheek as he walked us to the house.

"Tino! Stop it!"

He did it again.

"Oh my God. Please. You're hurting me." *And making me wet.* I was in his arms, wearing no underwear, and every spank he gave me squeezed a gush of arousal between my legs.

Fuck, I was wet for my fiancé's dad.

His palm landed on my butt one more time. "If you can't handle the pain, then you shouldn't be a naughty, bratty girl all the time."

I bit a moan. "Yes, Tino."

I didn't realize the way I moaned that except when his eyes darkened with desire. I had no clue how I turned into that deviant that leered at a man's junk, talked about spanking and nipples and underwear and moaned like a bitch in heat when I was around Tino.

Only Tino.

"Can you put me down now, please?" I asked as we entered the house.

He continued and headed for the stairs instead of my room. "Why?"

Because you make me wanna do very wrong things. I just sighed, my arms sliding to his back, feeling him up. "Where are you taking me?"

"My room."

I gaped at him. "W-why?"

He climbed up without answering, my heart banging with every step.

"Tino?"

"Shhhh."

A gasp fled my throat. "What the hell?"

He threw a casual glance at me. "What?"

"Say that again."

"Say what again?"

"That shhhh. Say it again."

He looked at me like I was insane. "I haven't said anything, Angelina. Has the sun hit your head already?"

"I'm not crazy. Say it again."

He put me down at the top of the stairs and touched my forehead with the back of his hand. "You're warm. This can't be the sun. You barely stayed out there. Get inside so I can check the wound."

"You? You'll check the wound?" The panic of him seeing my naked body made me forget about my demand. I was probably going crazy to think what I'd thought anyway. This was Tino. Marciano was dead. Yet whenever I was aroused, *he* managed to play a mind trick on me. There was no other explanation.

"Yes. You have a problem with that?" He opened his door and ushered me inside.

"Yes, I do. I'm completely naked under this dress."

"Nothing I haven't seen before."

Jesus. That didn't make me feel better or make this any less awkward. "I…I'd rather let Arancia do it. This is just…"

"Relax." He opened his wardrobe and got out a hundred shopping bags. "I bought you some things, underwear included."

"Oh. That's…uh…very thoughtful of you. Thank you, Tino. Is that…uh…why you brought me to your room?"

"Si, si. Why else?"

"Mhmm. Yeah. Of course."

He put the bags next to the bed—his bed. "Put on some panties so I can see you."

"So you can see me in panties?"

"So I can see the wound, Angelina."

Fuck. Did I say that out loud? Oh my God. "I…I'm fine. Really. It's not infected. There's no need—"

"Put on some panties or I'll just lift your dress when you're all naked underneath and—"

"All right! All right. Fine." It wasn't a possible infection that was making me imagine and say weird things. It was him being half naked, all wet and hot, while I stood in his room, where he slept, where he…

I sat on the edge of the bed and snooped inside the bags. There were all sorts of clothes in there. Shorts, t-shirts, dresses, swimsuits and underwear. I grabbed the first pair of panties I found and asked him to turn around.

He chuckled but did what I asked. Of course, I took all the time in the world to put on one pair of panties to marvel at his perfect, hot ass.

"You done?" He snorted.

I cleared my throat. "Yeah."

He spun and came my way. Then his hands slid up my thighs, meeting my butt as they hiked up the dress to the edge of my ribs. My body burned with shyness and arousal, but I didn't try to hide anything. The deviant only he brought in me wanted him to see.

He removed the dressing carefully and inspected the stitches. "It looks fine."

"I told you."

He put down my dress, and as his head tilted up, our gazes met for a long moment. Then mine fell to his lips, and my mind drifted to that memory when we almost kissed. "Did that moment happen or was it wishful thinking?"

"What moment?"

I grabbed his hand and placed it on the back of my head. "The one so similar to this one we're having now."

His fingers tangled in my hair, and his mouth drew closer, the heat of his breath making my head spin. "This moment?"

I had no clue where I got the guts to thread his wet hair with my fingers and pull him closer. "Yes." It was so wrong. Not just taboo and forbidden. It was destructively wrong. He was Leo's father. My fiancé's father. But fuck yes.

His breath teased me as our lips almost touched. My eyes fluttered closed, and my heart rocketed as I desperately waited for him to seal our kiss.

"No." Cruelly, brutally, his breath was no longer on my lips, and his hand left my hair, forcing me to leave his, too. "It didn't happen."

CHAPTER 45

Tino

She deserved that humiliation. She deserved that painful longing. She deserved the agony of wanting something so badly while knowing she couldn't get it.

We barely spoke for days. After Arancia removed the stitches, and the weather had cooled, Angel had spent her time exploring the island to kill time and to stay away from me as much as she could. I'd given her space by day, but at night...

She was sleeping soundly, and I resumed my previous routine of undressing her, missing her beautiful body. In the moonlight, her perfect tits were so sexy. I ached to suck those nipples she'd long taunted me with. My cock throbbed painfully for her. I wanted to touch every inch of her skin, mark her whole body up.

Carefully, I undid my pants before sliding them to my ankles, and then I kicked them off. I peeled away my shirt and had it join my pants as well. Once I was standing beside her in nothing but boxers and socks, I stroked myself through my underwear.

God, I fucking want her.

I decided to remove my boxers, too, my heavy erection aching, hot and pulsating in my grip. I was dying to push into every single one of her holes. To draw out pleasure and pain from her. I wanted to make her see who truly owned every part of her.

Fisting my cock, I licked my lips at the sight of her naked pussy. It looked so delicious I wanted to devour it. The thought fueled my desire for her. I pressed my lips to stifle my groans as with each rub, I got closer and closer to release.

I traced her pussy lips and dipped my finger inside a little. Then I licked my finger.

The taste tightened my balls. My cum spurted all over her pelvis.

I watched as my cum slid down on her pussy. With my fingertips, I dragged my seed along her stomach to the curves of her tits. I smeared it all over her nipples and my cock jerked alive when they hardened in response.

Surrendering to the urge to touch her pussy, I was hard again when a moan escaped her as my wet finger slid and circled her clit. Before, she had her own fingers to pleasure herself. Tonight she had me. She'd always have me.

Her body squirmed in her sleep. I pried her legs apart and pictured my tongue on her clit until she screamed my name.

Her breathing gained a more alert rhythm, so I dragged my finger out. I couldn't let her wake up and see me so weak for her like this. I stared at her stained, glistening tits and pussy until her breathing returned to normal speed. Then I fully dressed us both.

Suddenly, a lightning bolt hit the sky. There was nothing in the news about a storm coming. Merda. Thunder followed swiftly. She'd wake up now.

As if on cue, she bolted upright, mumbling a protest.

Cazzo.

Her head tilted in my direction and our eyes collided. "What the fuck? Who's there?" She retreated fast to the other side of the bed, and then she jumped out of it to flip the light switch.

I just stood there.

"The fuck, Tino! You almost gave me a heart attack. You gotta stop doing these things. What the hell are you doing here? In the dark like some creep?"

Touching the body I'd waited to have for years. Marking you mine the way it should be. "The storm. I thought you'd be scared."

She blinked, frowning. "You came down to stay with me during the storm?"

"Yes. Maybe make you some chamomile?"

Her stance relaxed, and she laughed under her breath. "I thought… How could you be like this?"

"Like what?"

"So kind and thoughtful and freaking beautiful but at the same time so…viciously cruel."

"I'm always viciously cruel even when I don't seem to be. Don't ever forget what's written on my chest, Angelina."

"I try. You don't make it easy, though."

A smile forced itself on my mouth. "Go back to bed. I'll go make you the chamomile, and I'll stay with you until you fall asleep."

She slid back under the sheets. "Thank you, Tino."

I went to the kitchen and returned with her drink. Clean. I wanted her sober. It was time she saw the real me for herself.

When I came back, she was cringing at the violent sounds outside. I walked around to the other side of the bed and sat next to her. She took the cup and thanked me again, her eyes a hundred wonderings.

I stretched my body beside her, resting my back against the headboard, and pulled the covers over me. I noticed the hitch to her breath when I did. I lifted my arm and extended it around her back without touching her. Then I nodded for her to come closer.

She stared at me in confusion for a second, but, with a twist to her lips, she did it anyway. She wanted to be in my arms as much as I wanted her to be. Her hair cascaded down to my abdomen as she placed her head on my shoulder.

She was warm, her smell hot as fuck. My cock pulsed as I inhaled her. My nostrils flared with every breath she took. I wanted to inhale her deep inside of me and never release her. I was completely addicted to Angelina Baldi. The bane of my existence. My absolute obsession.

"You're confusing me, you know?" she said.

"It's just a hug. One of many I've given you before and will continue to give you even when you're being a naughty brat."

She rolled her eyes up at me. "It's snuggling. In bed."

"I can leave if you don't want it."

A scoff exploded from her mouth. "You *know* I want it. I need it."

"Need it? Because of the thunder? Or because you miss my son and you're displacing, again?"

"Here comes the asshole in you again."

I reached for her ass and spanked her. The little yelp she did every time never ceased to amuse me. "He misses you, too, by the way. He said it a thousand times the last time I saw him. Unlike you, he's going bonkers without you home. That's what I hear, at least."

"I'm going bonkers here, too."

"Because you miss him?" I mocked. She'd barely mentioned him.

She swallowed. "Marrying Leo was a mistake, and you know it."

"You knew it, too. You still made it."

"After all what's happened, all that horror and loss and pain, if I'd known, I'd have given him up without a second thought."

"I wonder what Leo would say about that. The poor fuck is killing himself out there every day to retaliate for the girl who would give him up because she's scared of some bad guys. Like she didn't know bad guys would be a part of her life when she decided to marry into the Mob."

She withdrew and glanced at me with tears in her eyes. "Is it ever gonna stop? Are you ever gonna stop?"

"Stop what?"

"Punishing me. Isn't that what you're doing? Giving me a mental spanking?"

"For what?"

"Stop being such a dick. You know why."

My cock lurched as I spanked her again and left my hand on her ass. I couldn't help my greedy fingers. They wanted to touch her all over. "I don't. You have to say it."

She trembled, licking her lips, tears falling down her face. "For marrying your son when all I ever wanted is you."

CHAPTER 46

Lina

He was smiling, smirking, while I cried.

He must have thought I was still a confused little girl who knew shit. He'd ignore me, dismiss my feelings, pretend they never happened like he always did. "I'm not confused or displacing. I know what I feel now. I'm not a little girl anymore, Don Bellomo."

He squeezed my ass, pinching it with the fingers he forgot there after the last spank, punishing me for the *Don Bellomo* thing. "Oh

I'm aware that you're not a little girl anymore." His thumb brushed over my lower lip. "You don't know how long I've been waiting for you to become a woman."

The feeling of the roughness of his thumb brought back the memory of the one man who had ever touched me like that. I quivered at the touch, at the words, at the memory.

Like him, Tino did it more than once, brushing my lip back and forth, and my body reacted the same way all over again. I sucked in successive, short breaths, heat squirming through my body as I shuddered with every time he felt the texture of my lips.

He removed the cup from my hands, set it aside, and then both his hands were on my waist, pulling me onto his lap.

I gasped loudly as I felt the hardness poking me from his pants. "Is that…"

"My cock that's so hard for you? The cock your panties are staining with your wetness now? Yes."

I bit my lip so hard at the heavy throbs in my pussy. I bet my face was crimson now. My whole body was burning with shyness and arousal. If he said another dirty word, I'd come all over his pants.

"Are we… Is this happening?" I panted.

"If by this you mean," his hand went down to my ass and tugged at my drenched panties, and his other hand dove into my hair, yanking me toward him so he could whisper in my ear, "fucking your untouched pussy so hard, giving you one orgasm after another until you can't remember your name, then yes, it is happening, my sweet Angel."

I moaned his name so hard, my pussy clenching uncontrollably and… *Wait what?* "What did you just call me?"

He looked me in the eye. "My sweet Angel."

My heart skipped a beat. "Why would you call me that?"

"Because you like to hear it."

"What? What are you… What?"

"From *him*. You liked it, didn't you? You loved everything *he* did to you."

I shook my head, denying it. "Not anymore."

He grunted. "Va bene. If you say so." His hands traveled up my waist, feeling my sides and moving to my chest. The trail of fire he was leaving on my body pulled me back in the moment, kicking away all the dark thoughts, leaving only my need for this man.

My nipples hardened, and he stared, his tongue darting out, before he cupped my boobs and squeezed. Then his thumbs circled my nipples. They were painfully hard and felt strangely tight and dry as they pebbled up harder under his touch.

My whole skin tingled with a sudden dryness as I squirmed on top of him, something like a coat, a body mask that had dried out and needed to be removed. Maybe I didn't take a proper shower today. I'd been afraid to get water on the wound even after the stitches were removed.

How embarrassing. The first time he'd see my body... The first time a man would make love to me... He'd think I was disgusting.

"Would you...mmm...give me a minute?" His touch felt so fucking good. "I'll go freshen up."

"No need. You're beautiful just like this."

"But I was sleeping, remember? I need to, at least, brush my teeth."

His breath fell on my lips. "You don't need anything."

With that, He pulled me into his mouth. His lips pressed to mine, and my heart careened. He claimed my mouth with an odd familiarity, savoring me slowly and then passionately.

Just like my first kiss.

My only kiss.

Out of breath, I let his tongue part my lips as I'd let *him* before, and I moaned into Tino's lips helplessly exactly as I'd moaned for *him*.

What the hell? This can't be right. How can they feel exactly the same? Kiss the same way? Taste the same?

Fuck me, even sound the same?

Was this another one of the tricks my mind loved to pull on me? Was this the delusion caused by the imprint *he* had left on me, the mark, the scar that would never heal?

I yanked my head back, gasping for the breath Tino took away. I stared at him as if seeing him for the first time, shaking my head in disbelief.

He smirked. "You okay?"

"I really need that minute."

He laughed. "Va bene." His lips caressed my cheek as he started to unbutton his shirt. "Don't take too long."

I pulled up my panties, practically running to the bathroom, and shut the door. My chest heaved with labored breaths. I thought I'd have a panic attack.

"What's going on? What the fuck is going on?"

From the first moment I'd laid eyes on Tino, the man with the sunglasses at the bakery, my heart had thrashed in his presence and when I noticed he was the same build as *he* and had a beard like *he* did.

Only his accent dismissed the horrible assumption, but that *shhhh*, and that *my sweet Angel…* They didn't have an accent. They sounded exactly as I'd heard them from *him*.

Then there was that whisper, Tino's whisper before he approved of my marriage that felt exactly like one of *his* whispers.

And that day when Marciano tried to kidnap me, everything was weird, different. I couldn't believe it was *him* until I saw his apartment.

I stifled a gasp with my shaking hand as the million other signs I'd ignored spiraled in my head. How he knew my precise underwear size, how his restaurant had a Halloween birthday promo… That dinner was my seventeenth birthday present. He was there. He'd been there all along.

Could this possibly be true? Could Tino be *him*? Had been *him* all this time?

No. No, that didn't make any sense. This was Marciano's doing. His mindfucks were screwing me even after his death, and those wet dreams I'd been having were mixing delusions with reality.

The man waiting for me in bed, hard and hot for me, the man who desired me as much as I desired him even if we shouldn't have was Don Sebastiano Bellomo. My benefactor. The Mafia boss. My *ex* fiancé's dad.

But he was not my psycho murderous stalker. He was not the son of a bitch who thought he could buy me, who wanted to rape me.

I closed my eyes and tried to breathe, taking off my dress. "I won't let you ruin this for me, Marciano."

When I opened my eyes, I looked in the mirror to see what was stuck on my skin that caused the dryness. The strange coat was white and slick and covered my nipples, under my boobs, my pelvis and, when I took off my panties, I felt the same texture on top of my pussy.

"What the hell?" I rubbed a little of it on my fingers and smelled it. "Oh my God. That's fucking cum." My eyes widened in panic. This couldn't be my cum. That was someone else's cum all over my body. On my pussy.

My stomach lurched, and my eyes stared slowly at the bathroom door. No. No. Nononono.

How could I have been such an idiot? How could I have been so blind? I'd even caught him standing by my bedside in the dark.

Twice. Once with a fucking gun. How could I believe all his lies?

Tino was my murderous stalker.

Tino was *him*.

It's always been him.

What was I gonna do now? He was waiting for me in bed to fuck him. How the hell could I run? Where could I go?

I was in the middle of nowhere, stuck with my stalker, alone on an island only he knew how to leave. I couldn't even call for help.

My mind suddenly tried to convince me I was wrong about Tino, and it was all in my head. I was desperate to believe it, but I could no longer delude myself, not when I carefully opened the door just a crack and saw him in my bed, shirtless, inhaling my sheets like a sick creep and whispering with eyes rolled back, "My sweet Angel."

I pushed the door closed, careful not to make a sound, and opened my mouth wide with a silent scream. *I must find a way to get out of here.*

But how?

Think, Lina. Think.

The only thing I could come up with was buying myself some time until I figured something out. Until I could run away from this monster and his island.

Quickly, I turned on the water and looked for a razor. If I told him I just got my period, he wouldn't have sex with me. All I needed was some blood to make him believe—

The door creaked, and my heart fell to pieces with it. I froze in place as I saw his smirking face in the bathroom mirror.

His footsteps stopped right behind me, and he held my shuddering body from behind, the scruff of his beard pricking my face, the hardness of his bare cock on the nakedness of my back. "Hello, Angel. My sweet, sweet Angel."

CHAPTER 47

Lina

"**W**hat were you gonna do with this?" He yanked the razor out of my hand, his accent all gone. "You naughty, naughty girl."

My mouth went so dry I couldn't talk. Desperately, I shot a panicked glance around me, but I saw nothing that could serve as another weapon.

"Answer me, Angel."

"Please," I rasped, "please let me go."

"My answer to your insane request will always be the same. Never."

"It wasn't the Lanzas who attacked us at the wedding, right? You did it. You staged it to get me here away from Leo. You kidnapped me. You almost killed me."

"They weren't supposed to shoot you, only scare you so I could bring you here. With me where you belonged. The asshole who didn't know how to fucking aim is lying in pieces in a very dark grave."

My eyes squeezed with pain and fear. "What about my sister? Is she alive?"

"Of course she's alive. Why would I hurt Nicole? How many times do I have to tell you she's like a daughter to me?"

"Where is she?"

"Safe with Leo, like I said."

"Do they really know I'm alive?"

He exhaled a long breath. "Yes. For now. What I tell them later, though, is really up to you, Angel. If you behave, we'll all be one big happy family. If you don't…" He sighed.

My chest contracted at the horrid possibilities. "Please. Please, Tino, let me go. I don't want this."

He feigned shock. "No? Aren't I the same man you were drenching his pants as you rubbed yourself against his cock a minute ago?" His fingers twisted one of my nipples that, surprisingly, was hard. "What about this?" His fingers dropped between my legs and dove inside the gathered wetness. "And this?"

I cringed at the violation, my skin crawling.

"What did I say about lying to me?"

"I'm not lying. I wanted you before I…"

"Before you knew? What about when I was *him*?" His fingers sank deeper, finding my clit and rubbing it. "You didn't want me then? You didn't get wet for *me*? You didn't touch yourself thinking of *me*? You didn't come over and over and over picturing *my* cock fucking your sweet, little pussy? I'm the same man, Angel, the man you've always wanted, as Tino, as *him*."

I thought of all the times I'd masturbated, all the times I'd been naked in my room at the condo, at his mansion, when he must have been watching. All the nights he'd stripped me in my sleep and come all over my pussy. I moaned with the torturous feeling of his fingers inside me. They burned me with the pain of betrayal, yet my body was responding with the old naive, ignorant need. They mocked me with the pleasure they were stealing from me.

I squeezed his hand in an attempt to make him stop, but he only moved faster, teasing the engorged nub, hitting on the orgasm that had been building a few minutes ago.

"Stop! Maybe I wanted you then, but it was wrong. I should have never…" I shook, my voice thick with unshed tears. "You've been using me. I trusted you, and you betrayed me. I don't want you now!"

His hand wrapped around my throat, and he pushed me against the bathroom wall. "Don't say shit you'll regret later. You will always want me. Why, Angel?"

I just shook my head. I didn't know what he wanted me to say.

"Because you're mine. You will always be mine," he answered for me. "Do you understand me?"

I just nodded, too scared to even think about saying or doing anything other than what he wanted.

He released my throat. "Bellisimo. Now where were we? Ah." He circled my clit again, watching my stained-with-his-cum, naked body. "God, Angel. I can't get enough of watching your beautiful body. I want to see you come again for me, this time with my hand giving you the pleasure you need."

I resisted the only way I knew how. I let my back slide down the wall until I plopped on the floor, my knees drawn up to my chest where I hid my face, wrapping my arms around my legs. Then I let my long hair cover my shuddering body.

"Get up, Angel," he said in warning, a predatory edge to his tone.

I shook my head, tears escaping me.

"My sweet Angel, you have a choice to make. What we have can be delightful and sweet for you or it can be really painful. What's it gonna be?"

I trembled hard, sniveling with no tears. I believed him when he said he could make it really painful for me. I still wouldn't move.

"D'accordo. Have it your way." Suddenly, he reached for me and wrapped one arm around my waist and another under my knees. I whimpered and squirmed as he lifted me. "You're only gonna hurt yourself like this. I don't want your wound to reopen."

I struggled and fought as hard as I could, but his grip on me was ironclad. He placed me on the bed, but before he got on top of me, I rolled to the other side and scrambled for the door.

Flying down the stairs, I prayed, but no one listened. The front door was within reach when his grip yanked me away, tightened around me and squashed me so hard I couldn't breathe.

I kicked back, but my strength was nothing against his. He easily turned me around to face him. Was he gonna hit me? I braced myself for a smack on the face.

Instead, he took me into his arms, pulling me into one of his hugs that used to make me feel like I was in the safest place in the world, like nothing could ever hurt me as long as I was there. I buried my tears in his embrace, my naked body pressed against his, the smell of his cologne treacherous like everything else about him.

He wasn't hurting me, but he had me completely incapacitated. The only thing I could think of to defend myself was to bite him.

I did. I bit him in the chest. He growled and pulled my hair so hard I screamed and had to release him. Without letting go of my hair, he returned to incapacitate me with his other arm, his expression dark and angry, his blue eyes locked on me.

Suddenly, his face softened, a tender smile on his face, confusing me as he carried me back upstairs to his room. When he turned on the lights, panic froze the blood in my veins. At the four poles of his bed, there were cuffs.

"No. No!" I screamed, my limbs flailing. I was beat from our earlier struggle and the pain in my abdomen, and I was afraid if I put up more struggle, the wound would reopen, and I'd ruin my chances of trying to escape. But I didn't care now. This couldn't be happening.

He laid me on all fours, his weight on my back and his strength subduing my every move until he secured the cuffs on my wrists and ankles. I tugged at the chains hard and screamed when they wouldn't budge. "You can't do this to me!"

"Shhhh." He kissed my neck, and his hands caressed my body. "I didn't want to do this to you. You chose this, remember?"

My eyes squeezed shut. "Didn't you promise me when you took me I'd be seeing your face in broad daylight?" I said, biding my time.

"And I'll keep my promise, my sweet Angel. But first," his weight lifted off me before his heavy hand smacked my ass, "you have to be punished."

He spanked me until I wanted to pass out so I wouldn't feel the pain. He recited my mistakes one by one as his palms slapped and squeezed the tender flesh, starting with the time I'd thrown away his gifts and ending with when I said I didn't want him.

With every swat, the pain grew unbearable, but so was the throbbing in my pussy. He'd conditioned my mind and body to crave his cruelty, to respond as he wished, not as I did.

Dawn peeked from the windows, and I'd never been more terrified of the light. He uncuffed me, confident I no longer had the strength to fight or run. One of his hands was now on my butt cheek, soothing the soreness. His other hand explored my body.

When he reached my boobs, my nipples were hard. He felt me up before he squeezed. His touch, strangely, felt as good as earlier. He was the only man who ever touched me. The only man I really wanted to touch. I didn't know anything else.

He put me onto my back, and I sucked in a sharp hiss as my ass touched the sheets. "It's okay. I'll make it go away," he said.

"How?" I whimpered.

His body was on top of me, but he braced on his elbows, shifting his weight off me. So he wouldn't squish me? My great savior.

He left a trail of hot kisses from my chest to my stomach along the stained line where he'd marked me. Then his lips found my nipple and suckled. I trembled, pressure gathering between my legs. He did the same with my other nipple, and the pressure intensified.

He sniffed the smell of the wetness gathering in my pussy like a dog. I cried as his hand traveled between my thighs and felt the evidence of my arousal.

"Atta girl," he murmured, stroking me. Then his mouth reached where no one had ever touched.

I tried to resist, but he effortlessly spread my legs and lapped his tongue along my slit. "So fucking sweet."

The way his mouth moved against my clit seared me with pleasurable pain and inexplicable need. The throbbing between my legs and in my heart along with fear were taking my breath away.

I was surprised to find out I still had some resistance in me as I tried to keep him away, writhing and kicking. His response was a laugh, and his breath tortured my sensitive flesh. He easily stopped me from moving, bringing me back into submission so he could devour me. I squirmed against his tongue, making things worse, myself tangled in need even more.

My body tightened against my will. A wave of pleasure rippled in me so intense my toes curled. A climax like nothing I'd given myself before.

My first real orgasm a man had given me. And it was at the mouth of my stalker. My kidnapper.

I wanted it to finish so I could cry, but Tino was nowhere near done. He crawled up my body and kissed me with the same sensual violence I was used to from him now. His kiss grew hungrier, more animalistic. Not dancing the usual dance around mine, his tongue penetrated my mouth. His hand was rubbing my pussy again. My body tensed with fear and desire as his erection pushed between my thighs.

"Please," I whispered, crying, hoping he'd see my devastation and stop. "Please, Tino. You know I've never been with anyone. I don't want it like this. Please don't rape me, Tino."

His nostrils flared. "Rape you? How many times do I have to tell you I'm not like your father? I'm never gonna rape you. You're my sweet Angel. I can never do this to you." Then his eyes gleamed. "I'm gonna make love to your beautiful body in broad daylight as promised. Your body that is mine."

"But I didn't give it to you."

"Angel, you don't need to give me anything. You can't give what's not yours. You're already mine. You've always been mine."

"You're crazy," I whimpered.

"For you, my sweet Angel." He devoured my mouth, upping the speed of his rubbing. "I can't wait to be inside you. I promise I'm gonna make it feel so good." He ushered his erection toward my center.

I gasped as I stared down. Then I gulped when I saw the size of him, my fear doubling. This was gonna hurt. So fucking much.

He pushed inside me, inside the slick wetness that was only increasing, but my body resisted the foreign violation. He didn't heed my continuous pleas and pushed the tip in. It hurt. Seared. I screamed, pushing at him as hard as I could.

His eyes darkened as he groaned. "Cazzo, you're so tight, so fucking good. Relax, Angel. You're going to enjoy it if you just relax."

"It hurts, Tino. You're hurting me."

"Just at first. I promise." He pressed into me, and my flesh slowly parted, painfully stretching for him.

I writhed underneath him, my nails scratching at any part of his skin I could reach, but he wouldn't stop, slowly entering me, forcing me to take his length. He groaned something in Italian as he winced. Was he struggling? No. I knew he loved it so much, this violation that was tearing me apart.

He sucked my lips one by one, and then he pushed with one firm thrust. I cried out again, the stretch excruciating. I couldn't see, but I knew he'd just taken my virginity.

I couldn't believe this was happening to me. After all Nicky and I had been through, I lost my virginity like that. I was being raped like that.

He kept stretching me, asking me to relax, until I was painfully taking every inch of him. I fought the sobs, but the pain was unbearable. I wished I could have passed out until he was done. But I felt everything.

It was the most violating thing I'd ever experienced. And I was molested by my father and had been stalked by this psycho monster for six years.

"Easy, my sweet Angel," he murmured softly as if he was making love to me, not forcing himself inside of me, "I want you to enjoy this as much as I do."

How could I believe him when he was ripping me open? When he'd been lying to me all my life? He was raping me, and I couldn't do anything about it. Even if I could fight him off and escape this room, this house, where would I go? All I could do was take whatever this psycho wanted to do to me and my body.

Tears rolled down from my eyes. His lips kissed my tears, messing with me, lying to me. My untrustworthy body started to obey him, to relax in response to his kisses, to the soft lies of his sick touch. *No. Please don't.*

The hungry wolf began to move, pulling away from my body and then pushing himself back in. Making sure I wouldn't resist anymore, keeping my body at his command, he reached and rubbed my clit.

My eyes widened in terror when I felt it again. The unbelievable pleasure that gathered hot low in my belly that turned pain into something I should have never felt with this monster. I squirmed hard, mad at myself, trying to stop the treacherous response. I couldn't let him believe I wanted him.

I couldn't let *me* realize I still fucking wanted him, wanted his pain and abuse. His darkness that festered in my soul until it became one with it.

His thrusts grew harder, deeper, and I cried out, begging him to stop. The intensity of the pain and the pleasure mixed until the lines between them blurred, until the world was shut out, and there was only me and Tino and this sick, twisted, dark connection and pleasure our bodies craved.

I exploded, the orgasm ripping through my body with unmatched force. He groaned my name against my ear as he stretched me even wider. His cock throbbed inside of me, and a warm gush filled me as he, too, came.

Inside me. Bare.

A new horror took over me. I'd just had nonconsensual, unprotected sex with my stalker. The brutal Mafia boss who was supposed to be my father-in-law. The killer of my father. My captor.

Tino Bellomo had stolen my virginity, claimed my body and filled me with his thick cum, marking me up for life.

He collected me in his arms, kissing my forehead, holding me close. I cried in his embrace, seeking consolation and refuge from the very person who had just ripped me to shreds.

CHAPTER 48

Lina

I didn't know how I could sleep after what happened, but I did. My whole body was sore, and I had one nightmare after another, but I forced myself to stay in slumber. He might have been masturbating to me in my sleep, but he wouldn't fuck me then.

When I did wake up, thunder was still booming. It was as though the weather had changed overnight into this awfulness just like my life. I couldn't tell if it was morning or night. The windows were closed, and the lights were on. I was naked in his bed, my arms more strained than the rest of my body. One rattling tug was enough to tell me I was in cuffs again.

"Buonasera, my sweet Angel. Slept well?"

My head whipped toward his voice. He was sitting naked in a chair in the far corner of the room, an easel in front of him, and a brush in his hand. "What the fuck is this?"

"If you want me to spank you, you can just ask. You don't have to be a bad girl and make me angry like this."

"Where's the fucking fun in that?"

He chuckled, painting. "A year ago you barely cursed. What happened to you?"

"You. You happened to me."

"You know what? You're eighteen now. Swear all you want. It's kinda cute when it comes from you."

"Fuck you."

He cocked a brow at me. "Gladly, Angel. Let me finish this painting first."

I fought back the tears threatening to burst. Was this how I was gonna live from now on? A fucktoy for this psycho, used for his pleasure whenever he wanted?

"You look so sexy cuffed to my bed I had to paint it," he added.

I blinked. "What?"

He shifted the easel a little so I could see what he was working on. My naked body was sprawled naked in the painting, cuffed in submission. The details sick yet incredibly vivid. So alive. So real, even my wound was there.

I hated how much I loved it.

How much it turned me on.

The helplessness. The forced submission. The feeling of being used. The feeling of losing all control to a vicious monster like Tino.

I tore my eyes away, and he laughed. "So hot, vero?"

Anger rumbled in me. "What are you gonna do with that? Fuck your fist and come all over the canvas?"

His tongue darted and licked his lip as his predatory eyes devoured my nakedness. "I prefer to come all over a different canvas."

I cringed as I remembered all the times I'd woken up with his cum in my panties, thinking it was mine. Abruptly, my pussy throbbed, like a man fucking himself to watching your naked body in your sleep when you didn't know and then shooting his load all over your pussy and keeping it there was hot as fuck.

Another clenching throb.

Fuck.

He dropped the brush and prowled toward me, stroking his erection. I yanked at the chains before, in one move, he was on top of me.

Totally incapacitating me, he feasted on my skin with his lips, tongue, teeth, hands. My breath came out hard, and my body burned with the exasperating old need for him. "Stop. Stop touching me. Stop kissing me. Stop!"

"God, Angel. Why do you keep doing this? Do I have to dip my fingers in your pussy every time to show you how wet you are for me? You need me. I'm giving you what you've always needed. I'll always give you anything you need or want." He settled between my legs and kissed my mouth. "But seriously, this behavior needs to stop. It's exhausting. Before, you were a kid. You didn't know better. You had no clue what was best for you so I had to make those decisions for you. You're a grownup now. What's your excuse?"

I couldn't begin to fathom his logic. "What? What are you talking about? What decisions have you made for me?"

"Everything. Starting with that fucker Baldi. One of you had to off that bastard, but you were little girls. It was a hard choice for you to make, so I made it for you. Then there was the violin. Another choice I had to make when you were about to ruin your future picking the piano. And…" he parted my legs, his expression darkening, "there's the worst decision you've ever made, Leo. Look what I had to do to fix that. You couldn't make the right choice even if your life depended on it."

He held my thighs and started to push inside me. I cried out, my knees jerking. "Wait!"

"What now?" he grumbled, losing his patience.

"Look." I nodded at the stained sheets and the dried blood between my thighs. "I need a shower to clean all the blood first. Maybe change the sheets, too?"

I was only delaying the inevitable, but who knew? Maybe something would happen with time. Maybe he'd get distracted with something else. Maybe he'd get a heart attack all of a sudden and die.

He grunted, and then shifted on his elbows and uncuffed me. With a smile, his thumb caressed my cheek before he picked me up and headed for the bathroom.

He gave me a bath himself, thoroughly cleaning me up yet gently as if he was bathing a baby. My eyes traveled along his body—his gorgeous, muscular, tattooed body—and I couldn't help but stare. The angels on his body made more sense now. Despite everything, it made me feel…special.

Being the object of someone's obsession, someone as powerful and rich as a Mafia boss like Tino, was intense and dangerous and utterly frightening but…somehow beautiful. Like he was.

However, I couldn't see him as the man that lit up my life with care and protection. He wasn't the man that had me falling hard and fast. The man I'd long fantasized about, making love to in my dreams.

Yet there was a truth about my time with Tino Bellomo I couldn't deny. I'd never felt more cherished than when I was with him.

As if he couldn't help himself, he stopped moving the loofa over my thighs and leaned in, running his nose up my jaw. His scent surrounded me, and my pussy betrayed me for the millionth time. I was conditioned to crave him. It'd take a lot of time, a lot of healing, to reverse what he'd done to me.

If ever.

"You can touch me, Angel," he whispered. I know how much you want it. I want you to touch me, too."

"I don't want to touch you. I don't want you to touch me," I lied.

He dropped everything in his hand and grabbed my hair, whirling it around his fist and pushed me, my face against the bathroom wall. Without a word, he parted my legs and bent me over. Then he thrust his cock inside me without warning.

I screamed so hard, but it seemed to fuel him. He slammed into me harder, stretching me, his hands rough on my scalp and hips. With a loud, tight groan, he tugged at my hair, and his fingers dug into my flesh as his warm, thick seed exploded inside me.

"You're an animal," I sobbed.

His rapid breaths fell on my neck. "So lucky for you, Angel."

"Lucky?" I sobbed again.

"You don't know much, but you gotta know by now you like it rough, naughty girl. That's why you keep provoking me. You're a sucker for punishment, for pain. You're lucky you married *an animal* that can accommodate your needs."

My heart skipped a beat. "Married?"

He kissed my neck, still inside me. "Certo. I don't need a piece of paper or a wedding to make you my wife. Fuck, I wanted to propose to you since you were sixteen. I wish I had. It'd have saved us a lot of time and trouble.

But it's okay. We're here now. A man and his woman. That's all that matters."

"What you're saying is insane! Do you even love me, Tino?"

"Love?" He laughed hard. "Oh, Angel."

His scorn wounded me. "Yes, love, Tino. Love that makes people care for each other, not hurt each other."

"Didn't your father love you? And what did he do to you? Love, too, hurts, Angel. *You* hurt me, Angel."

"Leo loved me. He didn't hurt me."

"He was going to," he gritted. "You don't know the first thing about him or what he's capable of. One day you'll know that I saved you from him just like I always have."

"He can't be worse than you. Fuck, even my sicko father wasn't worse than you. At least, they loved me."

"Fuck their pathetic love. I once thought I loved you. I even confessed it in a whisper the moment I was giving you to him. But I know now I don't." Both his arms were now wrapping around me tightly, like a snake squeezing a prey. "What I feel for you is beyond any definition," he said, softer. "No, I don't love you, Angel. It's simply not a word that could describe what I feel for you because it's bigger than anything you or them had ever felt." He squeezed even tighter, and I could hardly breathe. "Call it love, possession, obsession, sickness, plain psycho shit, call it whatever you want. All you need to know is that it's true and real and stronger than anything you'll ever know."

He let out a long sigh before he pressed a deep kiss on my head. We were both trembling now, locked around each other, inside each other, not just our bodies but our souls, too.

CHAPTER 49

Tino

The light that had dimmed in her eyes glimmered again when she reconnected with her violin. I'd brought it back with me but decided not to give it to her until she behaved.

She was reluctant to touch it even though she wanted it so badly, just like she did with me. She didn't want to acknowledge the truth or validate my endless giving for her.

As always, I had to force her to do the right thing. I ordered her to play for me once and twice until she no longer resisted and our private recitals had become part of our routine.

I loved every note, every second of her performance as my eyes worshipped her naked body and my ears savored her beautiful music. She played just for me as I'd always dreamed, and it was everything I'd imagined and more. It was worth every agony in the wait.

When I wasn't making love to her or I was managing business in my office, she played for herself, willingly. That was when I decided to give her another reward.

I blindfolded her, and she thought I was going for kinky sex and started shaking. "Having sex while being blindfolded can be really fun and hot. We can try it later, but this isn't my intention now," I whispered in her ear.

"What do you want then?"

"I have a surprise for you. You're gonna love it."

She walked with me silently, and I led her into her old room—she slept in my room now—that I'd rearranged with the surprise I had for her.

I took off the blindfold. "Allora, what do you think?"

Angel squinted in the middle of the room at the shelves that replaced the bed and wardrobe. The desk in the right corner and the piano in the far left.

Her head tilted at me, her jaw hanging low. "What is this?"

"Your library and music room." I beckoned at the shelves. "I brought all these CDs and books for you when I came back. It's a vast collection, but they have all your favorites in classical music, practice pieces as well. Also, all your favorite romance reads among hundreds of other books are in there."

She gasped in surprise, a hint of a smile on the corner of her gaping mouth.

"Do you like it?" I asked, hoping she did.

"Like it? Tino, I'm having a Belle moment here."

"A Belle moment?"

"You know when Beast shows Belle the huge library in his castle? Books to her are like music to me, the one thing she loves the most, and he gives her that. It's her way of escaping. She's like, finally, a good thing in my eternal imprisonment."

"So I'm Beast in this moment? The cruel monster that is keeping you as his prisoner?"

Her jaw twisted. "Except you're no beast."

I chuckled. "Come here, Angel."

Slowly, she walked toward me, but she wasn't hesitant. For the first time since our first night as a couple, she wasn't reluctant to nestle in my embrace

I held her tight but gently, and then I bent my head to hers and took her lips between mine. Her lips moved with me, a small, shaky move, but I loved it. My desire for her flared so I grabbed her waist and put her on the desk.

"Tino, please."

"Right. This desk is for studying. I got all your schoolbooks for you here, too. I don't want you to fall behind. Anything you can't understand or need help with, I'm right here."

"School? Really? And you'll *tutor* me?"

"Certamente. You need your education." I turned toward the piano. "That old thing, though, we can use for other purposes."

She flustered as I carried her and placed her on the piano surface. "I-I thought you didn't want me to play the piano. How did you get one on the island anyway?"

"That old thing has been here for years, unused. I dusted it out and put it here so we can play together."

"You play the piano?"

"Used to. Just like with painting, I'd stopped when my wife died."

"And resumed when I came into your life?"

"Yes. You, my sweet Angel, have revived my passion for so many things I'd forsaken. You brought me back to life."

A small smile played with her lips. I started to unbutton my shirt, and the smile vanished. "Can we please not…"

"Why, Angel?"

She blushed. "I started my period this morning."

"Oh." Disappointment ran through me.

"I borrowed a tampon from Arancia. You can ask her if you think I'm lying."

"I don't need to ask her. I can see for myself. But I know you're not lying, and that's not why I'm disappointed."

"No?"

"You think some blood would stop me? I'll make love to your beautiful pussy even if it's shooting fire. I'm disappointed you got your period in the first place." I felt her belly and sighed. "I was hoping…have been praying—"

"Don't say it, Tino, please. Please!"

"Why, Angel?"

"Because it's disturbing and scary and sick. Your son was my fiancé. He was gonna be my husband. He still thinks he will be. You want to make me the mother of his sibling?"

"I want to give you everything and have everything with you."

"But I'm scared to death all the fucking time. *You* scare me to death, Tino. I'm only eighteen and my life is over. You kidnapped me from my husband. You raped me. You are imprisoning me here indefinitely. How can I want a baby with you?"

"He was never your husband, and I never raped you. I claimed what's mine!" I banged the piano surface, and she flinched.

I closed my eyes for a moment and sighed. Then I rubbed her arms gently. "Listen, when it comes to me, you have nothing to fear, Angel. Ever," I vowed. "I'm obsessive to a fault and possessive as fuck, but I'll always protect and care for you. Every single thought, every goddamned action of mine revolves around you, Angel. You don't understand how deep you've carved yourself inside me. I'm ready to give up anything and everything for you."

I filled my nose with her smell as I hugged her. Then I undressed her to her panties. I used my shirt to put under her and my pants on the floor for the mess we were about to make.

The sweet taste of her lips burned me as I devoured her. "You can't be scared of starting our family, Angel. Nobody else will ever have you because you're mine." I rubbed her pussy over the fabric of her panties. "Say it for me, Angel. Tell me who you belong to."

She only whispered a moan.

I pinched her nipple and loved how it hardened under my touch. "Say it."

Her moaning gasps were the only answer she was willing to give. I suckled her nipples before I pinched one again, my fingers rubbing her pussy faster. "Say. It. Who do you belong to, Angel?"

Her eyes squeezed, and a tear fled them. "You."

"You're gonna wear my ring and take my last name. Why, Angel?"

The heat from her pussy made my balls swell. The loud moan coming from her parted lips sent a pulse in my cock.

I slapped her ass when she didn't answer. "Why, Angel?"

"Because I'm yours."

"Fucking right you are. And I'm gonna come inside your pretty little pussy over and over until you're pregnant with my baby." I growled, the image of her pregnant hot as fuck. "Why, Angel?"

Her all moaning no answering act forced another slap on her ass from me.

"Because I'm yours, Tino."

"Atta girl," I praised and gave her a little choke while I upped the pace of my rubbing and suckled her engorged nipples.

She shuddered as an orgasm rippled through her. I loved to watch her come. I wished I'd been able to paint and capture it forever. But it'd take me a lifetime to capture every fraction, every contort of her face, every squeeze of her eyes, every twist of her lips... I'd film her, but I couldn't risk it being discovered or falling into any hands. That beautiful, sacred reaction was mine alone to watch.

When she was done, I freed my erection and took off her panties. Then I dragged the bloody tampon out of her pussy and smelled it. The scent of her orgasm, her pussy and her blood. "Mamma mia."

She watched me in awe. A good awe. She seemed surprised by my reaction yet relieved. She liked that I loved it. She liked that nothing could stop me from loving her body.

I immersed my finger in her pussy gently and kept my eyes on hers as I sucked her taste off my finger. She bit her lip, her pupils dilating and darkening with arousal. I took her hand and guided it to my throbbing cock. She trembled as she fisted it. It was the first time she touched it. I covered her fist with mine and stroked, showing her what to do.

Her little hand around my length made me feel even bigger, and the shade of pink in her cheeks as she rubbed my cock almost made me nut on the spot.

I cupped her ass and pulled her closer. Then I hooked her legs around my hips and stopped her hand so I wouldn't come in her fist. "Put my cock inside you, Angel."

She drew me in and pressed the tip to her opening. Fuck, that thick wetness set something wild in me. I thrust inside her deep, savoring her scream. Then I drew back, watching my shaft covered in her blood. She watched, too, and her eyes darkened some more. Why that turned us both on so much didn't matter. What mattered was that I was making love to her, and she was enjoying it the way she should be enjoying it.

I fucked her hard and fast. Her hands held on to my shoulders, and her tits bounced as I rocked into her. She moaned with my groans, her body choking the hell out of my cock.

She clenched around me with the force of her coming orgasm, and it set me over the edge. I came with a feral growl. She followed instantly. My cock throbbed out the rest of my release. As soon as I'd given her all I had,

I slid out and watched as my white seed ran back out of her glistening red pussy. It dripped on my pants on the floor, pooling between her thighs.

"You're so fucking hot, Angel. So fucking hot." I bent and kissed her belly. "Once your period is over, I'm gonna fuck you day and night until I put a baby in you. This is happening, my sweet Angel."

CHAPTER 50

Lina

The next day I woke up to an empty bed. Well, not exactly.

Normally, I'd wake up with Tino's arm wrapped around my waist or his hand cupping my breast or his cock snuggled between my legs. Sometimes we even slept with him inside me.

His possessive nature was over the top, and while it was sucking any sort of freedom and the illusion of ever having any out of me, it was easy to get used to, and sometimes delectable, even charming and attractive. In his possessive, obsessive embrace I was safe from everything.

Everything but him.

Today I woke up with one wrist cuffed—he no longer did that because why would he when he never left my side?—and no sign of Tino in the room.

I didn't like it.

Tino was the only person in the whole world I should be afraid of. The only man I needed protection from. He'd hurt me in ways no one else did. But I woke up alone in his bed and the first thought that came to my mind was that I couldn't bear the emptiness on his bedside. I needed him back here.

Where the hell was he? Did he leave again without telling me? Did he leave my side to sleep with Arancia? Was he with her now?

I yelled their names, tugging at the handcuffs, until footsteps scurried outside. Then a red head popped in from the door. She stared at my half naked body—I was only in my panties, and only because I was on my period—and cleared her throat. "Yes, Angelina?"

I didn't give a shit about her seeing me cuffed and naked like that. I'd been humiliated much more aggressively. "Where's Tino? Is he in your room?"

"No," she answered so casually as if it was okay for anyone to ask this question, and the answer would be a simple yes or no without any need for further explanation or any sort of guilt or shame.

I gave the chain another tug. "Then where is he?"

"Fishing. He'll be back in an hour or two." She pointed at his pillow. "He left you a note."

When I looked to the side, I saw the folded piece of paper. Then I saw a small jewelry box and a dress lying next to me. A white wedding dress.

I stared at them for long minutes without even opening the note. I was scared of what might have been written inside.

"Do you need to use the bathroom?" She waved at my wrist. "I have the key."

I just nodded.

She used her key and walked me to the bathroom. She wanted to go inside with me.

"Don't be ridiculous and wait outside. I'm not gonna run away. There's nowhere to go." This was a fucking island. Tino didn't have a boat here for me to steal, and I wasn't Noah or Tom Hanks. Even if I knew how to build a raft or a boat or whatever, how was I supposed to keep it from Tino and his guards? Would I just jump in the sea and swim for a hundred miles, hoping a ship would find me or I'd find the next island or town? The bodyguards were everywhere. They'd have caught me before I'd made it to the deep waters. Even if I did make it, the chances were sharks would find me way faster than a boat would.

There was no way out of here except by plane, which Tino flew himself, and I knew nothing about how to fly it. My chances to escape were limited to two miracles. I either stole a gun and threatened one of the bodyguards at gunpoint to fly me away—assuming they wouldn't incapacitate me in a couple of seconds because they were trained for this shit—or I found Tino's satellite phone and called for help.

However, my mind was occupied by another matter. The note on the bed, what was inside the box and the fucking white dress.

As I got out of the bathroom, the nuptial collection on the bed taunted me. I snatched the note and unfolded it.

Buongiorno, my sweet Angel.

Don't worry. I know you don't like it when I go. I'm still here, on the other side of the island, fishing. I left you a couple of things that would forever bind us, not that we need them. We're already bound as long as we both shall live.

When I return, I want to see you in them. You will wear my ring and take my name. Why, Angel?

"Because I'm yours," I murmured as if in a trance.

The next line replied as if he knew beyond doubt that would be my response.

Smiley face. *Atta girl.*

"Are you going to open it?" Arancia asked, a huge grin on her face, her toes curled as her eyes pinned to the ring box.

I squinted at her. "Why would you be excited about this?"

"Who wouldn't? I love weddings. Besides, we don't get much excitement here. When Tino told me there was going to be a wedding today I was so thrilled. I couldn't wait for you to wake up so I'd see the ring and the dress. I'll help with the hair and makeup. You're going to look favolosa."

"Aren't you sleeping with him?"

"What? Ewww. No kinkshaming, but I'm not into that."

"You don't have to lie to me about—"

"Oddio, Angelina. I can never sleep with Don Bellomo. He's my half-brother."

"What?! Why didn't he say so from the start?"

She rolled her eyes. "He can't introduce me as his sister. I'm one of Daddy Bellomo's bastards. It's a no-no della Famiglia."

"So he locks you up here instead?"

"No one is locked up here, Angel. I only come to the island when he tells me to. Like to clean up and check on the house or to help around when he or Leo came here on vacation, even when his wife was still alive. Other than that I live in Cavallino with my husband and my boy."

I laughed under my breath. "Wow."

"Can you open it now, per favore?" Her grin came back.

I laughed again at her excitement, at how gleeful I'd felt that Tino wasn't sleeping with her. "Can I get a robe or something first?"

"Oh, certo." She took off hers and gave it to me.

"Thanks." I shrugged into it and tied the belt before I sat on the bed and held the box.

My head was in a haze. My emotions were confused as ever. Tino was giving me his ring, ordering me to wear a white dress for him and take his last name.

As if he didn't need to ask first. As if I had no right to say anything but yes. Just like everything, he just took without permission.

I didn't know why that upset me. I didn't expect anything else from a man like him. And after what happened between us last night, I shouldn't be surprised. I touched him. I *let* him fuck me, and I enjoyed it as much as he did.

To him, that was already a big fat yes. Not that my yes would ever matter to him.

Leo's words echoed in my head all of a sudden. *Don Bellomo doesn't take no for an answer. He always gets what he wants. If he thinks something is his, nothing else matters. Nothing stops him from having it. Not even his own family.*

I opened the box, and Arancia gasped before me.

The ring was extraordinary and fabulous. A huge pink tourmaline stone—my birthstone just like the ones in earrings he'd gotten me for one of my birthdays—centered the ring, flanked by two dazzling diamonds.

My mind went blank. My eyes saw nothing but the mesmerizing beauty of the ring. I put it on, the size impeccable, the weight on my finger perfect. I thought it'd be heavy, but I assumed, like my violin, it was custom made to fit just me.

"Tino," I sighed.

"He's amazing, isn't he?"

I looked at her, not knowing what to say. Would an amazing man who cared so much about a girl kidnap her, almost killing her in the way? Would he rape her?

I rubbed my eyes, shaking my head. None of that made any difference now. It'd already happened, had been happening for weeks, but I'd given in to him. I gave him myself willingly last night.

And just like everything else I fought and refused to submit to but eventually gave him, I'd become his wife, and I'd carry his children. If I said no today, he'd drag me kicking and screaming until he made me realize it was what I wanted all along, too. So why fight?

Sick and wrong or not, Tino Bellomo was the only man I'd ever desired.

I half-smiled. "Is he really fishing?"

She chuckled and shook her head. "He's preparing the spot he chose for the wedding."

"That makes more sense."

I got the dress out of the clear bag and touched the fabric, so smooth and elegant and simple. Another designer dress, of course, that cost a year's salary. A beaded organza beach wedding dress with long chiffon sleeves that resembled...wings.

"It's so beautiful," she said in tears. "You'll look like an—"

"Angel. I'll look like an angel. *His* Angel."

Arancia got all her makeup products, hair straighteners and curling irons to the room and made me look even prettier than I was at my former wedding.

She got dressed in a green gown that looked incredible on her body, her red hair and tan giving the color an extra something. My thoughts went with Nicky. I wanted her here, even on that twisted, fucked up wedding. She never agreed to the first, and she'd have never agreed to this one, but I wished she could have been here. God, how much I missed her.

A man's voice came from downstairs, not Tino's, and he was speaking in fast Italian. Arancia went outside the room and said something in return.

"What's going on? Who's that?" I asked.

"One of the guards." She flashed her teeth at me. "It's time."

CHAPTER 51

Lina

The guests were the bodyguards. My bride's maid and the person ordained to marry us was Tino's illegitimate half-sister. My groom, the man standing by the beach looking at me as if hypnotized, as if in bliss, was the father of the man I was supposed to marry, the man who kidnapped me from his own son because he was so obsessed with me he could never let me go.

I walked down the aisle all by myself to marry the killer of my father, my captor, my stalker.

Something flicked inside me the second I reached Tino and our eyes locked. As if I'd just realized what was happening here for the first time, and that realization made me want to scream.

I'd been here at Tino's mercy and entirely isolated from the rest of the world until further notice. How much more time would I spend in captivity? A glorified sex slave?

My chest contracted like I was suffocating, like all the air at the beach wasn't enough for me to breathe.

"Angel?" Arancia's voice somehow penetrated the ringing in my ears. "Angel, stai bene?"

I finally managed to draw in some much-needed air, and I glanced at her. She was staring at me with a puzzled grimace, and Tino no longer had his awestruck gaze. His expression was dangerous, his dark blue eyes almost black like a fucking demon.

"Leave us," he said sharply.

Arancia blinked, taken aback by his tone. I'd never heard him speak like that before. Not to her, at least. I should be afraid, but at this moment, I didn't care about whatever punishment he'd have for me. Rage had built up in every muscle in my body, a volcano underneath my soul about to erupt.

Arancia and the bodyguards scampered away instantly, and I spiraled out of control.

My feet flew with the wind, my screaming and cursing echoing across the island. I didn't know where I was going, and I was certain he'd catch me and hurt me, but I couldn't bring myself to stop. All the anger, terror, humiliation, frustration and agony I'd felt since I set foot here boiled to the surface, erupting in fierce rage.

I didn't know how long I'd been running before ironclad arms bound me immobile from the back, capturing me in an embrace from which I'd never be free. I kicked and screamed until I could no longer stand, and my voice became aching rasps. I crumbled against him on the sand in defeat, tears running down my face.

"Why, Angel?" he whispered in my ear, the sinister, intoxicating darkness in his tone that imprisoned me and brought me down to my knees far more strong than his body. "You ruined our wedding."

And now it was time for my punishment. My skin tingled. My whole body responded to the pain that was to come with eagerness and anticipation. That heart wrenching fear and the violent delights that followed.

"I never wanted it," I whimpered.

"Then you don't fucking deserve it!" His hand fell heavily on the back of the dress and ripped at it. I cried out with every tear until the dress turned into scattered shreds flying with the wind, and I was a pile of sobs in only my underwear on the sand.

He fisted my hair and twisted my body so I'd face him. Then he pushed me against the sand and ripped off my bra and panties. He took off his suit and boxers and tossed them away, towering over me stark naked. His eyes looked at me like he wanted to devour me. The wolf that would tear out my soul and swallow it whole.

Helplessly, my gaze was drawn to the perfection his face and body and cock were, and I hated myself for craving him so much. It burned me up and ate my soul that I loved, fucking needed, the vicious cruelty of this predator. The pitch black darkness I'd learned to love.

I was in love with Tino Bellomo. I'd always been in love with him.

His grip tightened around my wrists as he lifted my arm above my head and yanked out the tampon. Then he thrust his erection into me, fucking me harder than ever, angrier, rougher. I bled around him, my gushes of arousal thicker than the blood. He pinched my nipples and bit them roughly, fucking me deeper with every scream of mine.

"Why, Angel?" he whispered as his erection swelled inside me.

I couldn't say it, unwilling to utter the irreversible. He'd taken everything from me by force. I wasn't going to give him the one thing he couldn't take. I wouldn't open up to the wolf. I couldn't let him know the real reason behind my fury was that I was fucking in love with him.

When I didn't reply, his expression darkened further. "Why?"

"I hate you. I hate you!"

His eyes became pits of blue fire as he pounded me. "You hate me?"

"Yes," I hissed, "I hate you!" I couldn't let him know the unthinkable truth.

Suddenly, he slid out of me and flipped me on my stomach. Then he walked to his belt and bent to grab it. He folded in in front of me, making me know what was to come. "I don't give a shit if you hate me. You're fucking mine whether you like it or not."

The lashes and whips of the belt descended heavily on my ass, each strike fire searing at my skin. His body crippled me from behind as I cried out in pain, but my body relaxed when his hardness poked my butt cheek, needing the sex that would follow.

When he was done, he tossed the belt away and slid inside me from behind with one thrust. He pulled my hair, yanking my head back so he'd consume me with a hungry kiss. I reveled in his taste. My backside was on fire, but it didn't lessen my need and desire for him one bit. It deepened it tenfold.

He was swollen inside me again, and I shuddered with delight that bordered on anguish. I bucked into him, taking him deeper, needing him to fuck me, to claim me in the most primitive way possible.

With a howl, he pulled out of me and flipped me. Then he came all over me, marking my body with his bloodstained cum.

He got off me, and just like that, without giving me the usual orgasm or bothering to pick me up to take me back to the house or even covering me up, he started down the beach, walking away from me without a word.

I used his clothes to cover up before I went back to the house, but he was gone with the roar of the plane.

CHAPTER 52

Lina

A week, the longest week of my life, had passed and Tino hadn't returned yet.

Arancia gave me a pitiful glance, hearing the question on my mouth before I asked it. "He'll be back, Angel. You know he will."

"I only want him back so he can take me home." My jaw twisted. "He obviously no longer wants me."

She snorted. "Yeah, sure."

"What? You don't believe me?"

"It doesn't matter what I believe, Angel."

"Stop calling me that." She'd been calling me Angel since I'd known who Tino really was. While I didn't mind before—because what was the point?—it agitated me now. "My name is Lina."

"Your name is Angel. That's what Don Bellomo calls you, and it stays that way. You know what? I think you like it much more than Lina."

"Fuck you, Arancia."

She strutted away in a white bikini. "You're not my type, *Angel*."

I growled. Fuck this whole fucking family.

I marched into the music room and picked up my violin. Shostakovich No. 10, Movement 2. I hit the chords with the anger roiling in me that suited this piece perfectly. Then, subconsciously, I switched to that Korean song in the Goblin OST show by Soyou.

I Miss You.

My eyes snapped shut as I swore, almost throwing the bow against the wall in frustration. How could I fucking miss him after all he'd done? How could his absence slice at me, ripping my soul to pieces like that?

How could I love him that much?

I restarted the angry piece, and again I switched to *I Miss You*, tears falling in abundance, desperation taking over me.

A distant roar flicked through me like a match lit in the dark. I ran to the window and saw it in the sky. Tino's plane.

He was back. He didn't abandon me. He came back for me.

I ran outside, my violin and bow still in my hand. I sprang to one of the beach chairs and pretended I'd been playing there all along. I wanted him to see me the first thing so he wouldn't just go inside the house and ignore me.

But when he landed, he still did exactly that, went inside and ignored me.

I dragged my pathetic sorry ass inside and headed upstairs for *our* room. Apparently, my dignity was taking a vacation.

He was taking off his shoes when I entered. I went to sit next to him on the bed, but he rose and went straight to the bathroom. Then I heard the water running.

Without thinking, I left the violin on the bed and entered the bathroom. Steam had gathered in the shower as water cascaded on him, on his beautiful curls and beard, on his tattoos and muscles, on his cock that jerked a little when he saw me.

He rolled his eyes and gave me his back. His marvelous ass.

I'd been denying myself the pleasure of enjoying his sexy body. Not anymore. If I had no choice but to be his, he was mine, too.

I stripped and walked into the shower with him, holding him from behind. "Did you miss me?"

He gazed at me over his shoulder, and I stared at his lips, the need to remind myself of his taste dominant. "When I miss you, you'll know," he said.

My hand slid down his hip and onto his pelvis until I filled my fist with his cock. "You mean when you shove this big cock inside my pussy and use me for your pleasure whenever you want?"

A muscle ticked in his jaw, and he blinked once. "Yeah."

I stroked him. "What about when I miss you?"

He blinked again, his chest rising with a deep breath. "I thought you hated me."

"I thought you could tell when I was lying."

He twisted and slammed me against the wall, his grip on my neck. "What the fuck do you want?"

"You know what I want. You've always known what I wanted before I did," I rasped.

"You want me to punish you."

"I want *you*, Don Bellomo."

His swat didn't hit my ass this time. It landed on my pussy. I bit a moan, the sting arousing as fuck. He did it again while choking me. I could come just like that. But I was greedy. I wanted more. Much more.

"I'm not on my period anymore."

"Cazzo." He let out a primitive sound, squeezing me harder, two fingers plunging inside me. "How many times have you touched yourself while I was gone?" he asked.

"Every day," I confessed. I'd gotten used to getting it daily from him, and then he cut me off cold turkey. It was unfair. "You?" I moaned with the pleasure his fingers dragged from me.

A hint of a smirk touched his mouth. "I never cheated on you, Angel." He understood my intentions perfectly. I was driving myself crazy thinking he'd be having sex all the time he was gone and wanted to know if he did. "Not once. Not since you were sixteen."

The revelation was perverted yet so sexy. He hadn't had sex with a woman for two years because of me. "Does that mean you're mine, too? Only mine?"

A smirk manifested on his lips before, abruptly, he gripped my waist, pushed me up, hooked my legs around his back and pushed his heavy erection inside me. "Does that answer your question?"

"No," I teased.

He swatted my pussy again, and I hissed. Then he started pounding me. "How about now?"

I was coherent enough to shake my head.

"Liar," he whispered, and his pounding became harder, more punishing. He was ruthlessly driving me higher and higher until I was screaming, my nails raking down his back as release hovered just beyond my reach.

Then, as he spanked my ass and returned to squeeze my neck while stretching me with his deep thrusts, I was finally there, my body crashing apart as a powerful orgasm swept through me.

He pulled out and flipped me over. Then he pushed back inside me, resuming fucking me from behind, his body large and strong. I was surrounded by him. The heat emanating from his skin. His incredible smell. The back and forth movement of his thick cock inside my body as the head bumped against my cervix with each thrust of his hips.

In this position, he went deeper, hitting every right spot, sucking gasps and hisses of both pleasure and pain out of my throat. "I touched myself every day while I was gone watching you come."

My inner muscles clenched helplessly around his shaft in another orgasm as he said that. A week or two ago that would have made me cringe, the idea of my stalker, watching me in the privacy of my bedroom without knowing while I was naked, touching myself, and jerk off to it, but now, it was one of the sexiest things I'd ever heard.

He groaned harshly, his cock pulsing and jerking within me, his pelvis grinding into my butt cheeks. It enhanced my own orgasm, drawing out my own pleasure, dragging it to last longer.

When he slipped out of me, he turned me and cupped my pussy, preventing any of his seed from spilling. He stared at me in a dare.

I wanted to protest, but I also didn't want to upset him anymore. I just got him back. Besides, there was something hot about a man wanting to get a woman pregnant. It meant he needed to dominate her in every way possible. It meant he wanted them to have a connection that couldn't be broken ever.

A sudden knock on the bathroom door interrupted our staring contest. I frowned. Who would dare interrupt Don Bellomo in the shower?

"Che cosa?" Tino asked.

A man spoke quickly in Italian. All I could make out from what he said was Leo's name.

"Che cazzo?" Tino jumped out of the shower, dragging me out with him.

"What's happening?" I asked.

"Leo has found out where I'm keeping you. He knows everything."

CHAPTER 53

Tino

"**I** have to get you out of here." I threw a towel at her and drew her out of the bathroom with me. Then I opened the wardrobe and got out two outfits, one for me and one for her. "Here. Put that on. We don't have time to pack."

She just stared at me while I jumped into my pants. I read her eyes, the stupid plan formulating in her head. We both looked at the bathroom door at the same time before she sprinted, jumped inside and locked herself up.

"You silly, silly girl." I banged on the door. "Open up."

She didn't make a sound. I didn't have time for this shit. "Get back. I don't want you to get hurt." Quickly, I kicked the door, smashing it open.

She backed up in the corner, the frightened little girl she'd always been. "You think he'll save you if he finds you?"

"Yes," she whimpered.

"You're wrong. You don't know him like I do. Leo is a danger to you, Angel."

"You keep saying that, but it doesn't make any sense. Leo is kind and funny and compassionate and—"

"A fucking killer!"

She grimaced, her lips trembling. "Only because you made him one."

She still didn't understand. "No, Angel. He's not the Mafia kind of killer. He's the kind that kills a girl because she doesn't want to be his girlfriend. Do you understand?"

Her head shook rapidly. "This can't be true. You're messing with my head again."

"Why would I need to mess with your head? You've already given yourself to me a minute ago, and I know you want me, Angel, not him."

"That's before I thought I had no choice or a chance to get out of here. Now Leo can come and take me home, and you're playing me so you can put me in another one of your prisons."

"The fuck, Angel? I really don't have time for this." I grabbed her and threw her over my shoulder. She banged her little fists on my back, but I silenced her with a spank or two. "You'll thank me later. As always."

I threw the towel over her body and grabbed her clothes and my guns on the way before I dashed down the stairs, yelling for my men and Arancia.

A roar of a motor came crashing from outside. I looked through the curtains and saw a speedboat darting to my shore. Merda. That couldn't be Leo, but he'd sent some of his crew to delay us.

My men rushed in to protect me. I told two of them to take Angel and Arancia, who had just rushed in, too, to the plane. I gave Arancia Angel's clothes and told her to get her dressed once they boarded.

"What about you?" Arancia panted as Angel squirmed and yelled when the men took hold of her.

"Don't worry about me." I looked at one of my men. "If I don't get back in ten minutes, you fly that plane and get them out of here, understood?"

"Si, Don Bellomo."

"No!" Angel suddenly shouted, and her eyes reached out to mine. "We can't leave without you."

Didn't she want to stay for Leo to save her from me? Now she couldn't leave without me? "Just go, Angel." I unlocked my gun and nodded for the men to go.

CHAPTER 54

Lina

We ran through the lush side of the island away from the beach, bullets echoing, my brain jumbled.

I'd totally surrendered to Tino as I realized I had deep feelings for him that would never go away, but then a chance to get out of his prison erupted, and I had to take it. After all, he kidnapped me and was planning on keeping me hidden forever. He couldn't blame me for fighting for my freedom.

But he told me his son's darkest secret, and everything changed. If what Tino said was true, it only meant one thing. Tino, in his twisted ways, had been trying to protect me from Leo all this time, not just trying to own me and take me away from him.

Tino killed my father to save me. He interfered before Leo and I hooked up to save me. He punched his son when he proposed to me to save me. He kidnapped me before I married Leo to save me.

But if Tino was lying, I would have every right to try to escape. Our relationship was toxic, to say the least. Even if I loved him, I was better off without him, far away from all the Bellomos.

I knew I should run for my life without looking back. I should be grateful that I was leaving here without him where there might be a bigger chance to escape everything and never having to be a prisoner, a slave at his mercy again.

The idea of Tino in danger, though, tore at me, and—I hated myself for this—toxic or not, leaving here alone without him terrified me more than anything.

What the fuck is happening to me?

The plane appeared in a walking distance, a couple of minutes away from the trail we followed. It wasn't easy to advance among the thick trees with only a towel wrapped around your body, and the sun diving west. A chill ran through me at the approaching night cold and the bellowing gunfight that wouldn't cease.

Another bellowing sound cracked in, this time coming from above. I looked up and I saw it.

A plane.

Leo's plane.

The bodyguards started to swear and urge us to speed.

"No! We can't leave now!" I screamed, my heart racing. "What if they hurt each other?"

The two men and Arancia cursed again and practically dragged me to the plane and shoved me inside.

"What the fuck is wrong with you? He's your brother. He's your boss."

"We have to follow his orders, signora," one of his bodyguards said as Arancia guided me to the bathroom so I could put on my clothes.

The bullets rained in the background as I finally got dressed. My heart squeezed with every shot. I heard the man talking outside. It was all Italian, but I could gather they were getting ready to fly as there were only two minutes left to Tino's deadline.

I listened for the gunshots. They weren't getting closer. If anything, they were getting farther. Tino wasn't coming to the plane. There was no way he could make it in time.

A knock on the bathroom door interrupted my thoughts. "Signora, are you okay?"

"Yeah. I'm coming out now."

The bullets suddenly died. There were no sounds coming from outside except for those of the wind and the distant beach. What did that mean? Was the fight over?

Or was *it* over?

No. Tino would never hurt Leo. Could I say the same about Leo?

My heart shrank. This couldn't be happening.

A second knock on the door disrupted me. I took a deep breath and opened the door. One of the men gestured for me to take my seat as we were about to take off.

"Can you please wait another five minutes?" I urged.

"Mi dispiace, signora. Don Bellomo said ten minutes only."

"At least, go look outside the plane door and fucking check if he's anywhere close." I was done being polite.

The second bodyguard popped his head out of the door, and then he glanced at me and shook his head.

"Please take your seat," the first one said.

I stared at Arancia, who was already in her seat waving for me to join her. *Okay. I can do this.*

I took one step, and with the next I faked a fall. When one of the men bent to help me up, I stole the gun in his belt and aimed at both of them. "I'm not leaving without Tino. You wanna stay here, fine, but don't try to stop me from going back."

They mumbled a few curses and threats. I didn't care about them or Arancia's pleas as she jumped off her seat. I just backed up slowly, my hands firm on the gun, the wind clashing against my back, ruffling my hair. Then I wheeled out of the plane and ran as fast as I could back to the beach.

Thank God the guards didn't try to stop me. They could have easily. I didn't know why they let me leave. Maybe they were afraid to hurt me, afraid I'd hurt them if I recklessly pulled the trigger without prior training, afraid I'd put a bullet in the plane body and break it or—I hoped—wanted me to go so it'd be an excuse for them to come back for me and Tino without being at fault.

Whatever it was, I was thankful. I couldn't let a father and son kill each other because of me. I couldn't let Tino die because of me.

When I arrived, it was getting darker, but I could still see the bodies and the blood scattered on the sand. All the men were dead, Leo's and Tino's. No sign of Tino or Leo themselves, though.

Voices in a heated argument and sounds of struggle streamed from inside the house all of a sudden. I rushed toward the front door, my breath catching, my heart hammering.

"You took her from me!"

"She was never yours. She's mine! Six years I've been taking care of her, waiting for her to grow, and you just—"

"I love her, and she loves me. She wants me!"

"She never wanted you. It was only when you lied to her that she agreed to be with you, thinking you saved her from Marciano when you faked the whole thing to make it look as if you did, thinking I'd been using her to get you made."

What? Oh my God.

"Isn't that the truth? You did use her to get me in the family business. Isn't that the only reason you agreed to bring her to the mansion?"

"No, Leo. I brought her home so I could be with her, so I could keep *you* away from her, to protect her from *you*. Why do you think I scared her like that at the theatre? Only so that she'd agree to come live with me where you didn't."

So Leo had been lying to me all this time. All the things that brought us closer were fake, staged to make me choose him.

"It doesn't matter. You know I'm not gonna let her go," Leo said. "You know I can't."

"Nobody understands you more than I do, Son. We're so much alike, Leo. You're obsessed with her like I am, but she was never yours."

"I don't care! Where is she?"

I stepped inside, and both their heads jerked toward me. "Right here."

"Lina!" Leo dashed toward me, a gun in his hand, but I stepped away, going to where Tino stood unarmed. I pointed my gun at Leo's. How the fuck could he pull a gun at his own dad?

"Fuck, Angel. Why did you come back?" For the first time ever, I heard a speck of fear in Tino's voice.

"I couldn't just leave you behind," I confessed. "And I needed to know the truth."

"Lina, I came here to save you from him. He's been lying about the Lanzas. *He* kidnapped you. *He* almost killed you."

"You lied to me, too," I said.

"Lina, I love you. Everything I did was because I love you. You're my wife."

"Not anymore."

Leo's eyes darkened. "What does that mean?"

"It means you should go back home. I don't need saving. Not from Tino." I meant every word. Tino had always been my savior. My dark, dark protector. I saw that now.

Leo raised his gun at Tino's head level. "What did you do to her? What the fuck did you do to her? You raped her, didn't you? You raped my wife and fucking brainwashed her!"

"Leo, please," I begged. "Just go."

"I'm not leaving here without you." His voice took a harsh turn, an edge of darkness I'd never heard from him before. "Come here."

"Or what? You're gonna kill me? Like that girl that said no to you?"

"Angel, no. Shut the fuck up," Tino said.

"You told her about Gloria?" Leo's jaw twisted. "Is that how you brainwashed her?"

"So it is true? You killed an innocent girl just because she couldn't love you back?" I asked in disbelief.

"She loved me back! She just didn't want to believe it. She chose to believe another man's lies and chose him because of it." Suddenly, he switched the gun direction and pointed it at my head. "Just like you did."

Bang!

"Noooooo!"

Thud.

Blood. I knew the texture of it by now when it covered my body, and the taste it left when I got some of it in my mouth. And the surge of panic that followed when I wondered if it was mine or somebody else's.

I glanced down, and my fear doubled. This wasn't my blood. It was Tino's.

I fell to my knees next to his body. "Tino! Tino!" I stared at the blood streaming out of his body, staining my hand as I pressed the hole in his chest, shuddering. "You can't die. You can't leave me. You can't leave me, Tino. You promised you'd never let me go." My head whipped at Leo as I pointed my gun at him. "What did you do? What did you do?! This is your father, you sick fuck!"

He aimed at me again. "What did *you* do? How could you choose him after all he's done to me, to my mom, to you? He was gonna kill you."

The memory of Tino standing by my bed with a gun in his hand flashed in my head. The situation was similar. He was about to shoot me dead so I wouldn't be with another man. Just like Leo did now.

Except Tino couldn't pull the trigger and Leo could. "So were you. He never did, though. It's you who just shot at me." And Tino had jumped and took the bullet for me. He'd die for me for real, not in a staged charade.

"Put the gun down, Lina."

I thought about shooting him with the goddamn gun in my hand I didn't know how to use. How hard could it be? All I needed to do is squeeze the trigger and empty the whole magazine in his body. But another idea came to me out of rage, out of desperation, out of the loss he should feel, too, for the rest of his life. Leo shouldn't die. He should suffer for a very long time. "Or what? You're gonna fire at me again? Do it. Shoot me. Shoot me and the baby inside me."

His eyes narrowed in shock. "Baby? You're pregnant?"

"Yeah. So go ahead. Kill me and your baby brother or sister just like Seppi did to your mom. I want you to live with that guilt. The guilt of killing your father and your sibling."

"Lina?"

"My name is Angel!"

My eyes flickered at another gun appearing from behind Leo. Then I saw the face of one of the two bodyguards from the plane. He swung his arm and hit Leo on the head with the back of his gun.

Leo dropped on the floor unconscious, and the second bodyguard took away all the guns on Leo's body.

"Signora, you okay?"

I nodded, trembling, tears frozen in my eyes as I looked at Tino's pale face. "But he's not breathing."

CHAPTER 55

Angel

Arancia patched Tino up as best she could before we flew to the nearest hospital that belonged to the Mafia to avoid the police.

The doctors weren't optimistic, even after they operated on him and took the bullet out. It hit very close to his heart, perforated his lung, and he'd lost a lot of blood.

Leo was sent to the Lanzas for safekeeping until his destiny was determined according to the Mafia laws. I called Nicky and told her I was safe. She was still in the mansion, guarded by Tino's men now.

Three days after the operation, and he hadn't woken up yet. I stayed by his bed, holding his hand, praying, waiting.

Arancia was surprised I didn't run away or try to call for help. I was surprised at myself, too. This was my only chance to go and start over away from all the pain and darkness. But the same reason I had to go back for Tino on the island was keeping me here.

"How can I live without you, Tino?" A tear dropped on his hand I was holding. "You're my savior, my lover. You can't leave me alone in this world. You're part of me. I need you. I love you. I've always loved you."

I kissed his hand and placed it on my cheek. Then I closed my eyes and prayed. "There's so much left for us to do together. We haven't jammed yet. Me on the violin and you on the piano…You know what? I bet I'm better than you at playing the piano. Actually, I don't think you can play at all. No? Well, you have to wake up and prove me wrong."

I hiccupped through the tears. "You have to wake up so we can have a decent wedding, one without any kind of blood for once. You have to wake up so you can make me pregnant for real or your son is gonna try to kill me again."

I opened my eyes and gazed at his features that even now were mesmerizingly beautiful. "If you wake up, I promise I'll behave. Well, not all the time. You know me. I like my spanking, and I think you like it, too. Don't you, Tino?"

A heated moan shivered on my lips in pain as I continued to cry. "You have to wake up so you can be with me." I kissed his hand again. "Please don't leave me."

"Never."

A gasp ripped from my throat at his slur. "Tino? Tino, are you up?"

Nothing happened for a second or two, and I thought I'd imagined it. Then his fingers moved faintly in my hand, squeezing.

I squeezed back, crying in relief. "You're awake. You're here."

I yelled for the doctors, and they hurried in with Arancia. They checked him and the monitors and assured me he was stable now.

The dark blue eyes smiled at me again, swallowing me in where I belonged, promising me the life I'd never thought I needed and turned out to be exactly what I dreamed.

When the doctors were done, they left me alone in the room with Tino.

"I thought you'd be gone by now," he said.

I smiled, shaking my head. "You won't get rid of me that easily."

"What about Leo?"

I heard the blame in his voice. "I'm sorry. I was an idiot. But that's our thing. I make a stupid mistake, and you save me from it."

"And punish you for it. I'm not gonna stop doing that."

"I hope so. It's the best part."

His lips stretched with a faint smile. "Come here, you naughty, naughty girl."

I nestled carefully into his arms and rested my head on his chest, as if I was the one that needed his care, that needed to heal.

"So about that baby I need to put in you…"

I laughed. "You heard that?"

"Every word."

My eyes glanced up at his. His gaze held me as his arms did. "I can't live without you either. Why, Angel?"

"Because I'm yours, and you're mine. Always."

He kissed my head, breathing in my hair. "Always, my sweet Angel."

The End

Thanks for Reading!

Looking for the epilogue?
You can download it here
https://bookhip.com/WTLBJV
As this beautiful story comes to an end, I hope you enjoyed this journey with me as much as I enjoyed writing it.

Please leave a review

Read other books in the series
The Italian Heartthrob
The Italian Marriage
The Italian Happy Ever After
The Italian Dom
The Italian Son

Also by N.J. Adel

Contemporary Romance
The Italian Heartthrob
The Italian Marriage
The Italian Happy Ever After
The Italian Dom
The Italian Son

Paranormal Reverse Harem
All the Teacher's Pet Beasts
All the Teacher's Little Belles
All the Teacher's Bad Boys
All the Teacher's Prisoners

Reverse Harem Erotic Romance
Her Royal Harem: Complete Box Set

Dark MC and Mafia Romance
Furore
Tirone
Dusty
Cameron
Night Skulls Mayhem

Author Bio

N. J. Adel, the author of The Italians, All the Teacher's Pets, Her Royal Harem, and The Night Skulls MC series, is a cross genre author. From chocolate to books and book boyfriends, she likes it DARK and SPICY.

Mafia bosses, psycho anti-heroes, bikers, rock stars, dirty Hollywood heartthrobs, supes, smexy guards and men who serve. She loves it all.

She is a loather of cats and thinks they are Satan's pets. She used to teach English by day and write fun smut by night with her German Shepherd, Leo. Now, she only writes the fun smut.

Made in the USA
Columbia, SC
15 April 2025

56673583R00283